DOES HE KNOW?

NEW YORK TIMES BESTSELLING AUTHOR
KAYLEE RYAN

Cover Design: Emily Wittig Designs
Editing: Hot Tree Editing
Proofreading: Deaton Author Services, Jo Thompson, Jess Hodge
Paperback Formatting: Integrity Formatting

KAYLEE RYAN

DOES
HE
KNOW?

ROMAN 1

EMERSON Age 19
ROMAN Age 29

THERE IS NOTHING QUITE LIKE sitting around a fire after a long day at the shop with the guys. It's a brisk spring evening here in Tennessee. When Forrest suggested a few beers at his place earlier today at the shop, we were all in. It's warm enough by the fire in just a hoodie.

Forrest is one of my best friends. One of four, actually. We're all from the same small town of Ashby, Tennessee. We've gone to school together since kindergarten, and I can't ever remember a time when it wasn't the five of us.

Our own little pack is what my mom used to say.

We were never overachievers in school. We got good enough grades to keep from failing and to keep our parents off our backs. We even attempted to form a band back in junior high, but we all quickly lost interest. Instead, we formed a plan. No college for us. We were going to open our own tattoo studio, make our own hours, work for ourselves, and say fuck you to anyone who didn't agree.

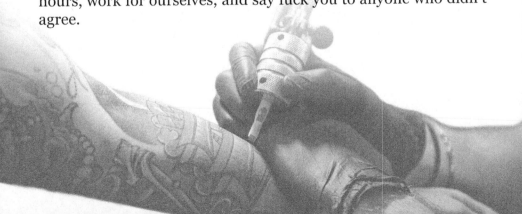

By the time we were twenty-three, we'd made that a reality. All five of us lived in a tiny two-bedroom apartment. We'd each had a minimum of two jobs, and we saved, working our asses to the bone to make our dream a reality. In addition to those two jobs, we all managed to snag an apprenticeship at surrounding tri-state tattoo studios, and the rest, as they say, is history.

"You know what I miss?" Lachlan asks.

"What's that?" Maddox answers.

"Real tits."

"What?" Legend asks, sputtering with laughter.

"How many of those have you had?" I ask him.

"You're cut off," Forrest chimes in.

"Come on, think about it. How long has it been since you've inked a nice set of real titties?" Lachlan asks.

"Is that something you keep track of?" Legend asks him.

"Yeah, I mean, I pay attention. The real ones are so much softer." Lachlan lifts his hands in front of him and pretends to squeeze a pair of fictional tits.

"Can't say that I miss them, but I prefer them," I admit. They all agree with mumbled replies.

"Six years," Maddox says. "We've inked a lot of tits since the day we opened our doors."

"And to many more." Legend raises his beer, and we all follow suit before taking long pulls.

The sound of the patio door sliding open draws our attention. We all turn to look, but it's Forrest who calls out, "Hey, little sis," to his sister, Emerson.

I shift in my seat and lean forward, placing my elbows on my knees. Emerson Huntley is a fucking knockout. She's also ten years my junior and one of my very best friend's little sister. However, that doesn't mean that my body doesn't react to seeing her.

I grew up with Emerson always being around. Forrest and Emerson's parents are alcoholics and sometimes hit the harder stuff. Forrest, being ten years older, has always stepped up. He's more of a parent to her than their actual parents.

When Emerson turned eighteen, she moved all of her things here, to his place, before she went off to college. She's not far. Just about three and a half hours. She's going to school in Lexington, Kentucky.

So, yeah, Emerson is always around. She was sixteen when I really started to take notice. She lost the braces. And those real tits Lachlan was just going on about? Hers made themselves known.

I immediately started to distance myself from her. The rest of the guys laugh and joke around with her, treating her like their pseudo-little sister. I tried like hell to do the same, but fuck those assholes must be blind as bats not to see the sexy-as-fuck woman she was becoming.

Somehow, in my quest to not perv on Forrest's little sister, I became the broody, grumpy asshole. Which is fine. Whatever I need to do to save face. I mean, sure, I hate being short with her. If she only knew the effect she had on me.

"I thought you were staying at Monroe's?" Forrest asks her.

She steps closer to the fire and holds her hands up, rubbing them together for warmth. "I was going to, but decided I wanted to sleep in my own bed. I leave to go back to school the day after tomorrow," she reminds him.

"You should have brought her with you," Maddox tells Emerson. "You know she misses me."

"Nope." Emerson pops the *p* in her reply. "None of you are allowed to hook up with my best friend. She's mine. Get your own."

"Come on, Em," Legend goads her. "We're family. Families share," he says, humor lacing his tone.

"Not happening," Emerson fires back.

"Well, can we at least get a damn hug? This is the first time I've gotten to see you since you've been home on spring break." Lachlan stands and saunters over to her, wrapping her in a hug.

"I know. Monroe and I went to Gatlinburg with a few friends from school for a couple of days before we came home."

"Stop hogging her." Maddox pulls Emerson from Lachlan before she's then passed to Legend, and then there's me.

I'm not a complete asshole. At least I try not to be where she's concerned. Just asshole enough to keep my distance. Not greeting her like the others would be noticeable, so I stand and hold my arms open.

"Hey, Rome," she whispers.

Is it just me or is there something different in her eyes when she looks at me? She steps into my embrace and wraps her arms around my waist. I release her quickly and take my seat by the fire, just like the others. The only difference is that I didn't want to let her go.

Fuck, she feels good in my arms.

"How's school?" I need to ask the question to remind myself that she's too damn young for me.

She smiles. "Good. I'm almost through the first year of my major."

"Surgical Tech, right?" I already know because I pay attention to her, even when I want everyone to think that I don't.

"Yeah, I wish I would have decided that my first year."

"You have plenty of time to join the workforce of society," Forrest tells her. "Just enjoy college life."

"Maybe don't enjoy it too much," Maddox adds, making her laugh.

"I already have one overprotective big brother," she reminds him.

Maddox shrugs. "You have five, Em. This isn't recent news."

She smiles and shakes her head. "Anyway, I just wanted to let you know I was here and that I'm going to bed."

"You sure you don't want to stay and join us?" Forrest offers.

"Nah, I'm going to read for a little while before bed. Night." She bends down and kisses Forrest on the cheek.

"Night, Em," he says as she retreats into the house.

"Have you heard from your parents?" Legend asks Forrest.

"Nah, not since the day Emerson turned eighteen, and I moved her out. She doesn't reach out to them either."

We're all quiet as we let that sink in. Out of the five of us, Forrest had it the worst. His parents were never really parents to either him or Emerson.

Maddox starts talking about scouting for a new location, and we get lost in shop talk. We've grown so much, and the current building we're in needs a lot of work. We're tossing around the idea of renovations or a new facility altogether. It's a big step, but one we all agree we need to take. We just have to decide in what direction we want to go. We could rent the building or sell it and use that money to put toward the new one.

"I say we go new," Legend speaks up.

"Yeah, the sale or rent will help with the new place," I agree.

"Vote?" Forrest asks. "Raise of hands for a new location." All five of us raise our hands. "Well, there we have it. Let's start looking for a new building or land. Do we all agree that we want to stay in Ashby?"

Again, we all agree. There might not be much in our small hometown, but it's ours, and most of us have family here that we don't want to leave.

"I gotta take a shit." Lachlan stands and tosses his empty bottle of beer into the recycling bin we moved out here next to the fire. Makes cleaning up a hell of a lot easier. We've learned over the years.

"Spray!" Forrest calls after him.

"I gotta piss," I grumble.

"Just use my bathroom upstairs in my room," Forrest tells me. "It's too fucking cold to piss out here. Your dick might fall off."

I stand and amble my way to the back door. He's right. Once you step away from the fire, the chill in the air hits you.

I shiver as I pull open the patio door and step into the warm house. I hear the exhaust fan going in the half bath downstairs as my foot lands on the first step. I keep my steps light, not wanting to bother Emerson if she's already asleep.

Once I reach the landing, I see a soft glow of light coming from her room. The door is cracked open. There's a small enough opening that I could look through, but I talk myself out of peeking inside, until I hear my name. At least, I think I hear my name.

I freeze. I'm not even sure if I'm breathing as I listen.

"Rome." A soft, breathy moan greets my ears, and my cock is instantly hard as steel.

I know that this is wrong. All. Kinds. Of. Wrong. However, the temptation is too strong. I have to know. I have to bear witness to what's going on behind that door.

Cautiously, I take another step and peek inside. And what I see—fuck me, I'll never be able to unsee it.

I move a little closer, so I can get a better look. I'm going to fucking hell, but dammit, I have to. I just have to.

Peeping through the crack in the door, I see Emerson lying on her bed. She's wearing a tight white tank top that does nothing to hide the fact that her nipples are hard. Her panties are around her thighs, and her hand... motherfuck... her hand is where I wish mine could be.

She moans, and I act on instinct.

Slowly, I push open her bedroom door, step inside her room, and close the door behind me. The audible click has Emerson opening her eyes. I don't know what the fuck I'm doing, and I don't know what I expected, but her heated gaze locking with my own, and her hand continuing to massage her clit is not it.

Her mouth opens in surprise, forming a perfect *O*, and I can't help but wonder how those lips would feel wrapped around my cock. She didn't expect me, but she's not stopping. She rubs at her clit while her eyes undress me. Her eyes are usually a bright green, but right now, the desire-filled orbs are almost black.

Reaching behind me, I flip the lock on her bedroom door before leaning my back against it. I've had a handful of beers. I'm not drunk, but I'm not sober either. What I am is going out of my fucking mind. I shouldn't be here, but I can't make myself walk away. I need her to tell me to walk away, but she makes no move to do so.

Tearing my eyes from hers, I focus on her hand as she slides a finger inside.

It's more than I can take.

I need relief.

Popping open the button on my jeans, I tear down the zipper and pull out my cock. She gasps, which has my eyes flashing to hers. Her dark-brown hair is fanned out over her pillow, and her eyes, so fucking dark and burning with desire, watch me.

"Don't stop." My voice is gritty and barely a whisper. It doesn't matter because she hears me. Her hand once again starts to move, and so does mine.

My sweatshirt is in the way. I pause, ripping it over my head and letting it fall to the floor. I take my cock back in my hand, lean back against the door, and begin to stroke. I squeeze hard as my hand glides from root to tip and back again.

I'm dry and wish that I could run my hands over her wet pussy, but I keep my feet planted where they are. Instead, I lift my hand and spit and get back to business.

Time seems to stand still as I get lost in the sight before me.

I've never seen a woman more beautiful.

She's too young for me.

She's my best friend's little sister.

We could get caught.

My mind races with a million thoughts, but there is only one that matters.

Release. Release with Emerson's eyes on me.

Her hand starts to pump faster as she adds a second finger, and my hand pumps faster. I match her stroke for stroke. Her face is flushed, and her chest rises and falls with each labored breath she pulls into her lungs.

Her back arches off the bed, and I feel the familiar tingle in the base of my spine. My balls tighten, and I know I'm not going to last much longer. I want to tell her that. I want to tell her to rub her clit and come for me.

Come. For. Me.

But I don't. We both remain silent, our eyes roaming over every inch of each other as we both chase our orgasm.

"Rome..." she whispers my name, but it's not just a whisper. Her voice cracks, her chest rises and falls even faster, and her hand moves to her clit. She rubs furiously, her head shaking from side to side. Her legs start to fall closed, and I grunt my disapproval.

Like the good girl that she is, she forces them back open, letting me see all of her. Her pussy is wet, and I'd give anything to have a taste. Just one taste.

My hand pumps faster, as does hers. She bites down on her bottom lip as her body shakes with the desire crashing through her veins. Seeing her like this is all it takes, and I'm blowing all over my hand, dripping onto her bedroom floor. When I'm finally spent, I tuck my cock back into my jeans and pull my T-shirt out of my hoodie. I clean up as best as I can before pulling my sweatshirt back on.

I glance down at the shirt in my hands and realize I've fucked up. I'm going to have to toss it, hide it, something. I can't carry this back out to the backyard.

"Mine." Her voice is barely a whisper that I'm surprised I heard it over the drum session rivaling a rock concert that's going on in my chest.

Mine.

I'm not attached to the shirt, and there is something insanely hot knowing that she wants to keep it. On shaking legs, I stand to my full height and walk to where she's lying on her bed. I hand her the shirt as I memorize everything about her.

Her flushed skin.

Her hard nipples.

Her scent.

I broke the rules. I crossed a line that I can never uncross. I know that this will be the last time.

I can do better than sneaking into her room and stroking my cock for her. I need to do better. Forrest and Emerson both deserve that. However, I can't resist when I bend my head and place my lips to her temple.

"Good girl," I say gruffly before turning and walking out of the room. I pull the door closed as softly as I can before I haul ass down the hall and into the bathroom. Inside, I engage the lock and brace my hands on the counter.

I hang my head because I can't look at myself.

I fucked up. I should have kept on walking.

Not only did I violate her privacy, but I know that I'll never be able to forget this night. I also broke the bro code, and yeah, I'm fucked in so many ways.

Turning on the faucet, I wash my hands before splashing water on my face. I have to get out of here. I've been up here far too long to just be taking a piss. I need to leave and to be honest, I'm not sure that I can. How do I walk past her door, knowing what's waiting behind it? How do I face her? How do I face my friends?

I've been drinking, and I was going to stay here, but I can't do that now. I just can't. Besides, I'm completely sober after that. Whatever it was that just happened.

Turning off the light, I open the door and step out into the hallway. I force myself to walk past her bedroom door and keep my eyes straight ahead. With each step, I fight the urge to go back to her, but I know that's not possible.

One fuckup is all that I'm allowed. The memory will have to last me because that is never happening again.

When I reach the kitchen, the guys are all coming inside. "Your guts shutting down too?" Lachlan asks me.

I nod and place my hand on my stomach. Not because of some kind of gut issue—well, maybe it is. My gut is churning with guilt and desire.

"I called an Uber," Lachlan says. "I'd rather shit at my place if that's how this night is going to go."

"I'll split it with you." I sound miserable because I am. I'm trying not to look guilty, but even with this churning, with this heaviness of what I've done sitting on my chest, I wouldn't change a single fucking minute of tonight.

Not unless it meant more time with her.

EMERSON 2

EMERSON Age 19
ROMAN Age 29

STEPPING OUT OF THE SHOWER, I hear my phone ringing. I quickly wrap my hair in a towel, then grab one to tie around my body before opening the door and rushing to where my phone is plugged in on the nightstand beside my bed.

I smile when I see my best friend Monroe's smiling face. "I just left you not even an hour ago," I tease.

"Shut it," she fires back with absolutely no heat in her tone. "Have you seen him yet?"

I roll my eyes even though she can't see me. "No." I don't have to ask her who she's talking about. I know she means Roman, one of my brother's best friends, the man I can't stop thinking about.

Monroe and I have been inseparable since kindergarten, and I don't hide anything from her. This is why as soon as I caught my breath after our mutual space-sharing masturbation session, I called her to tell her what had happened.

That night is also why I've been both dreading and anxiously awaiting summer break from college. I don't want to face Roman. I don't want to see the remorse in his eyes. I don't want to be his living regret.

On the flip side of that, I do want to see him.

I want to see if that night was just a drunken mishap or if there could be something there. Not to mention I've missed my big brother.

Forrest has always been there for me, checking in and ensuring I have everything I need. The day I turned eighteen, he showed up at our parents' place with his four best friends, Legend, Roman, Maddox, and Lachlan, and moved me in with him. That was the best day of my life. I owe my big brother everything, so this request to come home to see him, even though I'd rather avoid his best friend, was an easy one to grant.

"Damn," Monroe mutters. "I was hoping he would be there."

"Do you wish that torture on me?" I ask her. I'm only partially serious about that question. It's torture to see him and not have him, not that I need to explain that to my best friend. She knows me well enough to understand my meaning.

"You know I don't," she counters. "However, I can't wait to see how he reacts."

"Roe, we've been over this. He's going to look at me with regret, possibly corner me and threaten me never to speak of that night, or he's just going to ignore it all." Including me, but I don't say that.

"Or, he might want another go? Maybe watching just does it for him." I can picture her shrugging, her long black curly hair bouncing with the movement.

I hear the front door close and heavy footfalls on the hardwood floors. "Forrest is home. I just got out of the shower, so I'm going to get dressed and go hug my brother."

"Oh, hug him for me too." Her tone is sassy and flirty. "Make sure you tell him it's from me. And if his sexy besties are there, they get a hug from me too, 'K?"

I can't help but laugh at her. Monroe has flirted with Forrest and his friends for years. She's not interested in my brother, but she loves to get under his skin. He thinks of her as a second little sister. As far as the rest of the guys, I can't be sure.

"I'll leave that up to you. I'm not flirting with my brother for you."

"What about the others? They're all fine as hell. I mean, Roman is obviously yours. The whole 'watch me crank my shaft' display makes that a given, but the other three are no relation to you, so...." She lets her voice trail off.

"Not flirting with any of them for you." Especially Roman, but I don't say that out loud.

"Party pooper," she retorts. "I was going to ask you to send a picture of that vein that pops out on Forrest's forehead."

"That's all you, Roe, and you know it. That's an in-person kind of reaction."

"Fine." She heaves a heavy sigh. "I'll just have to do it myself. Not tonight. My mom is already making dinner, and I'm exhausted from the drive."

We left Kentucky early this morning. We both had cars with us at school, so we did a mini-caravan type of thing. Stopping at all the same stops for gas, food, and bathroom breaks. Forrest was very happy to hear this. He then proceeded to brag about how he taught me well. He's not just bragging like any big brother would do. Forrest has been a parent to me, more so than our parents. He's protective, sometimes too much so, but I love him for it. It's nice to know I have someone in my corner other than my bestie who cares.

"Me too. I plan to talk to Forrest for a few and then crash."

"Tomorrow?" she asks.

"Yeah, I'll see you tomorrow. Night."

"Night." Tossing my phone onto my bed, I slip into a pair of sleep shorts and a tank top. I don't bother with a bra. Instead, I grab an oversized flannel from my closet and pull it around me to ward off the chill of the air-conditioning. I don't bother to do anything other than brush out my hair, pull it up in a messy knot, and call it good.

Tearing open my bedroom door, I rush down the stairs. It's been way too long since I've wrapped my arms around my big brother. Before my foot hits the bottom step, I'm calling out for him. "Forrest! Forty!" I add his nickname that only I use. I was irritated at twelve when he kept calling me kid and started calling him Forty, telling him he was old. He hated it, which only made me love it even more.

I hear a noise in the kitchen, so I head in that direction. However, as soon as I pass the threshold, my bare feet skid to a stop. Standing in the kitchen, looking hotter than should be legal, is Roman Bailey.

He stares at me.

I stare at him.

"Emerson." His voice is deep. Gruff. Sexy as hell.

"Rome." I manage to find my voice. "Where's Forrest?"

"He had a client run late. He didn't want you to come home to an empty house." He places his hands on the counter. The tattoos on his arms seem to come to life as his muscles flex with his grip.

I can't help but think about that night. The way his fist gripped his cock. The veins in his arms did a similar dance that night. One might say they put on a show for me while we were putting on a show for each other. And the piercing... damn, I wasn't expecting that, but it was hot as hell.

"I've been home for a while. I took a shower," I say lamely. Not that he couldn't already tell from my wet hair. Feeling self-conscious in front of this Adonis of a man, I reach up to tighten the wet knot of hair on top of my head.

"Looks like you forgot some of your clothes." His voice is tight, and his eyes stay riveted to my chest.

Shit.

When I reached up to my hair, my flannel came open. I forgot all about forgoing a bra in a hurry to see my big brother. My instincts tell me to rush to close my flannel, but I can't bring myself to do it. Not with the way he's looking at me.

There's hunger in his eyes. It's a look I told myself for years that I was imagining. I repeated that mantra after that night he slipped into my room during spring break, but right here, right now, there is no mistaking he likes what he sees.

He sees me.

Sure, it's just my tits that have him enthralled, but I expected indifference. "I was just coming down to say hi and hug my brother before going to bed."

"Is that how you dress at college? Your bare tits beneath a thin piece of fabric not leaving anything to the imagination?" There's bitterness in his tone.

"How I dress isn't your concern," I fire back.

"The hell it's not." He stands to his full height and glares at my chest before his gaze captures mine once more. His green eyes are blazing with something I can't name.

"I must have missed that memo," I say sweetly.

"Emerson." My name is a growl, and it sends heat pooling between my thighs. I ignore it.

"Roman," I retort.

He moves around the counter, but I'm too slow. I turn to run back to my room, but Roman is there. I step backward until my back rests against the kitchen island. His hands cage me in as his green eyes blaze with his stare.

I hold his gaze, refusing to be the first of us to look away. Not that it matters. Roman changes the game when one of his hands slips beneath my thin tank top. He traces just above the waistband of my shorts with his index finger.

My chest rises and falls with each labored breath, but still, I hold his gaze. He steps in closer, the heat from his body wrapping around me like a warm embrace. When he bends his head, I lick my lips, certain he's about to kiss me. His eyes flash to my lips and then back again.

Two can play this game.

I stand up, which pushes our bodies together. We're so close, I'm not sure where he ends and I begin. His hand slides around to the small of my back as he holds me close. His eyes remain locked on mine.

His head falls forward, and his lips hover above mine. His hot breath breezes across my skin, causing goose bumps to race down my spine. In my mind, I'm willing him to kiss me. With my eyes, I dare him, my body tempting his. I'm about to make a move, taking what I want—a kiss from the man I've crushed on since I was old enough to be interested. However, just as I work up the nerve to take what I've always craved, the front door crashes open.

"Emmy!" Forrest calls out for me. "Get your ass down here!" He's laughing, and I can't help but smile too. I've missed him.

Roman's hand drops from my body, and he takes several steps back. I watch as he runs his tattooed hand through his unruly jet-black hair. He moves back to the opposite side of the island while on shaking legs, I manage to perch my ass on a bar stool.

"Close your shirt," Roman grits out.

I look down and see my hard nipples poking through. "Your fault," I sass before grabbing both sides of the flannel and wrapping it around me.

"You better answer him," Roman reminds me.

I swallow, licking my lips. "In here, Forty!"

My brother's heavy footfalls echo throughout the house. "There she is." Forrest grins as he stalks toward me and wraps his arms around me in a crushing hug.

Hot tears prick my eyes. I owe my big brother so much. He's always been my protector and my biggest cheerleader. "I missed you, Forty," I murmur softly.

"I miss you too, Emmy." He pulls back and nods at Roman. "Thanks for greeting her, man. That last client was a pain in my ass."

"It's always the new ones." Roman chuckles.

"Don't I know it," Forrest fires back before he turns his attention back to me. "Are you hungry? I can order something."

"No, just tired from the drive."

"Any troubles?"

"Nope. We did a mini-caravan, stopping at the same times, following each other closely."

"There's something I want to ask you. I was waiting to do it in person. We've been meaning to hire someone to work the desk, take appointments, cash out customers, that sort of thing."

"Then you'd just be up shit creek again once I go back to school."

"I know." He sighs. "But that gives us time to hire someone while you're there helping out, taking some of those tasks so we can interview. You can help too. I feel like I never get to see you anymore. Working with us all summer will be great."

"I live here," I remind him with a soft laugh.

"I know, but I work long-ass hours, and it would be nice for us to work together. Next summer, you'll be graduated and off to do great things in the operating room."

"I'm going to be a surgical tech, not a surgeon." I shake my head at my brother, always my biggest cheerleader. I spent my first year of college doing my prerequisites and this past year, and next is my concentrated curriculum.

He shrugs. "You're doing big things, little sister. I just worry, and I know once you graduate, I'll get to see you even less."

"I'm a big girl now, Forty." I hold my arms open, and he leans in for another hug. "You don't have to worry so much, big bro. You've done your job. I know how to throw a punch, and I know how to adult because of you."

He gives me a sympathetic look. It's hard to believe that we turned out the way that we did with the parents we were blessed with.

"Well, we're having a party for your birthday at the end of the summer before you head back to college. No arguments." He points his index finger at me. "I don't care how old you are. You will always be my little sister. I want to do this for you, Emmy."

"I don't need a party." I tell him the same thing every single year. However, every single year he insists on throwing me one.

"You're turning twenty. We have to celebrate that."

"It's just another day, Forrest." I chuckle.

"You're no longer a teenager," he reminds me.

My face heats. Embarrassment washes over me. My brothers and his friends are all the same age. They're ten years older than me. The last thing I want is to remind Roman of our age difference.

"Just another day," I say again.

"It's going down, little sister." Forrest grins.

"I'll be here," I assure him. Not because I want or need a birthday party, but because he's my big brother, and after everything he's done for me, the least I can do is show up for a party he's having in my honor.

Forrest grins. "I knew I'd wear you down."

"On that note, I'm heading to bed. I'm exhausted." I stand and give my brother one more hug. "Night," I mumble before looking over my shoulder at Roman. His eyes are already locked on mine. "Night, Rome." I smile sweetly and turn back around, walking toward the stairs.

"Night," his deep, gruff voice replies.

I grin, feeling like I might have the upper hand where Roman is concerned.

Once in my room, I shut the door, grab my phone from the nightstand, flop down on my bed, and text Monroe.

Me:	I saw him.
Monroe:	Tell me everything.
Me:	I told them I was going to bed. Too much to text.
Monroe:	Not cool, Em. Not cool. You can't tell me that you saw him and then leave me hanging.
Me:	Fine, but I have to whisper.
Monroe:	Go to the bathroom. That will help muffle the sound.

Sliding off the bed, I walk to the en suite bathroom, shutting and locking the door behind me. I already showered, so I can't turn the water on as a distraction. I'm just going to have to talk quietly. Not that I'm not allowed to talk on the phone. I realize I'm acting like that's the case and shake my head at the absurdity of it. That's what the man resorts me to. Acting like a kid afraid to get in trouble for being on the phone.

I dial Monroe, and she answers immediately. "Hello."

"Hey," I whisper.

"Tell me everything." She repeats the same words she said in her text message.

She wants the details, and I need to talk about this. About him. So that's exactly what I do. I start at the beginning and tell her everything that has transpired since our earlier phone conversation.

"He wants you, Em. I told you that hot piece of tattooed, muscled man meat wants you."

I don't reply because I'm not sure that she's right, but then I'm not sure if she's wrong either. The way he touched me. The possessive hold he had on me. The way his green eyes blazed with what could only be described as desire… it's got me reeling.

The last time when I was home on spring break, and we had our mutual self-love incident, he was drinking. I chalked it up to a night to remember and one he would either forget or want to forget, but now I'm not so sure. He's bossy and seemed to be pissed about my clothing choice, but that could be because I'm his best friend's little sister. But he's never touched me like that before.

"You know I'm right," Monroe says, pulling me out of my thoughts.

"He's so damn confusing. He's never been like this with me before." I don't elaborate because Monroe already knows what I'm referring to.

"He's always watched you, Em. When he thinks no one is paying attention, he can't take his eyes off you. I've been trying to tell you that for a while now."

"I know, but you're my best friend. I thought you were just supporting my crush and trying to make me feel good."

A hearty, carefree laugh trickles down the line. That is everything that encompasses my best friend. "I'm your best friend, which means I will always be honest with you, even when the truth hurts. He's into you."

"Forrest is his best friend. All five of them have been thick as thieves since they were little. There is no way he will risk his friendship with my brother. And we both know me dating a man ten years my senior, brother's best friend or not, Forrest will blow a damn gasket."

"We need to find him a woman to keep him distracted." She snickers.

"No, this is crazy talk. He was probably seconds away from warning me to never breathe a word to my brother or anyone about what happened that night, but Forrest came in before he could."

"I want it to go on the official best friend record that I'm team Roman and Emerson, and when that team unites, I get to say I told you so."

I laugh because there is a huge part of me that hopes that she's right. "Love you, Roe."

"Love you too, Em. I'll see you tomorrow."

"Night." I end the call and turn off the light, making my way back to my bed in the dark. I lie awake for hours, despite my exhaustion, trying to make sense of what's happening. I don't come up with a good explanation before sleep claims me.

ROMAN 3

My HEART FEELS LIKE A bass drum beating in my chest. What the fuck am I doing? I can't have her, no matter how bad I wish I could. Forrest was seconds away from catching us doing— Fuck me. I don't know how far I would have let it go.

I grip my fists at my sides, my hands still warm from the touch of her soft skin.

Emerson has dominated my mind since that night. The one that I try not to think about but fail every damn day. It's a constant loop that I can't seem to turn off. What's worse is that I don't really want to turn it off. The way her skin flushed, the way her fingers worked her pretty pink pussy. Fuck me, I never want to forget that night, but for my sanity, I know that I need to.

Forrest is one of my best friends.

The two of them didn't have the best home life, and he's been her pseudo-parent for as long as I can remember. I'm ten years her senior, and I don't do relationships. I never have, and he knows that. So, for him to find out that I did what I did, yeah, he'd kick my ass, and I'd have to let him.

"Thanks for meeting her, man," Forrest says. He walks to the fridge and pulls out a beer. He offers me one, and I wave him off. I definitely don't need to be drinking right now. I'm already making questionable decisions sober.

The last time I drank around her... yeah, it's best I stay sober. "No problem," I say, my voice gruff. I clear my throat. "Not that I needed to. You were literally right behind me." I'm annoyed, but I try to keep it out of my voice. I'm not frustrated that he asked me. I'm irritated that he showed up when he did. His timing saved me from crossing yet another line where Emerson is concerned, but I'm still pissed that he did.

I really wanted to cross that fucking line.

It wasn't a problem. In fact, I'd been wracking my brain trying to think of a reason to stop by here tonight just to get a glimpse of her. As soon as I found out she was coming home today, seeing her was all I could think about.

Who am I kidding? I've been thinking about her far longer than just after our little tryst when she was home for spring break. That was just the first time I acted on what I've been feeling. I didn't know how she would react, and I knew it was wrong, but I was still jonesing for a fix of Emerson, and the alcohol dulled my decision-making skills. Let's go with that.

Thankfully, the client Forrest was working on was a pussy. He insisted he was man enough for a full sleeve on his first round of ink ever. Forrest tried like hell to talk him out of it, but the big man insisted he could handle it.

He couldn't.

Normally, that would annoy the fuck out of me, but he's not my client, and it worked out for me in the end. His need for continued multiple breaks was a win for me. I got to see her. To touch her warm, soft skin, and— No. I shake out of my thoughts. I have to shut this down.

Now.

Permanently.

"I wasn't sure how much longer we were going to go. He pussed out and scheduled another visit in two weeks. I didn't hide my irritation that he didn't listen to a word I said before we started. I should have refused to do it. Lesson learned."

I chuckle. "I know you tried to warn him."

"Yeah, I should have put my foot down, but it is what it is." He shrugs.

"Well, I'm going to head home," I tell him.

"No need to rush off. You sure you don't want a beer?" He raises his again to entice me.

"Nah, I'm tanked. I'm going home to shower and crash."

"All right, man. I'll see you at the shop tomorrow. I'm planning on a little get-together this weekend so Em can catch up with everyone. Probably Saturday after we close down the shop."

I nod. "I'll be here." I deserve a pat on the back for keeping my voice even and not giving anything away.

With a wave, I start for the front door. I pause at the bottom of the stairs. My eyes search for her even though I know she's not just going to be standing there waiting for me to pass by. Pissed off that I'm desperate for even the smallest glimpse of her, I quietly close the door behind me as I step outside. I tell myself it's the polite thing to do, but in all reality, I don't want to wake her if she's sleeping.

In my truck, I stare up at what I know to be her bedroom window. It's dark, so I know she's sleeping. She's tucked in safe and sound, where I can't get to her. It's what's best, but my hands itch to touch her, to watch her bring herself pleasure. My cock thickens, just like it always does when I think about that night. Ignoring it and the pain of the pressure of my cock against my zipper is causing, I back my truck out of the drive and head toward my own place across town.

Pulling into my driveway, I shut off the engine and stare at my home. It's a small ranch style with dark-gray siding. It has two bedrooms and two bathrooms and is under twelve hundred square feet, but it's just me. I can afford a bigger place. Hell, the shop is thriving. It's not about not being able to afford it. I'm a single guy. My buddies stop by, but that's it. There are no women who come here. This is my space, and that's that. The only one of us who has a big place is Forrest. He bought it to give Emerson a home.

Climbing out of the truck, I make my way into the dark house. The motion sensor night-light comes on as I lock the door back behind me and go straight to my room. I'm already stripped out of my shirt, and my shoes are kicked off by the time I reach my en suite.

Flipping on the light, I reach in and turn on the water before stripping out of the rest of my clothes. I tell myself that I'm not going to get myself off to her. Not again. This has to stop. I can't keep imagining her lying on her bed, naked for me. Her body flushed, and those smooth legs of hers wide open, putting her pussy on display for me. I know it's wrong. I need to control these urges, but here in my home, behind these walls, it's just me.

Me and my thoughts.

Me and my memories.

I wash my hair and face and move to my body. My cock throbs, begging for release. If I don't do something about it, I'm not getting any sleep tonight. Squirting some body wash in my hand, I grip my cock and moan as I lurch forward, resting my other palm flat against the shower wall.

Closing my eyes, I try to pull up an image that isn't her, but my mind is blank. She's the only thing I see. I grit my teeth as my hand strokes from root to tip. The head of my cock is sensitive due to my piercing, and that just leads me to think about whether or not she would like it. I know it increases pleasure for both of us, and I want to give that to her.

Damn it.

"Emerson." I moan her name, and my balls tighten. I should be embarrassed. That's all it takes for me to go from "almost there" to "ready to coat the shower walls with my cum," but I'm not embarrassed. I'm turned the fuck on.

I pump faster, letting images of her play on repeat, and there it is. I shoot off like a rocket, keeping my eyes closed, not wanting to let the images of her go just yet. I stand under the hot spray, letting the water rain down on me.

It's been months since I've been laid.

Months.

Up until she came home for spring break, I was doing fine. I was able to pretend like she wasn't the most beautiful creature I've ever laid eyes on. I still had the occasional hookup, nothing crazy, but I haven't even looked at another woman since that night.

She broke my cock.

I can't get it up for anyone but her. The guys and I go out for a beer and the ladies swarm. They tend to do that, thinking they're walking on the wild side when they see our ink. Usually, there's a stir of something, and if I'm feeling it, I'll indulge. Since that night—nothing. Not a single twitch of my cock if it's not her.

Emerson Huntley has me beguiled.

That translates to *I'm fucked*. She's my best friend's little sister. *Little* is the keyword, as she's ten years younger than me, and I have no business thinking about her bent over her brother's kitchen island, but here we are.

I need to do something to get her out of my head. It's just a funk. It has to be. Forrest, and the rest of the guys, we've been tight since kindergarten. I can't ruin a lifelong friendship because my cock wants her attention.

Who am I kidding? *I* want her attention.

When the water finally turns cold, I twist the handle and step out of the shower. Quickly, I dry off and slip into a pair of boxer briefs before climbing into bed. I stare up at the dark ceiling, willing sleep to claim me. When I finally manage to fall, I dream of her.

As tattoo artists, we keep crazy hours. Some early mornings, but a lot of late nights and weekends. We have to be available when our clients are. It's nice, though, because we get to make our own schedules, and if we need time off for whatever reason, we take it. The five of us are equal partners in the shop, and none of us abuse the luxury. However, today is a day I wish that I would have canceled my clients and stayed locked up in my house.

Emerson is here. She wasn't supposed to start until next week, but apparently, she was bored, so here she is. All five foot six of her, with her long brown hair, her big green eyes, and looking sexy as fuck.

So, now, here I am, sitting in my room, staring down at my sketchpad. I have a client coming in about twenty minutes, and I'm making some final tweaks to his design. However, I can't concentrate with the sound of her laughter flowing throughout the building. It pisses me off that Legend, Maddox, and Lachlan are out there chatting her up. I know they all see her as a little sister. At least they better fucking see her that way, but it still pisses me off.

I know that I could go out there and join them, but I don't trust myself to keep my hands off her. I grip my pen a little tighter. I swear I can still feel the softness of her skin from last night.

There's a knock on my door, and I look up to find Emerson standing there. She has a small pad of paper in her hands. "Hey, Rome." Her voice is soft and almost timid. I want to pull her into my arms and kiss the hell out of her.

"Em." My voice is gritty.

"I'm going to run and grab lunch. Do you want something?"

You. "Sure. Just grab me anything," I say as I reach into my back pocket for my wallet. I pull out two twenties and hand them to her. "Yours is on me." I clear my throat. "For going to get it."

"You don't have to do that. Forrest already—" she starts, but I lift my head to stare at her.

"Use my money to buy your lunch, Emerson." I don't know why I'm making a big deal out of this. It's just lunch, and he's her brother, but there's something deep inside me that wants to know that I took care of her today.

"Thank you, Roman," she says, using my full name.

I nod and avert my gaze back to my sketch. Hopefully, my client will be here before she gets back, and I can get lost in my work. I try like hell to block out everything but the task at hand. It's working until Maddox knocks on my door.

"Hey," he says, sticking his head inside. "I'm manning the phones while Em's off getting lunch. Your client is running twenty minutes behind. You don't have anything after on the books."

"Yeah, that's fine." He nods and disappears to relay the message to my client. George is a longtime client of mine. He's an attorney by trade, but beneath his suits, he's covered in ink. We're doing a tribute piece to his grandma, who just passed away. She was ninety-nine. So, we're going to put her face in the center of one nine and her name, date of birth, and date of death in the center of the other. It's definitely unique, and portraits are always fun to do. I love to see my clients' faces light up when they see an exact drawing of their loved ones forever inked onto their skin.

One final adjustment and the design is ready. I'm sure George is going to love it. He already saw the preliminary when he stopped in a few weeks ago. I needed to measure the open area he had available on his lower back to make sure the design would fit.

Standing, I stretch out my sore muscles, knowing I'm going to be hunched over the chair for a good four to six hours, depending on how it goes. Not that I'm complaining. I love this job. Not one day has ever actually felt like work.

The chime over the door sounds, and from the commotion and chatter, it sounds like Emerson is back with lunch. I should go out there, but I stay in my room, pretending to be straightening up when there is nothing that needs to be straightened. We run a tight ship as far as cleanliness and organization go. This is our brand, our image, and the guys and me, we take that seriously.

"I'm back," her sweet voice says. I turn to face her as she steps into the room. "You said to get whatever, so I got you a mushroom hoagie with pickle and onion and french fries." She places the food on my desk, the one that's far away from my drafting table. "I hope that's still your favorite."

I nod. "Thanks."

"Oh, I got you a sweet tea as well. Be right back." She rushes out of the room and comes back with a bottle of sweet tea and a handful of napkins. She places them next to my food.

I should wait until she leaves, but I'm starving for her and for nutrients, and I have a client on his way. I need to eat quickly. So instead of doing what I know I should do, I take a step toward her. She makes no effort to leave as her pretty eyes follow my every move.

Her hair has fallen into her eyes, but she doesn't move to fix it, and I can't stop my hand from reaching out and tucking the silky strands behind her ear. My index finger lingers as I trace her soft cheek.

Fuck me, how is her skin so damn soft?

"Thanks for lunch." My voice is low and does nothing to hide what she does to me.

I watch her throat as she swallows hard. "You're welcome."

I take another step, bringing us closer together. She licks her lips, and I can't help but wonder what they taste like. I bite down on my bottom lip to keep from leaning in and finding out.

"Is it still one of your favorites?" There's something in her voice, something that sounds an awful lot like hope.

"Yeah, baby girl, it's still one of my favorites," I assure her.

She nods, and I lean in, bending my head, bringing us closer together. I want to taste her more than I want my next breath. My voice of reason is gone. It has a tendency to do that when she's this close. I don't think about what's right and what's wrong. All I can think about is how badly I want her.

The door chimes, and it's like a bucket of cold water. Standing to my full height, I take a small step back. I take another and another until I'm backed up against my table. Emerson still stands there, her chest rising and falling rapidly with each breath she pulls into her lungs. She's just as affected as I am, yet neither one of us are willing to talk about it.

I have to stop this.

I have to get this desire I have for her under control.

"You should go," I tell her. Her face drops, and I can see the sadness wash over her before she schools her features. She reaches into her pocket and pulls out some cash. "Keep the change," I tell her. I just need her to go. I need to calm the fuck down and get my cock under control so that I can do my damn job.

Her mask is firmly back in place. She appears to be unaffected. My cock is rock hard, and there is no hiding what she does to me, but I bet if I were to slide my hands inside her panties, she'd be dripping for me.

Fuck.

Do not think about her wet pussy.

"I'll send your client in," she says, her voice void of emotion.

"No," I snap. I gentle my voice. "Give me ten. I'll come out and get him." I didn't mean to snap at her, but fuck me. No one needs to see me like this.

Emerson nods and turns, leaving me alone in my room. Closing my eyes, I will my cock to deflate. Once I have myself somewhat under control, I scarf down my lunch and go get my client.

EMERSON

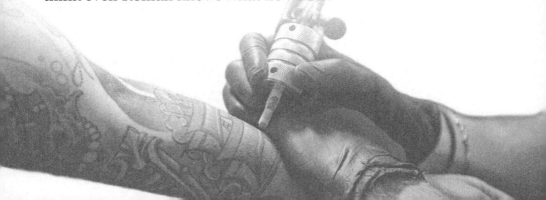

"ARE YOU ON YOUR WAY?" I ask Monroe as I sift through my closet. I'm trying to find something sexy to wear tonight, but I don't want it to look like I'm trying too hard.

"I just got into my car, and I'm bringing options."

"Thanks," I tell her.

"You've been evasive all week," she reminds me. "I'm going to need details before I give up the goods."

"That's unfair." Not really. Monroe and I tell each other everything, and I've yet to tell her about my run-in with Roman at the shop on Monday. I don't know how, but we managed not to be alone together again the rest of the week, partly because I kept his schedule full and partly because I made sure to always know where he was and disappear if needed. I've found some creative places in the shop to hide.

It's not that I don't want to be alone with him, but this push-and-pull thing we've been doing is confusing as hell. Does he want me? Does he want to push me away? Honestly, I'm not sure. I don't think even Roman knows what he wants.

What I do know is that my brother insists on having a little welcome home get-together tonight at our place, and I plan to look my best. Do I think something will happen? No. Do I hope that something happens? Yes. Most certainly, yes. Hence the reason my bestie is bringing me options.

"There's not really anything to tell. I've been avoiding him as much as I can this week while we're both at the shop."

"Uh-huh," she replies, not at all convinced that I'm telling the truth.

"Fine." I sigh. "There might have been a small little run-in, but it was nothing. All it did was leave me even more confused."

"Did he kiss you?" There's excitement in her tone.

"Nope."

"Did you kiss him?"

"No. I thought maybe he might, but then a customer walked in, and the chime of the door pulled him out of wherever he was in his head, and he pushed me away. Again."

"Girl, you know you should just take my advice and take what you want."

Monroe has been telling me the same thing ever since I confessed about the night he slipped into my room during spring break. She thinks I need to show him that he's what I want.

"I don't know," I tell her. "It's going to be all kinds of complicated. He's so much older than me, and Forrest is one of his best friends. I need to just let this go." I say the words, but even as I think them, I know I can't. I don't know what it is, but I've always had a thing for Roman.

"Age is just a number. Besides, it's only ten years. You're both legal adults."

"I'm not so sure he sees it that way," I tell her.

"He didn't seem to have an issue watching you pet your kitty."

"Monroe!" I scold. She's barely containing her laughter, and I can't help but join her.

"I'm pulling in," she says.

"I'll meet you at the door." Ending the call, I toss my phone on the bed and bound down the stairs. When I pull open the front door, she's already making her way up the steps with a huge duffel bag tossed over her shoulder.

"Did I forget to mention I'm staying here tonight?" she asks.

"You did, but I assumed that you would be." I step back, giving her room to walk inside, before shutting the door behind her.

"How much time do we have?" she asks.

"Forrest and the guys cut their schedules short tonight, so an hour tops." They do appointments only on weekends for the most part, and apparently, my big brother made sure they all knew this would be my welcome home weekend, so to speak, and all five of them made arrangements to be here.

"Well, your hair is on point, so we just need to find you an outfit." With that, she turns and starts up the stairs with her big-ass duffel bag on her shoulder. "So, I think casual sexy is the way to go," she says once we're in my room.

"Agreed. I don't want to look like I'm trying too hard. But I want him to notice."

"Try these on." She tosses me a pair of shorts.

"Oh, these are cute. When did you get these?"

"Yesterday when Mom and I went shopping." She keeps digging and pulls out a black ribbed tank top. "This too, with your black flip-flops. We're going to be around the pool after all, oh, and your white bikini. Your tan is fire, and it will make you look even tanner."

Reaching into my dresser, I pull out the white bikini she's referring to. We both bought one during our spring break shopping trip with her mom. I got white, and Monroe got a bright pink. She's right. The colors do make our tans pop.

"Are you sure I shouldn't wear my black one?" I ask, pulling it from my dresser as well.

"Nope. White one. Virginal." She winks.

"Um, I'm trying to get him to want me, not remind him how much younger than him I am."

"Trust me on this. Men want what they can't have."

"Pretty sure he can have me." I laugh.

"Work with me here, Em." Monroe shakes her head. "It's the illusion. You look hot and sexy and unobtainable. Yes, that's the word I was looking for."

"All right." I nod. "What about you? What are you wearing?"

"I have those same shorts in black," she says, pulling them out of her bag. "My same bikini in pink, and a white tank and white flip-flops."

"And which one of the guys is your target for the night? Please don't say my brother," I'm quick to add.

"The only one off the table for me is Rome." She winks.

"I don't think they can handle you," I tell her with a chuckle as I scoop my clothes up off the bed and head to the bathroom. It's not that I don't want to change in front of Monroe. We've done it countless times, but I need a minute. Just one or five, however long it takes me to change to get my emotions in check.

I can only hope that tonight pushes this thing I have for my brother's best friend in one direction or the other. Either I give up because he's pushing me away, or something happens between us, and I fight for what I want. My belly flops with nerves, but I'm ready. Regardless of the outcome, this back and forth, although fun, is hell on my nerves.

An hour later, Monroe and I are in the kitchen snacking on vegetables and dip while Forrest is on his fourth slice of pizza. "Did you eat lunch today?" I tease.

"I'm a growing boy, little sister." He grins, taking another huge bite. "Don't worry. There's plenty."

I look at the seven large pizza boxes. "Who all did you invite?" I ask him.

"Just the guys and the two of you."

"And you thought we needed seven large pizzas?" Monroe asks, her amusement showing in her tone.

"One for each of us, one for the two of you to share, and an extra." Forrest shrugs.

"When have you ever seen me or Monroe eat an entire large pizza on our own?" I ask him, eyebrows raised in challenge.

"You need to eat more. You're going to wither away to nothing," he tells me. His eyes flash to Monroe. "Both of you." He scowls, as if the thought of us losing weight bothers him.

"I gained weight when I moved to college," I tell him, shaking my head.

"Well, good." He nods. "Good. I like to know you're being taken care of."

I soften at his words, and suddenly, I need a hug from my big brother. Sliding off the stool, I round the counter where he's standing over the open pizza box that we now know is all his and wrap my arms around his waist.

"Love you," I whisper.

"Love you too," he says, pressing his lips to the top of my head.

"What's going on?"

I don't have to turn to look over my shoulder to see that Roman is the one who asked the question. Instead, I stand tall and release my hold on my brother, making my way back to the opposite side of the kitchen island, reclaiming my stool next to Monroe. I take my time opening a box of pizza and pulling out a slice for each of us, placing them on a napkin before I allow myself to look up.

Roman's eyes are locked on me. "Everything all right?" he asks. His eyes flash to Forrest, who's eating another slice of pizza, and then back to me.

"Of course," I say brightly. He doesn't ask me to elaborate, and I don't plan to. The last thing I need is to remind him that my brother thinks he still has to take care of me.

"Are you hungry?" Monroe asks him, breaking our staring contest. I quickly pick up my slice of pizza and take a bite as she continues, "Apparently, Forrest bought one for each of us and one for those who aren't stuffed from the first."

"Did I hear pizza?" Lachlan asks. He comes walking into the kitchen holding two six-packs of Smirnoff Raspberry. He sets them on the corner of the island, pulls one out, twists the cap, and hands it to me before he repeats the process of handing one to Monroe.

"Take it easy," Forrest warns. He's got the overprotective big brother look down to a science.

"You do realize we've been away at college, right?" Monroe challenges him.

"I don't want to hear about it. You two are only allowed to drink when you're with one of us." He waves his hand around the room, and that's when I realize that Legend and Maddox are also here.

"We're big girls," Monroe tells him. "Do you need me to show you?" She stands from her stool and saunters to where my brother stands on the other side of the kitchen island. She places her hand on his shoulder and lightly runs her fingers down his arm. I bite down on the inside of my cheek to keep from laughing.

"Monroe." There's warning in Forrest's tone, but that doesn't stop my best friend.

"Forrest," she purrs. Yes, she purrs and continues on with the slow trek of her hand sliding down his arm.

"He's about to blow a gasket." Legend laughs as he swoops in and snags Monroe around the waist, hoisting her up on his shoulders and running out of the kitchen. Their combined laughter leaves a trail behind them.

"She's like a sister," Forrest says, his eyes holding mine.

I lose my battle with my laughter as I hold my hands in the air defensively. "Hey, I don't care who or what you do. Just know that if you hurt her, I'm gonna be pissed."

Forrest's gaze burns into mine. "You'd be good with me dating your best friend?" he asks. I can tell by the tone of his voice he's completely surprised by my response.

"I mean, do you ever really 'date?'" I ask, adding air quotations as I say the word date.

Forrest rolls his eyes. "You know what I mean, brat."

I shrug. "You're both consenting adults. What you decide to do or not do with one another isn't my business. However, she's my best friend and will continue to be, so if you decide to go there, just remember that she's still going to be around when you're done with her."

"What makes you think I'd be done with her?"

"I don't know for sure, but that's how it's going to be. She's my best friend and will always be." I can feel Roman's eyes on me. Not just his, but Lachlan and Maddox are watching me too. Legend and Monroe are still in the other room, laughing at whatever antics they're up to while I hold my brother's stare.

"I don't want Monroe," he says, his voice soft. "She's truly like a little sister to me. I don't see her that way."

I finally break his stare and move my eyes to the other guys. Maddox winks, Lachlan is grinning like he knows the secret to world hunger and doesn't plan on telling a soul. And then there's Roman. His green eyes are filled with something I can't name. His look is serious and one of contemplation.

"That goes for all of you as well, and that one." I nod toward Legend, who has his arm slung over Monroe's shoulders as they enter the room. She has her arm around his waist, and they're both smiling.

"What goes for me?" Legend asks.

"If any of you sleep with Monroe, you need to understand that she's here to stay."

"Ride or die." Monroe holds her hand up for a high-five, and I lean in and slap my hand against hers.

"Oh, is that an option?" Legend tugs Monroe a little closer to his chest. "You want to go a couple of rounds, Roe?" he asks her.

"Meh," she says, and the room erupts with laughter.

"Y'all better eat before this pizza gets cold." With that, I grab another slice and place it on a napkin and hand it off to Monroe before grabbing another for myself.

The guys all gather around and dig in. There are five of them and two of us, all placed around the kitchen island. Somehow, Roman ends up beside me. His arm brushes mine every time he reaches for another slice or for his beer. My body is on high alert just being close to him, but the constant brush of his arm has me squirming in my seat.

"So, one more year?" Maddox asks as he wipes his mouth, tossing his napkin into Forrest's empty pizza box.

"Yes."

"I'm ready to be done," Monroe announces.

"You and me both."

"You're moving back home, right?" Lachlan asks. "Both of you are coming back to Ashby, right?"

I nod. "That was the plan. I've already got some feelers out for jobs. You do too, right?" I ask Monroe.

"Yeah, that would be the ideal situation. We're only a twenty-minute drive to Nashville. We can still live here and make that commute easy enough."

"That's what I was thinking too. Of course, closer to home is always good."

"Unless we meet men to sweep us off our feet, and we'll end up moving wherever they're going." She winks at me, and I have to fight from rolling my eyes. She's trying to get a rise out of... well, all of them would be my guess.

"Let's not start talking crazy," Forrest tells her.

"You know it's a possibility. She's going to get married and maybe even move away one day. There's not much... variety in this small town."

"You're both too young to be thinking about marriage." Forrest scowls.

"We're two adult women who are not too young to talk about anything." There's an undercurrent of innuendo in her tone.

"You can't even legally drink," Forrest fires back at her.

"No, but we can serve our country, we can vote, we can live on our own, have sex and babies, and a host of other things. In the eyes of the law, we are adults."

I cringe and sink onto the stool. This is not how I envisioned this conversation going. I get what she's trying to do. She's trying to make a point that the difference in years between us shouldn't matter to Roman, but I'm worried it will have the opposite effect.

I chance a look to my right, where he stands to find his eyes on me. I hold his stare until it becomes too much, too intense, and I have to look away. I can't help but wonder what he would do if I kissed him. Right here. Right now. In front of everyone around us. Would he kiss me back? I've asked myself that question countless times over the years, but the yearning to feel his lips on mine has never been this strong.

"No. Nope. Not happening." Forrest steps back and grabs another beer from the refrigerator. "We are not talking about either of you getting married and having babies. Maybe in, like, ten or fifteen years from now." He twists off the cap of his beer and takes a long pull.

"You're delusional if you think either of us will wait ten to fifteen years. We don't want to be single for the rest of our lives. We want to find someone to love," Monroe says, and I can practically see the hearts in her eyes as she glances at me, then at Roman.

Her declaration isn't for herself. Sure, she wants to be married and have kids one day, but she knows that for me if I had a choice, that man, the one to change my last name and give me babies, would be Roman. Not this year or even next, but as my best friend, she knows what's in my heart.

I give her a soft smile before sliding off my stool and starting to clean up.

ROMAN 5

THE CHILL OF THE NIGHT air is masked by the roaring fire. I pretend to be enthralled by the flames, but I'm not. It's the only way I can keep my eyes off her. Emerson is sitting diagonally from me in a lawn chair. Her bare legs are folded beneath her, and the oversized Everlasting Ink sweatshirt she wears is stretched over them to help protect her from the cold.

"We should play truth or dare," Monroe suggests.

"Bet," Legend says, leaning forward in his chair.

"I'm in," Maddox agrees.

"You know I love me a good game of truth or dare," Lachlan says, rubbing his hands together with glee.

"Are we teenagers?" Forrest asks.

"We are grown adults who can do whatever the hell we want," Monroe sasses him.

Forrest grins as he raises his hands in defense. "Retract the claws, woman. Fine, we can play." He shrugs as if it's no big deal, and I groan. I was hoping Forrest would shut this down. As protective as he is of Emerson and even Monroe, I was certain he would.

"I'll go first," Monroe announces, and none of us argue.

It's not lost on me that Emerson and I are the only ones who didn't agree to this, but no one seems to care. I guess we didn't outwardly object either.

"All right," Monroe says, tapping her index finger against her chin. She's sitting in a chair next to Emerson, dressed similarly. Her legs, too, are covered by an oversized sweatshirt. This one has the name of their college on it, and it's way too big to be her own. "Lachlan." Monroe grins. "Truth or dare?"

"Truth," Lachlan answers.

"If you had to kiss one person sitting around this fire, who would you choose?"

"Come on!" Forrest protests.

"Chill out, Huntley," Monroe scolds him. "This is all in good fun. We're all friends here and adults."

Forrest points at Emerson. "My little sister." He then points that same finger at Monroe. "Pseudo little sister," he grumbles.

"Not my sisters, bro." Lachlan laughs. I can't see Forrest's face, but I imagine he's glaring at our friend. "All right, I'm going to have to go with... Legend," Lachlan says, barely containing his laughter. "Look at those plump lips. Totally kissable. All the ladies are raging about it."

"Right?" Monroe chimes in.

"My turn. Monroe, truth or dare?"

"Dare." Monroe smirks.

"I dare you to kiss Legend," Lachlan says immediately.

"Oh, I'll give you a full report." She winks as she stands, stretching out her legs. She moves to stand in front of Legend. He watches her like a lion and its prey as she leans over, places her hands on his shoulders, and presses her lips to his.

It's not just a peck on the lips. This is more, and if the way Legend slides his hand behind her neck, holding her close is any indication, they might be at it for a minute.

I avert my gaze, my eyes roaming over Emerson to find her watching me. She licks her lips, and my cock twitches in my jeans. Fuck me, why does this woman, the one person who's off limits, have this kind of effect on me?

"Damn!" Maddox shouts.

Monroe stands to her full height and turns to look at Lachlan. "Definitely worth the hype." She grins as she saunters back to her chair, tucking her legs back under her and stretching the hoodie over them to keep her warm.

I can't help but crack a smile when I see the shocked look on Legend's face. He wasn't expecting Monroe to lay one on him like that, but he should have. That girl is a spitfire if I've ever seen one.

"Our boy needs a minute," Lachlan teases.

Legend clears his throat. "Forrest, truth or dare?"

"Truth." Forrest is quick to answer.

"Have you ever sent a dick pic?"

"Yep," Forrest says, lifting his beer to his lips.

"Forrest!" Emerson scolds her brother, but she's laughing, so it's not the lashing I'm sure she intended for it to be.

"She asked for it," he explains.

"Nothing wrong with a good dick pic," Monroe chimes in.

Like I said, spitfire.

"Maddox, truth or dare?" Forrest asks, continuing on with the game.

"Truth."

"Yell the first word that comes to your mind."

"Pussy!" Maddox calls out, and we all crack up laughing.

"Is that all you think about?" Emerson asks him.

"Yes." He nods, and there's not a single ounce of hesitation in his answer. "Emerson, truth or dare?" Maddox asks, and I sit up straighter in my chair. Leaning forward, I rest my elbows on my knees, and for the first time tonight, it's okay to keep my eyes trained on her.

"Dare." She grins.

Fuck.

Maddox takes his time, looking around the fire at each of us before he turns his attention back to Emerson. "I dare you to give Roman a lap dance for a full minute."

My body freezes. I want to scream out no, that I can't handle that. I can't handle that delicious body of hers taunting me in front of them. In front of her brother, my lips remain sealed.

"Easy," Emerson says, standing.

"I can't watch this." Forrest stands as well. "Anyone need a beer?" Legend and Lachlan raise their hands while the rest of us decline. He stalks off toward the house, and it's not until the patio door opens and closes, do Emerson's eyes meet mine.

"Who's got the music?" Emerson asks, her gaze still locked with mine.

"I got you," Maddox tells her.

I assume he's tugging his phone out of his pocket to queue up some music, but I can't be sure because I can't take my eyes off the beauty who's taking small, calculated steps toward me. When she reaches me, she smiles, and I know with that one look, I'm fucked.

On instinct, I widen my legs, allowing her room to step between them. My hands itch to grip her hips and pull her onto my lap, but instead, I grasp the arms of the chair I'm sitting in. I can do this. I can resist this woman. I *have* to resist her.

"Ready, Em?" Maddox asks.

"I'm ready," she calls back, never taking her eyes off mine.

When "Freak Me" by Silk starts to play, I bite down on my cheek. It's been years since I've heard this song, and I'll give Maddox credit. It's perfect for this moment. For the way I feel about her.

Panic rises in my chest. Does he know I want her? I don't have time to dwell on it when she starts to seductively dance for me. She sways her hips in a slow, seductive roll as she lifts her arms in the air.

The oversized sweatshirt hides her body, but that's okay. I know what lies beneath, pure sin. My eyes roam over every inch of her until I reach her gaze. She's watching me intently. The song continues to play, but I barely hear it as she turns. She thrusts her hips back, and her ass makes contact with my lap. I'm hard as steel, and with the way she grinds against me, she likes it. I continue to clutch the arms of the chair, but my patience is wearing thin. I want to hold her hips and thrust up into her. However, I remain still as she continues to have her way with me.

This is the longest sixty seconds of my life.

"Time!" Maddox calls, and the cheers erupt as the music cuts off.

Emerson stands to her full height and makes her way back to her chair without a second glance at me. She tucks her legs back beneath her, but she doesn't drag her hoodie back over her for warmth. I'm burning up with desire for her, and I can only hope that she's just as affected. I shouldn't think that way. I shouldn't want her to feel anything, but the asshole in me craves the knowledge like a bee craves honey.

"Good, I missed it," Forrest says, passing out the beers to those who wanted one and taking his seat. "I think we've had enough truth or dare for one night," he says.

"I have a client in the morning, so I need to jet," Maddox says, standing.

"You good to drive?" Monroe asks him.

"Yeah, it's been a few hours, and I only had two."

"I'm out too," Lachlan says, and Legend stands with him.

"You're my ride," Legend reminds us.

"You good to drive?" Monroe repeats her previous question.

"We're good. Didn't touch the new one." He points to the unopened bottle of beer sitting in the cupholder of his chair. "It's been hours since I had one."

"What about you, Roe? You good?" Legend asks her.

"I'm staying here tonight, but yeah, I'm good." She offers him a smile.

"Catch you all later," they say as the three of them make their way around the side of the house to leave.

"Rome?" Emerson's sweet voice calls out to me. "How about you? Are you good to drive?"

I want to say no. I wish that I'd had more than that one single beer with dinner so I would have an excuse to stay. Not that anything would happen, but I'd be here with her to look out for her. I know that she's had four of her wine coolers. Yes, I counted, and no, I don't give a fuck that it's none of my business. "I'm good. Just had one with dinner."

"I gotta piss. Are you two coming inside?" Forrest asks the girls.

"In a little while," Monroe answers.

"Yeah, I think we'll let the fire burn down a little more," Emerson adds.

Forrest holds his fist out for me. "See you," he says before turning and disappearing into the house.

The quiet surrounds us. I should get up and leave, but I can't make myself commit to the act. All I want to do is sit out here in her presence until she's ready for bed. Time passes as we make idle chitchat. They talk about being excited about their final year of college and moving back home. I comment where appropriate, adding myself to their conversation.

"I think I'm going to head in." Monroe yawns, and it's fake as fuck. "I'm taking the guest room," she tells Emerson. She stands and gives her friend a hug and then does the same to me. "Be good to her," she whispers in my ear before she, too, disappears inside. Her words don't surprise me. These two are two halves of a whole. I wasn't sure if she knew about our night, but now I'm certain Emerson told her.

The silence surrounds us. I'm sitting off in the shadows of the fire to the right of the back door. It would take someone walking outside a few moments to notice me. "Come sit next to me." I'm pushing for trouble, knowing she's pure temptation, but she's been too far away all damn night. I just want her close. I can keep my hands to myself.

Maybe.

Emerson doesn't hesitate to stand and walk around the fire. She grabs the chair her brother was sitting in and moves it closer before curling up in a ball.

"Are you cold?" I ask. I'm a dick. I should let her go inside.

"Nah, just preventive," she says, pointing to the sweatshirt pulled over her knees.

"Have you ever given a lap dance like that before?" The question is out before I can think better of it.

"Yeah, we play truth or dare back at school a lot. That's always one of the dares the guys make." There's humor in her voice, but it does nothing to quell the rage I'm feeling. The thought of her dancing like that for someone who's not me has me wanting to punch the nameless, faceless bastard in the face.

"Hey." She reaches over and places her hand on my arm. "It's always just in fun. Nothing more, nothing less."

"Be careful," I grit out. "If anyone tries anything, you tell me."

She smiles softly. "I'm a big girl, Rome. I can handle it."

"You don't have to handle it. One phone call, baby girl"—I point to my chest—"I'm there."

She climbs to her knees, leans over her chair into mine, and presses her lips to my cheek. "I have a big brother, Roman. I don't need another."

"Trust me. I know we're not related." My voice is low and gravelly. If she only knew the thoughts I have of her, she would know her statement is irrelevant.

"Why the concern?"

She's baiting me, and I'm letting her. "Because the thought of someone else touching you boils my blood." I close my eyes, tilting my head back. The words are out there, and I can't take them back.

"Who's allowed to touch me, Rome?"

"No one."

"That's hardly fair. Am I allowed to tell you that no one is allowed to touch you?"

Opening my eyes, I turn my head to look at her. "There is no one, Em. Not since that night, and hell, I might as well go for broke and put it all out there. Not since long before that night."

"Why?" The word is whispered, but I hear it loud and clear.

"You know why."

"Tell me anyway."

Sitting forward, I turn sideways, giving her my full attention. Her long brown hair is pulled up in a messy knot on the top of her head. Loose tendrils hang down, and she looks so damn sexy. If I confess, that changes things. I can feel it deep in my bones. If I tell her that she's all I can think about, all I dream about, that changes this. Whatever *this* is.

"You."

She sucks in a sharp breath, and there's nothing I want more than to pull her onto my lap and kiss her. But I can't. *We* can't.

"Rome."

"You're sexy as fuck," I tell her. Now that I've started talking, I can't seem to shut the hell up.

"That night—" She pauses, collecting her thoughts. "When you came into my room."

"What about it?"

"Why did you?"

"Because I wanted you."

"You didn't even touch me." If I'm not mistaken, there's hurt in her tone.

"You're my best friend's little sister, Em. I'm ten years older than you. I'm not good for you."

"Isn't that my choice to make?"

"No." I shake my head. "We can't do this."

"You don't want me anymore?" The question tugs at something hidden inside my chest.

"I want you," I rasp.

"You want me, but you don't want me? I'm confused, Roman. You're going to need to spell this out for me. You tell me that you don't think of anyone but me, that there has been no one, but the next breath, you're telling me that we can't do this. Tell me why?"

"Because it's wrong. Forrest is one of my best friends, and you're ten years younger than me."

Why can't she see that? No matter how bright this flame is that burns between us, we can't act on it.

"I'm not hearing anything that convinces me."

"That night, I let my desire get the better of me. I never should have slipped into your room, but when I heard you—" I swallow hard. "I had to, baby girl."

"So you used me?"

"No." My voice is hard. "You were playing with your pussy, and you said my name, Em. My. Fucking. Name." I pause, getting my emotions under control. "You were all I'd been thinking about, and then when I passed by your door and you called out for me, there was nothing and no one on this earth that could have kept me standing in that hallway."

"Not even my brother?" she challenges.

"I— Fuck, Em, I don't think so. I knew it was wrong, but I needed to see you."

"You touched yourself."

I nod. We were both there that night. There is no need to spell it out. Besides, I don't need to. Every second plays on repeat in my mind like a damn commercial.

"I wanted to touch you."

Fuck me. I should have left when the others did.

"I wanted you to touch me."

I can feel my control slipping.

"I wanted that too." My confession hangs between us. It's heavy, like a muggy afternoon. I wanted to touch her. I wanted to fucking devour her.

I still want to touch her.

I *still* want to devour her.

"Show me."

Slowly, I shake my head. "I can't."

Doesn't she see how hard this is for me? Can she not see how twisted up inside I am over needing her? She's right here, and I can't do a single fucking thing about it.

"You can."

"Dammit, Emerson. I fucking can't."

"Why?"

"Why?" I laugh humorlessly. Leaning over, I bring my face mere inches from hers. Unable to resist, I cradle her face in the palm of my hand. "Because once I start, I'll never be able to stop."

"Then don't stop."

"Fuck, you are a dangerous kind of temptation."

"I don't want to tempt you, Rome. I just want to be with you." She leans into my hand, and I know I have to get up and walk away. If I don't, I'm going to do something that will ruin my friendship with her brother. I should say that I'll do something that I regret, but I know with everything that I am, that I would never, *will* never, regret any moment shared with her.

Knowing that it's wrong but unable to resist, I lean in and press my lips to her forehead. "The fire's burned out, and it's cold out here. Let's get you inside." I stand and offer her my hand, which she takes. I lace our fingers together and lead her to the back door. "Lock up behind me."

"Rome."

This time it's both of my hands that cup her cheeks. I tilt her head up so that she's looking at me. "If there was ever someone that I would risk it all for, it would be you." I kiss her forehead one more time before dropping my hands and stepping away. "Go on inside."

I can see the sadness in her eyes, and if I'm not mistaken, a little anger too. I expect her to fight me, but she does as I ask, stepping inside. She locks the door and turns out the lights. I stand here staring through the patio door into the darkness of the kitchen, wishing like hell that I was on the other side, following her to her room.

EMERSON

THE WEEKS ARE FLYING BY. It's been three since the bonfire celebration of me being home for the summer. It's also been three weeks since Roman and I have barely said more than a few words to one another. If it's not about the shop, we don't discuss it.

It's driving me insane.

He's stubborn and sexy, and did I say stubborn? I don't know how to get through to him. What this is between us should be just that—between us. My brother shouldn't even factor in. We're both adults and can make our own choices. I know that Forrest is protective, but he has to let me live my life.

I understand that they're best friends, but at the end of the day, we have to live for ourselves. If growing up with two alcoholics as parents has taught me anything, it's that. I used to stress and worry about them constantly, but they never spared me another thought. I'm not saying that you shouldn't care about others, but you have to do what's best for you.

What if what's best for Roman and myself is us being together?

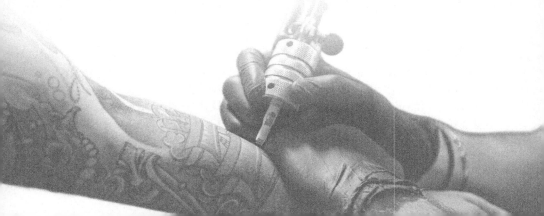

"I'm out," my brother says, walking up to the desk, cell phone and keys in hand. "You coming straight home after work?"

"I'm not sure yet. I might swing by Monroe's. We talked about taking a late-night swim."

"She's welcome to swim at our place. I bought that house partially because it had a pool for you." He grins.

"I know. I'll let you know where I end up." I love my big brother and all that he's done to take care of me and help me with a car, college, and a safe place to live. I feel guilt creeping in that I'm lusting after his best friend. I understand how Roman feels, but I still believe we can make our own choices.

"Be safe." He leans in and gives me a hug, and then he's out the door.

The shop is quieter than usual today, with only two of the guys here now that Forrest is gone. Legend is working on a back piece that will take up the remainder of his day, and Roman is starting a sleeve for a client that will take several sessions. He has nothing on his books after this, so it's a slow afternoon for me.

I don't mind. It gives me time to clean and work on getting things more organized. It's also mid-June, so I need to get an ad posted for my replacement. I leave for school in August, and it would be nice if we could find someone soon so that I can get them trained and know that I'm leaving the guys in good hands.

With the quiet of the shop, I'm able to clean the entire break room and sweep the lobby. I'll wait to mop until after all the clients are gone. I even went as far as cleaning out the refrigerator. The shelves are sparkling, and all the science experiments the guys were growing have been tossed into the trash.

I'm bending over, grabbing more appointment cards from the storage shelf behind the desk, when the chime on the door rings. I finish my task and stand to find a man standing at the counter. "Welcome to Everlasting Ink. How can I help you?"

"I came in for some ink, but leaving with you might be a better option." He rakes his eyes over my body.

I keep a polite smile on my face, even though I'd love nothing more than to tell this asshole to kick rocks and find a different tattoo studio. However, instead, I remain cordial and smile. "I'm afraid that's not possible. Do you have an artist here that you work with?"

"You." This time his eyes travel to my tits and stay there.

"If you're here for a tattoo, we can talk about that. Anything else, I'm going to have to ask you to leave." My voice is firm, and the nice girl persona has been dropped. I'm over this asshole.

"Come on, sweet thang, let's go grab a drink." He reaches over the counter as if he's going to touch me, but pulls his hand back.

The words are barely out of his mouth when I feel the heat at my back, and two strong arms cage me in as Roman braces his hands on the counter. "Hey, baby girl," he says huskily.

I take a step back, bringing me closer to Roman. "Hey, Rome." He wraps one strong arm around my waist, and the other falls to his side.

"What can I do for you?" Roman asks the man, keeping his hold on me.

"I was just telling the lady here I'd like some ink." The guy stands taller, not that he has any chance of going up against Roman.

"Ink, you say?" Roman asks.

"Yeah, looking to get my Harley on my bicep." He points to his bare bicep thanks to his sleeveless T-shirt.

"I hear there's a good shop across town." Roman's words are said casually, but I can feel the tension in his body.

"Heard this place was the best," the man says. His eyes drop to my tits again. "Lots of... nice help." He cackles but starts to cough. Looks like Mr. Asshole needs to lay off the cigarettes.

"You're right," Roman tells him. "We are the best." The hand that's not wrapped around me points to the wall with all the awards the guys have won over the years.

"That's why I'm here," the guy replies, his eyes again flashing to me.

"I didn't catch your name." I can tell by the tone of Roman's voice and the way his body stiffens that he's about to lose his patience.

"Name's Jerry." Asshole, I mean Jerry, thrusts his hand out toward Roman, who doesn't move to shake his hand.

"Jerry, this is how this is going to go. You're going to turn around and walk out of my shop. If I see you in here again, I'll call the police and have you escorted. If I have to file a restraining order, I will."

"The fuck?" Jerry replies, his voice rising. "Do you treat all of your customers like this?" he asks.

"No. We cater to our clients, but those clients respect our employees."

"Come on, man. She's a dime piece," he says, his eyes again taking me in.

"She's a beautiful woman, and she's mine. If I see you looking at her, hell, if I hear you're thinking about her, you and I are going to have problems."

"It's a free country. I can look."

"You. Will. Not. Look. At. Her," Roman grits out. His grip on my waist tightens.

I lean into him and place my hand over his arm that's wrapped around me. Immediately, some of the tension eases in his hold. I don't say a word, deciding to let him handle it on his own.

"She's not worth it," Jerry sneers as he turns and rushes out the door.

I remain standing, my body pressed tightly against his, and wait. I can feel the rapid rise and fall of Roman's chest with each breath. My heart is racing, not because of the incident. Jerry isn't the first asshole to hit on me, and I'm sure he won't be the last. No, my heart feels like it could explode because of the way he's holding me. I can't tell you how many times I've wished for this to happen. I just wish it was under different circumstances.

"Rome?" I ask hesitantly.

He buries his face in my neck, and I shiver at the contact as his hot breath hits my skin. My eyes drift closed as I take in the moment. I wish more than anything that this was us. That I really was his and that this embrace was out of the love that we share, not his anger at a man who was being rude.

Voices carry from Legend's room, and Roman pulls away. "If he comes back, you tell me." His green eyes bore into mine.

"I had it handled." I should just say thank you, but I truly did have it handled. The guy was rude, but he wasn't hurting me.

"Emerson."

"Roman."

He steps forward and moves my hair behind my shoulder. "If he comes back, you come and get me. If I'm not here, you get one of the guys. He's not welcome here."

"You can't run off every customer. That's rude."

"He was being inappropriate with you. I won't stand for that, and you know damn well that the rest of the guys would back me up on that."

"Do you think that's the first time I've had to deal with an inappropriate creep like that?"

His jaw clenches. "Not here."

"Whatever." I roll my eyes and turn away from him. It's a mere few seconds before I feel the heat of his body pressed against me for the second time.

"Did you roll your eyes at me?" he asks. This time, instead of burying his face in my neck, he kisses me there. It's brief and just a soft peck, but I felt it. Heat pools between my thighs. I tilt my head to give him access, but he takes it no further. I want to scream and yell and demand that he give in to this. That he gives into us, but I keep my thoughts to myself. The stubborn ass won't listen, so there's no point in holding my breath. I'm going to have to find new ways to tempt him.

I make a mental note to brainstorm with Monroe later. My best friend is team Emerson and Roman, so I know she'll be happy to toss out what I'm sure will be ridiculous, over-the-top ideas, but skating around each other at work isn't working.

It's doing nothing to diminish the chemistry between us.

I still want him.

He still wants me.

We're at an impasse.

"Don't you have a client to get back to?" It takes acting skills I never knew I possessed to pretend as if his touch doesn't affect me.

"Do you know what I want to do to that sassy mouth of yours?"

"Show me." My words bring him back to the present, and he pulls away.

"I mean it, Emerson. If he comes in again, you get one of us and let us handle it."

"You're the boss," I say, waving him off.

He disappears back into his room. I hear him asking his client if he's ready to go again, and I slump against the counter. I can still feel his front pressed to my back and his arms wrapped around me. I can feel the ghost of his kiss on my neck, and it makes me want to scream in frustration. Reaching for my phone, I text Monroe.

Me: I need a plan.

Monroe: For?

Me: Roman.

Monroe: Finally. I have so many ideas.

I chuckle at her reply. I expect nothing less from my best friend.

Me: My place or yours after work?

Monroe: Mine. We can't risk being overheard.

Monroe: Just stay here tonight.

Me: I'll run home and grab a few things. I should be there by eight-ish.

Monroe: I'll start making a list.

I laugh as I place my phone face down on the counter and get back to work.

At fifteen minutes after eight, I'm pulling into Monroe's driveway. I'm barely out of my car when the front door opens, and she waves me inside.

"How was your day, dear?" she asks sweetly, making me laugh.

"I have so much to tell you."

"Well, before you start, Mom made this taco hashbrown stuff in the Crock-Pot. I don't know what all is in it, but it's so freaking good. Go change into your suit. I'll make you a bowl and meet you outside at the pool."

"Thanks, Roe." I give her a hug.

"What are besties for?" She heads toward the kitchen while I make my way up to get changed in the spare room I use when I stay over.

"Here." Monroe hands me a bowl of something that smells fabulous as I take the lounger next to hers. "Tell me what happened."

So, that's what I do. In between scarfing down the delicious dinner, I tell her about my day and Roman going all protective.

"He wants you."

"I know!" I place my empty bowl on the table next to me and take a drink of water. "He told me so, but he's not doing anything about it. Monroe, he called me his. I mean, I know he was just saying it to get his point across to the creepy guy who was leering at me, but my heart doesn't know that." I reach up to rub my chest. "I want to be his."

"So we need to step up our game."

"We?"

She waves her hand between us. "We. Best friends, package deal. No exceptions."

I smile and laugh. "I love you."

"Love you too. Now, I think we should start with how you dress at work."

"What's wrong with how I dress for work?"

"Nothing, but there are a few things that you can do to entice him. You know, like choosing the jeans that look like they've been painted on, or the shorts that are a little too short, oh, and low-cut shirts and tank tops. Oh, and I think you should start wearing your hair up more. He kisses your neck, and when he sees it, that's all that he will be able to think about."

"So you want me to dress more provocatively? That should be great for all the creeps that come into the shop."

"You have five big brothers. Okay, make that four big brothers and one Alphahole who's too damn stubborn to take what he wants from you. Not a single one of them will let you get hurt."

"It's not that I'm worried about getting hurt. I just don't want to give them more ammunition."

"It won't be forever. My guess is that Roman will crack sooner rather than later."

"I don't want to manipulate him, Roe."

"It's not manipulation. Consider it an incentive."

"Either way, I just want to be me. I want to dress how I want to dress, and if that's not enough, then I'll just have to find a way to move on from him."

"I made a list on my phone, but I'm afraid you're going to shoot them all down." She laughs.

"Let's hear them."

"Seduce him, lock him in his room and strip for him, show up at his house naked in nothing but a trench coat, you know, things like that." She barely contains her laughter.

"I can't do any of that, Monroe!" I laugh as well.

"Just be you, Emerson. He wants you. He's admitted as much. He's going to crack. You just have to be patient."

"I know. There's a part of me that wants to wait for him forever. Then there's another part that says I deserve better. That I shouldn't just be ready and willing when he finally pulls his head out of his ass."

"Maybe so. You're the only one who can decide that. I think you owe it to yourself to give this a little time. The two of you shared a hot moment, and then you left to go back to school. It's only been a few weeks since you've been home. Rome wasn't built in a day." She winks.

"No, he was not."

"That's not what I meant, but it does fit."

I think about what she said, and I know she's right. I need to give this time. "I'll give it the summer," I tell her. "If he's not on board with whatever this is between us by then, I'll know it's time for me to move on."

"Maybe moving on is what needs to happen for him to see what he's losing?"

"Possibly. I guess if he's not over this 'we can't be together' nonsense by the time we head back to school, we'll find out."

"Come on, let's take a swim."

I nod my agreement, and we make our way to the pool.

"What about you? I know you were talking to Henry. Have the two of you caught up since we've been home for the summer?"

"Nah, he was in it for the sex. Which I didn't give him. It's his loss." She shrugs.

"You deserve better," I tell her.

"So do you." She gives me a pointed look.

"I know I do. I'm not going to wait for him forever. He's either going to decide I'm worth the risk, or I'm not. It's going to hurt because he's been my crush for years, but I don't want to play this game. Not with him. Not with anyone."

"Whatever happens, I'll be here."

"Same," I tell her.

We spend the rest of the night talking about anything and everything. We both want to move home once we graduate, so we've been tossing around the idea of getting an apartment together here in Ashby. I want to be close to my brother and even the guys. No matter what does or doesn't happen with Roman, he's still always been a huge part of my life. I don't want that to change.

Monroe wants to stay around Ashby too. She's close with her parents and her grandma, and she knows that time isn't promised and wants to be near them. So we make plans for our future. In the back of my mind, there's this hope that my path will change and include Roman, but if not, that's okay. *I'll* be okay.

Time heals broken hearts. At least that's the saying, and I send up a silent prayer that it's the truth.

ROMAN 7

"WHAT'S BEEN GOING ON WITH you lately?" Forrest asks.

We're sitting on his back deck, watching Monroe, Emerson, Lachlan, and Maddox play a game of chicken in the pool. Legend is floating on an inner tube that looks like a donut, being the referee. At least he's supposed to be. I think he's asleep.

"What do you mean?" I keep my eyes on the pool. Thankfully, I'm still wearing sunglasses to hide who is holding my attention. The sun is starting to set, so that won't be the case much longer.

"You've been quiet, not going out as much."

I knew this conversation was coming with one, if not all, my friends. "Just not feeling it." I can't exactly tell him I jacked off while I watched his little sister getting herself off at the same time, and now she's all I can think about. I need to find a way to let this obsession with her go.

Okay, so I'm not obsessed with her in the literal sense, but she is all that I think about and dream about, and yeah, I've not been going out because I have no interest to. Not if Emerson isn't going to be there. I'm very aware I'm crossing the best friend no-go zone, but at least I haven't taken things too far.

"Dry spell." He nods as if he knows the feeling.

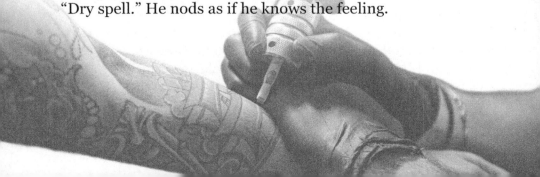

"You've been staying in a lot lately too." It's a weak attempt to take the heat off me.

"Yeah," he agrees. "When Em is home, I try to. She's going to be leaving to go back to school at the end of the summer. Fuck, that's just mere weeks away, and I want to spend time with her." He releases a heavy sigh. "Our parents haven't even reached out to her. To either of us. We haven't seen or spoken to them since the day I picked her up to move her in with me. I'm all she has, and I want her to feel loved and wanted."

My chest tightens when I think about Emerson not feeling those emotions. I want that for her just as badly as Forrest does. "Makes sense," I finally say. As his best friend, I needed to reply. As the man who can't stop thinking about his sister, I just want to be the one to make her feel that way.

"I need a beer," Lachlan says as he dumps Emerson into the pool. She sputters with laughter as she surfaces. "Rome! Take over for me while I sit this one out." He shakes his head, and water flies everywhere.

"Come on!" Emerson yells at me. "We're undefeated. I'm a sure thing."

Something tells me we're not just talking about a game of chicken in the pool. "You better stick with Lach," I call back to her. Her face drops for a few seconds, but she quickly masks her disappointment.

"Oh, I get it," Maddox calls out. "You're scared."

Forrest chuckles from his seat next to mine while Lachlan takes the one next to him. "They're never going to let you live it down, saying you were too scared to get beat if you don't go out there."

"Legend can do it."

"Nah, he's toasted," Lachlan explains. "He's been hitting that bottle of Crown since he got here. All he can do is float." He laughs.

I should be excited that I get to have my hands on her, and I am, but I don't know if I can hide how much I want her. I guess my only saving grace is that I'll be in the water, so I'll be able to hide my body's reaction to her. We've played this game hundreds of times in years past. This won't be the first time Emerson and I are on the same side. It will, however, be the first time since I realized she's not a little girl anymore. Not even close.

Slowly, I climb from my chair, pull my phone and keys out of my pocket, toss them on the ground, and make my way to the pool. Emerson watches me the entire time. She's smiling widely, and I can't stop the corner of my mouth from lifting as well. That's the effect this woman has on me.

Standing at the deep end, I dive in, letting the water cool my heated skin. I'm one of those people who can open their eyes when they swim underwater, so that's what I do. I swim toward Emerson and sneak up behind her, wrapping my arms around her legs. I stand with her, laughing, as she tries to fight her way out of my hold. She's wiggling so much that she manages to turn in my arms so that we're now facing one another.

She's laughing and smiling down at me, and my chest constricts. Carefully, I let her slide down my body and back into the water. She hisses in a sharp breath when she feels the evidence of what having her wet, nearly naked body against mine does to me.

She turns to face Monroe, and they talk shit about who's going to win. I'm standing far enough away from her that no one will notice, so I dip down under the water to my shoulders and reach out, placing my hands on her hips just below the surface.

"You're going down, Huntley," Monroe taunts.

Emerson looks over her shoulder at me. "Rome won't let me down."

That statement, although directed at her best friend regarding the game, does something to me. I know it has a double meaning, and I'll always be there for her, but I can't be there for her the way we both wish I could. Forrest and the guys, we've been tight since kindergarten. I can't screw that up by breaking the bro code and dating his little sister.

I just can't.

"Let's do this!" Maddox dips down underwater to allow Monroe to climb onto his shoulders.

I stand and move in close to Emerson, while she turns to face me. "Ready, baby girl?" I ask softly. My words are for her ears only. Legend is passed out on his donut, and Monroe and Maddox are too busy laughing as she tries to get on his shoulders to care what we're doing, and the others are too far away to hear.

"For you? Always." She flashes me a saucy grin before moving to stand behind me. She places her hands on my shoulders, and I dip below the surface of the water, letting her climb on. She taps my head once she's settled, letting me know she's ready for me to stand. Thankfully, my waist is still below the water.

We repeat this process a handful of times over the next hour. Before we know it, Forrest is calling out that it's time to eat. I stay in the pool longer than the others, because I need a minute. I push all thoughts of Emerson out of my mind, willing my cock to cooperate. When I'm finally presentable, I climb out of the pool and grab a towel, and make myself a plate.

"Shots!" Forrest calls, and everyone cheers. Everyone except for me, that is. I've had three beers since dinner. Once I saw how fast Emerson and Monroe were tossing back shots, I decided it was time for me to stop drinking. The sudden urgency to take care of her, to make sure she's okay, hits me like a ton of bricks. It makes no sense, because she's safe here. Even if all five of us guys were passed out cold, she would be safe. Yet, here I am still sipping on a bottle of water.

"You might want to slow down," I tell the group. I'm talking to all of them.

"Party pooper." Monroe sticks her tongue out at me as she wobbles on her stool. Legend, having caught his second wind, is there to wrap his arms around her. She plants a sloppy kiss on his cheek in thanks and takes the shot glass Forrest offers her.

"You sure you don't want in, Ro?" Maddox laughs. "We have two Roes." He bends over at the waist, holding his stomach. Everyone joins him. Well, everyone but me. They're all toasted, and I could tell them the sky was black, and they'd think it was hilarious. I'm not laughing at the two Roes comment, but I am fighting a smile at this drunken group. It might be fun for me to be the only sober one. Boy, am I going to have some stories to tell?

"He's not Ro. He's Rome," Emerson pipes up. "This is Roe." She leans over to give her friend a one-armed hug, and teeters on her stool. I shoot to my feet, and I'm there in time to catch her before she falls. She peers up at me under long lashes. Her eyes are bloodshot, both from the alcohol and the chlorine in the pool. I can tell she wants to say something, but even in her drunken state, she realizes it's not a good idea. Not with our friends and her brother within earshot.

"You good?" I ask her.

"Yeah. Yep. Yepper." She bobs her head.

"You sure?" I ask, not bothering to hide my smile.

She reaches out and places her hands on my chest, patting lightly. "I'm good, big guy."

Slowly, I step away from her, and her hands fall back to her sides. She blinks a few times and then focuses on the shot glass in front of her. She lifts it to her lips.

"Maybe you should skip this one," I tell her.

"What? No, It's In—Inde—it's that day." She laughs.

"It's firecracker day," Monroe offers helpfully.

"It's more than that." I know before I'm even finished, there is no point in arguing with them. Sober, they know exactly what Independence Day is. I know they're trashed and not thinking properly. I don't even know why I said it, other than to stand here next to her and keep talking.

"I can't feel my tongue," Lachlan says.

I glance over my shoulder and see him sprawled out on the couch. "Thank fuck we all agreed to stay here tonight," I mutter under my breath. Forrest is the only one of us who has a home big enough to house us all comfortably. That's why we always end up here. He bought this place as soon as he could afford to. He wanted Emerson to have a home where she felt like she had her own space and could live freely. Not one where she was hiding in a room the size of a crackerjack box from her parents, or staying locked in to avoid them.

The dull ache is back in my chest when I think about the life they both had growing up. I hate that for them.

I turn back to Emerson, pointing an index finger at her. "You stay there. I'm going to get Lachlan to bed."

"Are you going to put me to bed too?" she asks.

I lean in close, placing my lips to her ear. "Behave." Turning on my heel, I move toward Lachlan. "Come on, Lach." I help him stand and lead him upstairs to one of the spare rooms.

Forrest's house has four bedrooms, and a fully finished basement, so there are plenty of places for everyone. I get Lachlan settled in one of the twin beds in the spare bedroom, and head back downstairs. Maddox is slumped over the kitchen table, and I sigh. Maybe being the only sober one isn't as amusing as I thought it would be.

One by one, I help the rest of the guys. Maddox ends upstairs with Lachlan in the second twin bed. They're small, but better than trying to sleep on the couch. I guide Legend down to the basement and help Forrest to his first-floor master.

When I make it back to the kitchen, the girls are looking pretty haggard. "I need sleep," Monroe mumbles.

"You sleeping with Em?" I ask her.

"No. My room." She holds her hands up for me to pick her up, and I laugh. Bending, I toss her over my shoulder. She giggles as she bounces against my back on our way upstairs. I take her to the other room. The one she normally stays in. Part of me was hoping she would stay with Emerson for two reasons. It will keep me out of her room—not that I would take advantage of her drunken state—and two, I could stay in this room to listen for Emerson in case she needs something or gets sick. I should have taken Lachlan or Maddox to the basement. There's another bed down there, but that's too far away from her.

Looks like I'll be sleeping on the couch downstairs.

I get Monroe in her bed, and turn to step out of the room.

"Roman," she calls.

I stop and turn to look at her. The room is dark, but I can still make out her form lying in the bed. "Take care of her."

Something about her request rocks me as if I've been sucker punched. Of course I'll take care of her. I want to be the man to take care of her, but I fucking can't be. At least not the way I wish I could, but tonight, I can make sure she's okay. That's what Monroe is trying to tell me, but her words they bring forward a longing so deep I know it will never disappear.

"Always." I nod even though I'm sure she can't see me, and leave the door cracked slightly open. I tell myself I'm only worried about taking care of Emerson, but they're all my family. Even Monroe. She's always been there, and she's like a little sister to me. I'd do anything for any of them.

When I make it back downstairs, Emerson is no longer sitting at the island. My eyes scan the room, and I find her lying on the couch. I make my way to her and kneel. Lifting my hand, I push her hair back out of her eyes. "You okay, baby girl?"

"I drank too much."

I chuckle softly. "Yeah, you did. You're going to be feeling it tomorrow."

"Ugh," she groans.

"You ready for bed?" I wish I was asking her that so she would be joining me as we sleep, but again, that's a wish that will never be granted. I have to hold strong. I have to keep reminding myself that she's too young for me, and that her brother would cut off my balls if he found out I touched her. Hell, if he could read my mind, he'd cut off my balls.

"Will you carry me?"

"Yeah, baby. I'll carry you."

I lift her into my arms, bridal style, and she wraps her arms around my neck. She nestles into my chest, and I freeze. Something in my chest feels as though it clicks into place. I shake off the feeling and carry her up to her room.

Once in her room, instead of placing her on her bed, I sit with her in my arms. Her eyes are closed and her breathing is even. Everyone in this house is passed out, and I know it's wrong, but I just want a few minutes with her. To hold her and curse the fact that there are so many obstacles in our way. I can admit that if she weren't my best friend's little sister, the age difference is something I could get past. She's an adult, and knows her own mind, but luck unfortunately is not on our side.

I don't know how long I sit here, but I need to go. Standing, I place her on the bed and pull off her shoes. I tug the blankets up over her and lean down to press my lips to her forehead. "Night, baby girl."

I turn to walk away when her hand reaches out and snags my wrist. "Stay."

I peer down at her with nothing but the moonlight shining through the blinds. "I can't." The words feel like sandpaper on my tongue.

"Just until I fall asleep."

I'm crossing a line and I know it, but I also know that with that soft plea of hers, I can't say no. I tell myself it's because I'm worried about her. She might get sick and need me. I tell myself that if Forrest or anyone else walks in, that will be my story of why I'm in her bed. However, as I kick off my shoes and lie down next to her, she curls up against my chest, and I wrap my arm around her. This is more than just watching out for her. It's wrong, but fuck me, I can't seem to make myself stand and leave.

Several minutes pass by and her breathing evens out. I need to get up and go downstairs, and I will. I just need five more minutes of this time with her, and then I'll go. My lips press to the top of her head.

"You make it impossible for me to resist you," I whisper into the darkness of the room. "I know we can't be together, but I still want you. I want you more than I've ever wanted anything." I kiss the top of her head again, because at this moment, I can speak freely, and that's a gift I'm not passing up on. "Something tells me you're going to turn my world upside down, and fuck me, Emerson. I'm scared as hell that I'm going to let you." The confession falls easily from my lips, and it's not until this moment that I know it's true.

I've never felt this connection with anyone before in my life. She's different, and that's a blessing and a curse. I'm going to try to fight whatever this is, but as she rests peacefully in my arms, her hand gripping my shirt, I know it's impractical.

I can already feel myself falling.

EMERSON

I'M NERVOUS. I DON'T KNOW why, but I am. He's one of the best, but it's not his skill that has my palms sweating. When I think about approaching Roman and asking him to give me a tattoo that I've been wanting for a while, I'm scared to death.

I know he's just Roman, the guy I've known and crushed on for years. My brother's best friend, and my... well, he's not really my anything, but I wish he were.

Things have been weird between us. It's the end of July, and I leave to go back to school in a couple of weeks. I really want this tattoo, and I know I could ask any of the other guys, or my brother, to do it, but I want it to be Roman. They're all super talented, but I want it to be him. Besides, that will give us some time together. Maybe we can talk, and it will pull us out of this state of limbo we seem to be in.

He wants me.

I want him.

He says that doesn't matter and refuses to consider we could be more.

Yada, yada, yada.

Forrest and I already have matching anchor tattoos. He gave me mine on my eighteenth birthday, on the same weekend I moved in with him. He had Legend do his. Mine is on my ankle, and his is on his forearm. It's a symbol of staying grounded, and knowing that we always have a home, an anchor with one another.

I can still remember that day. I was nervous about asking him. I don't know why; he was excited to give me my first tattoo. When I told him why I wanted the anchor, he teared up and called out for Legend, who was the only other person in the shop at the time and told him to get to work on his drawing, and that he was next once mine was finished. As siblings, we are anchored together by love, and in life, we know that we always have a home in each other.

Tonight, it's just Roman and me at the shop. His last client was running late, and Roman said he would stay. He told me to lock up and go home, but I didn't listen. Instead, I've been sitting here at the counter working up the nerve to ask him to ink my drawing on my hip.

Forrest taught me to draw. He's by far more talented than I will ever be, but this drawing I've been working on for well over a year. I can't tell you how many times I've started over, or how many drafts I have. A few weeks ago, I finally came up with a version that I'm in love with.

The hum of the tattoo gun ceases, and I sit up straight. Glancing at the clock, I see that the three-hour session is over. I wipe my sweaty palms on the ass of my jean shorts. I know the worst he can say is no, but I really want this design, and I want more than anything for Roman to be the one to give it to me. It's a piece of me, and a piece of him that I'll have always, no matter how this weird in between thing we have going on ends.

"Thanks for coming in, Scott," Roman says, as he follows his customer to the front desk. "Hey, baby girl. I thought you were going home?" He tilts his head to the side to study me.

I pretend like my heart isn't racing just because he called me baby girl. I love it. It feels intimate, and he's the only person to ever call me that. The term of endearment makes me feel like his.

"I know, but I wanted to stay in case you needed me." That's only part of the truth, but there's no way I'm going to ask for this tattoo in front of his customer. The chance of him rejecting me is high, and I don't need anyone to bear witness to that humiliation, even if they are a complete stranger to me.

Roman stares at me for a few long, torturous heartbeats before turning his attention back to his client. "Em will get you taken care of. We'll need to give you a few weeks to heal, and then we can finish some of the shading. I would suggest booking now. The schedule tends to fill up quickly."

"Thanks again, Rome." The two shake hands and Roman disappears into his room. I quickly run Scott's credit card, book his next appointment with Roman, and walk him to the door. I turn the lock, switch off the Open sign, and turn off the lights in the lobby.

My knees are wobbly as I reach his door, where I knock lightly on the frame. He glances up, and his green eyes hold my gaze, but he doesn't speak.

"Hey." I clear my throat. "I have a favor."

"What's up?" he asks.

"I've been wanting another tattoo, and I was hoping you would be willing to give it to me."

"You know Forrest will be pissed that you didn't ask him."

"He gave me my first." I nod toward my ankle and my anchor tattoo.

"Doesn't matter. He's still going to be pissed."

I shrug. "I love my brother, Rome. He's everything to me, but I'm also an adult. I get to make my own choices in this life, and I choose you. I want you to be the one to do this for me."

He pauses. I'm sure he's letting my words roll around in that gorgeous head of his. We both know that my little speech is about more than just him giving me a tattoo. "Do you even know what you want?"

"I do. I'll be right back." I turn, rush back to the desk, grab my sketch, the final one that I'm in love with, and race back to his room. I hand him the drawing and step back. This is stressful, letting someone who is as talented as Roman look at my art. I've worked so hard on this, and the fear of him tearing apart the design is real. Not that he would ever be mean, but putting yourself out there is always scary, no matter who you're with.

"Who drew this?"

"I did."

His head snaps up, and those green eyes of his are burning with an emotion I can't name.

"I've been working on it for over a year, and I finally have it how I want it." I'm rambling, but he's not saying anything. He finally pulls his gaze back to the drawing, and he's just staring at it.

"This is really good, Emerson."

He rarely uses my full name.

"Thank you." I can feel the blush coating my cheeks. "I want it on my left hip, and I want you to do it." My voice is strong and clear. Not holding a hint of the anxiety that's coursing through my veins.

"You really want to face the wrath of your brother?"

"It's one of you. As long as it's someone from Everlasting Ink, from his circle, he's going to be okay with it. If he's not?" I shrug. "That's his issue, not mine. You're who I choose." I hold my breath as I wait for him to decide.

"When?" His voice is gruff.

"Tonight. It's just us, and it's still early enough. Unless, I mean, if you have plans, we can schedule another time?" I'm quick to offer.

"No plans, Em."

Hope swells in my chest. "Does that mean you'll do it?"

Slowly, he nods as his eyes find mine. "I'll do it."

I don't think. I close the distance between us and launch myself into his arms. He catches me easily. I wrap my arms around his neck and my legs around his waist. I cling to him, burying my face in his neck. After weeks of back and forth, and him pushing me away, I was certain he was going to tell me no.

"Thank you, Rome. Thank you. Thank you. Thank you." I lift my head so that he can see the sincerity in my eyes.

"It's really fucking hard for me to say no to you, baby girl," he says softly. His hands are gripping my thighs, holding me to him.

"You tell me no on a daily basis."

"Not without difficulty."

"So, I'm wearing you down?" I grin.

The corner of his mouth lifts in a smile. "With this. You wore me down with this."

"I'll take my wins where I can get them. Can we do it now? Tonight?" I ask eagerly.

"Can you sit through a few hours?"

"Yes." I don't hesitate with my answer.

"Then, yeah, we'll do it tonight. Let me get this set up and we'll get to work."

"Thank you." I kiss his cheek, and his hands grip my thighs a little harder. He doesn't reply, but he nods, and I know that's as good of a reply as I'm going to get. He stares deep into my eyes, and his head leans in.

He's going to kiss me.

I lick my suddenly dry-as-the-Sahara lips in preparation. He leans in a little closer, so I close my eyes, but it's not his lips I feel, but his forehead pressed to mine. "This is going to be by far the hardest thing I've ever done in my entire life." His confession is murmured, but I hear every word loud and clear.

"Why?" I know why. He feels this magnetism between us, but he refuses to do anything about it.

"You know why, baby girl," he husks.

I grind my hips against him, and he grunts, his fingers digging deeper into my bare thighs. "Stop fighting this."

"I can't. This is wrong, Em. You know he would never approve of us."

"It's not up to him. He'll either have to get on board, or be pissed off and miserable the rest of his life."

"He's my business partner, one of my best friends, and your older brother. He knows me. They all do better than anyone, and they know I don't date. Add in that I'm a decade older than you, and they'll all be grabbing their pitchforks."

I wish he would just listen. Just give this, give *us* a chance. "Not when they see how good we are together."

"There are no guarantees in life, Em. We can't predict the future. We don't know how giving in to these desires will end."

"You would never hurt me, Roman. I know that, you know that, and they will too." My tone is soft, but I hope he can hear my need for him to give in to this thing between us in my voice.

"Not intentionally." He lifts his head and his eyes find mine. "Never." That single word is said with so much conviction, it brings tears to my eyes.

"It's not fair, Rome. We both want this. Why are we letting everyone in our lives keep us from something that has the potential to change our lives?"

"It would change my life. You—" He shakes his head and takes a steadying breath. "They're our family, baby girl. We can't make them choose."

"They don't have to choose. You said it. They're our family. They choose us. We can choose us too."

"It's not that easy." He presses a kiss to my forehead, which takes me by surprise.

"Roman." My voice is laced with a little bit of sadness, longing, and pleading, all wrapped up in one.

He slowly lowers me to my feet, and I don't miss the feel of his hard cock as I slide down his body. He's denying us both what we want, but maybe, just maybe, I can convince him to give us a shot. Baby steps and all that.

Each time we're together, he gives me more. Today, he held me close and kissed my forehead. We're slowly making forward progress, and as long as that happens, I'll keep trying. I know what I want.

I want Roman.

I ignore the fact that he's hard from our interaction. It's difficult, but it's for the best. I still need him to give me my tattoo, and it has to be him. That's how I saw this going down in my head, and once I set my mind to something, it's hard to change it.

"I'm going to run out and grab us some food while you get the transfer ready. I'll be right back." I turn on my heel and race out of the room. I stop to grab my purse and keys and push out the door. I know what all five of the guys like to eat, so it's easy for me when I pull into Subway to get Roman his usual. Two subs, two bags of chips, and two large drinks later, I'm using my key to unlock the front door.

Roman rushes out of his room to help take the food and drinks from my hands, and waits for me to lock the door before leading us back to the small break room. "Did you take cash with you out of the drawer?" he asks, as he starts to unload our food.

"No. This is on me. I'm paying for my tattoo too." I give him a pointed look, and he rolls his eyes.

He reaches into his pocket and hands me two twenties. "This is for dinner, and no way in hell are you paying for ink."

"Dinner wasn't nearly that much, Rome. I've got it. Let me do something nice for you." I don't debate over paying for the ink. I know he won't give in. I'll just have to think of something nice to do for him to make up for it.

"You have college expenses. You're not paying." He shoves both twenties into my purse and gives me a look that dares me to argue with him.

I sigh, because I know better too.

All five of them are like that when it comes to me. Can a girl not do something nice for her friends and her brother? I get it. They make more than me, but I'm not destitute. I work as a waitress back at college, against my brother's advice. He insisted I let him cover the cost of everything that I need, but no way could I do that. Forrest has helped me so much, bought me a car, and moved me in with him, and so much more. I needed to pull my weight, and I have, even though he continues to grumble about it.

I have a feeling it won't matter how old I am. Forrest is always going to see me as that little girl he'd take to his place for the weekend once he moved out, to give me a break from our alcoholic parents.

We're quiet as we eat. I don't make small talk. I don't want to give Roman any type of ammunition to change his mind about this. I barely touch my six-inch sub, while he devours his twelve inch in what seems like a few bites.

"You not hungry?" he asks, noticing that I'm picking at my food.

"Too excited to eat."

"You want this that bad?"

"Yes." I stand and start cleaning up our mess, wrapping up my sandwich and placing it in the refrigerator for later. "Ready?" I ask when I turn to face him. He's leaning against the counter, feet crossed at the ankles, watching me.

"I'm ready," he finally says, before heading down the hall to his room with me on his heels.

"Have a seat on the table," he says without looking at me. "Left hip?" he asks.

"Yes." My pulse is pounding, and my palms are back to sweating. I can't believe he said yes. After over a year of perfecting this design, it's finally going to be a permanent part of me.

"Maybe we should call your brother," he suggests.

"What part of I'm an adult do you not understand?"

"He's going to wonder where you are if you don't come home. They know the hours of the shop, baby girl."

I roll my eyes and huff out a breath. He's right. I hate it, but he's right.

"Hand me my bag." I point to where my purse is sitting across the room on the desk. He does as I ask, and hands me my phone. I start to type out a text, but I know my brother, and he's going to call me anyway. I might as well get this over with. I dial his number and place the call on speaker so that Roman can be privy to the conversation. This is just delaying us. I swear if my brother messes this up for me, I'll be pissed.

"Hey, kid."

"Hi, Forty."

"Are you on your way home?"

Roman gives me an "I told you so" look, and I roll my eyes, which only makes him grin. "No. I'm still at the shop."

"Is everything okay?"

"Everything is fine. I'm actually going to have Roman give me a tattoo." There is nothing but silence that greets me on the other end. "Forrest?"

"Do you know what you want?"

"Yes. It's my own design. I've been working on it for over a year now."

"You know I'll do it for you."

"I know, but my plan is to get ink from each of you." That's not really my plan, but the idea popped into my head, and I'm rolling with it, hoping that it will help ease my brother's bruised ego.

"Really? I didn't know that."

"Yeah, it's something I think would be cool. A piece from each of you."

"I was your first," Forrest boasts proudly.

"Obviously."

"Can I come and watch?"

Shit. "No. I want it to be a surprise. You know Rome will take good care of me. Right, Rome?"

He clears his throat. "Always."

"Well, I can't wait to see it. Is this a one-session deal?"

"Yeah," Roman answers. "A few hours if she can stand it."

"She did great when I worked on her. I think she can do it."

"Thanks, Forty. Now, I gotta go. I've been dying to have this done, and it's time to get to work. Well, for Rome to get to work." I laugh.

Forrest chuckles. "All right. I'll wait up for you. Call me before you leave so I know you're on your way home."

"Love you, big brother."

"Love you too, kid." I end the call and hand Roman my phone. "Ready?"

He nods. "I'm going to need you to slip off your shorts."

My heart gallops in my chest. I knew that this was going to happen. Regardless of that knowledge, getting undressed with him when it's just the two of us here shoots a thrill through me.

ROMAN 9

OUT OF ALL THE TIMES I imagined getting Emerson out of her pants, this wasn't on the list. I turn my head and begin setting up my machine and the ink, because I can't watch her strip out of those tiny jean shorts she's wearing.

Uncapping the bottle of ink, I notice there is a slight tremble in my hands. Fuck me, I wasn't nervous when I did my first piece all those years ago, but the knowledge that I'm going to have my hands all over her soft skin, even if mine will be gloved, is wreaking havoc on me.

I should have said no. That would have been the right thing to do, but dammit, I just couldn't do it. When she looks at me with those sparkling green eyes of hers, I don't stand a chance at refusing her.

Basically, I'm fucked.

"What about my panties?" I hear her soft voice ask from behind me.

I swallow thickly. I'm going to have to turn around and verify the exact placement of where she wants this tattoo before I can answer that question. Squaring my shoulders, I turn to face her. My cock instantly perks up at the sight before me.

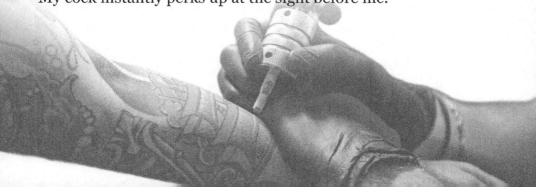

Emerson is sitting on the edge of my table in nothing but her black tank top and a pair of dark purple lace panties. She's fucking beautiful. Every part of that night, all those months ago, comes rushing back. The way she played with her pretty pussy as her eyes held mine. The arch of her back when her orgasm tore through her, and the heated look of her stare as she watched me stroke my cock.

I'm in so much fucking trouble.

I clear my throat. "Where do you want it?" My voice is gravelly.

She leans to the side. "I was thinking here." She points to her hip, and sure enough, it's going to require her to lose the panties. I don't even try to talk her out of the placement, because this drawing is outstanding, and this on her skin is going to be sexy as fuck.

The placement is perfect.

She is perfect.

"Panties need to go." The words come out as a gruff command, more than an answer to her question, but she doesn't seem to mind.

She doesn't blink an eye as she shimmies one side, then the other over her hips and down her legs. Once she's finished, she flashes me a grin, because yeah, I'm watching her every move. I'm just looking. There's nothing wrong with looking. At least that's what I keep telling myself to make this better. If Forrest knew, he'd kick my ass.

"Can you take care of these for me?" she asks.

Before I know what's happening, her panties—correction, her thong—is flying toward me, landing on my chest. On instinct, I reach up to grab them to keep them from falling to the floor. I can smell her on the fabric. I don't know how in the hell I'm going to make it out of this session keeping my hands to myself.

I've never craved a woman the way I crave Emerson.

I fist the slip of fabric as if it were my lifeline. I stand motionless as I fight like hell to maintain my composure. My need for her rolls through my veins like a summer storm. I count backward from twenty in my head, and then repeat that process before I shake out of my Emerson daze.

I tuck the thong into my back pocket and turn my back to her. "Lie back," I say, my voice thick.

I grab my phone and pull up a country play list because I know that's what she likes, and set the volume low. Just loud enough to hear over the hum of my tattoo gun, but not so loud we can't talk. I should probably crank it up, but I can't do that. I need to be able to hear her reactions to make sure she's comfortable at all times. The thought of hurting her, even though it's something she signed up for, has my gut twisted in knots.

"Are we adding any colors?"

"No. I want it black and gray."

I nod, letting her know I heard her. I suspected that's what she was going to say, as that's how she drew it, but I wanted to make sure. I want this to be perfect for her.

Pulling on my gloves, I grab the razor and get to work shaving the area. Once that's done, and the skin is clean, I change my gloves and transfer the design.

"Go take a look and make sure it's where you want it."

"I don't need to." She holds my gaze. "I trust you, Rome."

It's as if she reached inside me and fisted my heart in the palm of her hand. She may as well have done it with how tight my chest squeezes at her words. The look in her eyes. It's deeper than just this tattoo and we both know it.

"You sure?" I can feel the slight tremble in my hands. Not from nerves, but from the need to take her into my arms. I have to snap out of this. "Are you comfortable?"

"Very." She offers me a smile that lights up the entire room.

When I pick up my gun, the trembling stops. This is what I do best. A tattoo gun in my hand is where I feel most at home.

"First line," I say, letting her know that I'm starting. She's a fucking rock star and doesn't even flinch. "You doing okay?"

"I'm fine, Rome. I promise, if I need a break, I'll tell you."

"Okay, baby girl," I reply, my voice soft.

I get to work, and for the first forty minutes or so, we're both quiet. She doesn't move a muscle while my cock throbs behind my zipper. I've tattooed some exquisite women in my day. I've had my hands on asses, tits. You name it, I've done it. But none of them have ever affected me like Emerson.

"He doesn't have to know."

I lift the gun from her skin. "Who doesn't have to know?"

"Forrest."

"Em." I sigh because I don't want to lie to my best friend, but telling her no gets increasingly difficult every single day.

"We could keep this between us. Just to see where it's going to go. Maybe you'll tire of me. I mean, I know you're not much on relationships."

"Not because I'm against them, Emerson. I've never found anyone worth the effort."

"Maybe I will be."

"You're everything." I don't think before I speak, but I don't want to take the words back either. I mean it. She's everything. I've never felt this way, never been this worked up over a woman, and I know with just the small sliver of contact we've had that if I were to ever feel her from the inside, game over.

"You can't do that." Her voice is soft, but the emotion I hear tells me she's irritated. "You can't say things like that to me. You can't sit there and tell me that I'm everything but refuse me. That's not fair, Rome."

"I know, baby girl, but that's how it has to be."

She ignores me. I watch as she closes her eyes and pretends like I'm not sitting right here next to her.

I get back to work and for the rest of the session, she remains still, eyes closed. If I didn't know better, I'd think she was sleeping. When I finish and clean her up, I take the opportunity to stare at her. I meant it when I told her she was everything. I just don't know how I can have her and not lose my best friend.

If Forrest wasn't her brother, I would have already caved. I won't be the reason she loses the only family she has in her life. She has me and the guys, and Monroe, but I won't come between brother and sister. I can't.

Her eyes flutter open.

"You can look," I say, scooting back in my wheeled chair to give her room to climb off the table. I tear off my gloves and toss them on the small stand. I'll need another pair to clean up, but I can deal with that in a minute. Right now, I need to see her reaction. She stretches and climbs to her feet, and I watch as her bare ass pads across my room to look into the full-length mirror hanging on the wall.

I close my eyes and focus on breathing, but only for a few seconds.

I'm just looking. Looking never hurt anyone. I'm not breaking any kind of rules if I'm just looking.

"Rome." Her voice cracks. "I love it so much. Thank you." She rushes across the room and flings her arms around my shoulders. My hands automatically go to the back of her thighs. I'm aware of the fact that she's naked below the waist, and it wouldn't take much for me to move my hand a few inches, and I could feel her. I'd bet anything she's wet for me. She's just as affected by me as I am her. It's a curse we've both been blessed with.

We both want someone we can't have.

She pulls back, so she can see my face. Her arms are wrapped around my neck. She remains standing between my thighs, and I don't let her go. I should, but I just need a little more time. The feel of her soft skin beneath my fingertips is heaven.

"Will you try? For me? Can we just see where this goes?"

"Emerson, if things were different, if Forrest wasn't your brother, you would already be mine. I can't risk you losing your family over me."

"I won't lose him." She shakes her head. She's adamant that Forrest would be okay with us being together, but I have a different opinion on the matter. "This is our choice. Not his."

"I would risk it for you. I'd risk losing my best friend to make you mine, but I won't risk your relationship with your brother. I know the bond the two of you have, and I won't be the reason you lose that." The thought of him being upset with her, and in turn causing her pain, guts me.

"That's up to me. If Forrest wants to be an ass about it, then let him. He's the one that will have to live with the fact that he ruined the relationship with his sister because he's a stubborn ass. We don't choose who we love, Rome."

My heart gallops in my chest. The beat is so fast I'm fearful it might explode.

Love. That's not a word that any of us toss around casually. Surely, she meant it as a matter of speaking in regard to dating. She's not in love with me. She can't be. She needs to save that love for a man who her brother will approve of. One I'll hate because he gets to be with her and I don't. One that better watch his back because if he ever hurts her, he'll have me to answer to.

"He's protective of you."

"I know. I love my brother. I'll never be able to repay him for all he's done for me, but that doesn't give him the right to make my choices for me."

I don't say anything because she's right, but that doesn't mean he's not going to be pissed if we were to take this farther.

"So, that's it. Just no? You tell me I'm everything and that if Forrest wasn't my brother, you'd risk his friendship. That's it. No further discussion?"

"We can't." Those two words feel like glass slicing my tongue.

She nods. "Okay then. When you see me with someone else, I want you to remember this moment. I want you to remember that you didn't want me bad enough to fight for me." She tries to step out of my hold, but my fingers dig into her bare skin.

"Don't." It's a warning, but I'm not sure what of. The threat that I won't fight for her, or that she's going to find someone else. I know I just thought that same thing, but it's different when it comes from her lips.

Can I handle that?

Can I sit back and watch as another man holds her, kisses her, and gets to be a part of her everyday life?

If the panic that's rising inside me is any indication, the answer is no. I won't survive that.

"Don't what? Live my life? Move on? You can't expect me to stay in limbo like this. Roman, I care about you. I want this with you. I'll fight whoever we have to fight who doesn't agree, but I can't do that on my own. I can't do that without you being in this with me. So, yes, I'm going to live my life. I'm going to move on, and just like my brother, there isn't a damn thing you can say about it."

Mine.

Mine.

Mine.

That one word repeats over and over in my mind, and I don't think. I act.

The action has me lifting her onto my lap, sliding one hand behind her neck and pulling her mouth to mine. The instant our lips touch, I know I'm sunk. I know that there will never be another woman on this earth for me.

I nip at her bottom lip, and she gasps, which allows me entrance into her mouth. Her taste explodes on my tongue as I explore her. I keep a firm grip on her neck, holding her to me, because I am not ready to end this. My other hand grips her bare ass. She rocks her hips against my hard cock. Even through my jeans, I can feel the friction that move causes. I'm mindful of the fresh ink on her hip.

This kiss has months of built-up desire and tension. I've wanted this for so long... to taste her. To have my hands all over her. I don't know if I'm going to be able to stop. Not just tonight, but ever. One taste and I'm addicted.

I don't know how long I kiss her. What I do know is when I finally pull away, we're both panting, and Emerson's lips are bruised and swollen. I rest my forehead against hers, while I let the reality of what just happened settle in.

I crossed the line.

Not the invisible one I've already crossed with her. This is the real one. I blew the line apart. It no longer exists. I just pushed us into a situation that's going to be messy as fuck, but sitting here with this goddess wrapped around me, the taste of her lips still on mine, I can't seem to find it inside of me to care.

"Rome?"

For the first time since all of this started, I hear actual worry in her voice.

I cradle her cheeks and hold her gaze. "What's wrong, baby girl?"

"You kissed me."

I smile. "I did."

"What does that mean?"

"Honestly, I don't know, Em. I know that the thought of someone other than me kissing you has rage boiling in my veins."

"You want me?" Her softly spoken words would have brought me to my knees had I not already been sitting.

"I want you. It's never been about that. Me wanting to be with you has never been the issue. I don't know how your brother will react, and I'll be damned if I'm the man in your life that causes you to be estranged from the only family in your corner."

"Then we don't tell him." Her words are rushed. "We see how this goes. We can do that. We're adults. We make our own choices, and we can keep this between us."

"I don't know if I'm going to be able to do that. Now that I've tasted these lips—" I trace my thumb over her bottom lip. "I don't know that I'll be able to stay away." It's true. I've fought this for so long, and I only have so much control.

"We can do this. We'll take our time and see where it goes, and then we can go from there. It doesn't have to be anything serious." She says the words, but I know deep in my soul that it can never be anything but serious between us. For her and for me.

"You're not a dirty little secret, Emerson."

"No. I know that. I just... this might be something, or it might be nothing. I go back to school in a couple of weeks, and that's a long time for you to wait for—" She peers down at my lap.

"Hey." I wait for her eyes to find mine. "If we're doing this, it's just you." I don't tell her it's only been her for far too long. That the only action my cock has gotten in the past far too many months is the palm of my hand.

"I know that's a long time and I wouldn't expect—" she starts, but I kiss her to shut her up.

"That's not who I am. You know that. Right, baby girl? Tell me you know cheating is not what I'm about."

"But we're not really together."

"No one touches you but me." I kiss her softly. "No one touches me but you." I kiss her again, getting lost in the fact that if I'm going to hell and ruining a friendship, and potentially her relationship with her brother, we might as well go all in.

I kiss her until her phone rings, which has us pulling apart.

She stands on shaking legs and retrieves her phone from the desk. "Hey, Forty," she answers. "Yeah, we just finished up. I'm going to stay while Rome cleans up his station, and he's going to walk me to my car."

I smile, because that's not a lie. I do need to clean up, and she knows that none of us would let her walk out of here at night on her own. Ashby is a safe town, but you can never be too careful.

"All right, I'll text you when I'm on my way." She pauses. "Love you too." She ends the call and tosses her phone on the desk. "I guess we should probably clean up, and I should head home. He's waiting up to see my ink."

"Let me take a picture. Just for me, not for anyone else, and I need to wrap you up before you get dressed." I do just that. I keep my movements as professional as possible when all I really want to do is bury my face between her thighs.

"Thank you for this." She nods toward her ink then takes the thong I return to her, so she can slip it back on.

"I have some gym shorts out in my truck. Let me go get them so you don't have to put those tight shorts back on."

"I'm okay."

I step up next to her and kiss her forehead. "Let me take care of you." I grab my keys from the desk and rush out to my truck to grab the shorts I keep on days I hit the gym when I leave.

Back inside, I hand her the shorts and start to clean up. Fifteen minutes later, I'm walking her to her car. "Cameras," I remind her.

Her shoulders sag, but she smiles as if nothing is amiss. "I'll see you tomorrow?"

"Text me when you get home? Better yet, it's late. I'll follow you."

"You don't have to do that."

"I never do anything I don't want to do. Buckle up." I wait for her to do so before closing the door and tapping on the roof. Quickly, I jog to my truck and flash my lights for her, letting her know I'm ready to go.

EMERSON 10

I BARELY SLEPT A WINK last night. As soon as I got home, I was able to modestly pull down Roman's shorts to show my brother my tattoo. He was also touched and immediately knew the significance of the tattoo. Lilies have always been my favorite. However, what some might not know is that's the flower my big brother has given me every single year on my birthday for as long as I can remember. It was wrapped, but he still praised me for the design, and reassured me that Roman did good work.

Not that he needed to.

All five of them are incredible artists, and any one of them would have killed this ink, but for me, it had to be Roman.

Even with the lack of sleep, I'm energized for the day. Today is one of the rare days that all five guys are in the shop. I don't foresee any stolen kisses, but just being around him is enough for me. I'm a little nervous that he might have changed his mind, but that's not Roman. He's one of those men that if he gives you his word, that's gospel.

I bounce downstairs to find the kitchen empty. There is a note on the dry erase board of the fridge from Forrest telling me he went to the shop early to finish a design for a client, and that there's cash on the counter to stop and pick up pastries for everyone.

I've got to admit. Working for the guys has been fun. I'll be sad to leave them when I go back to college, but I'm excited about this final year. I'm ready to get a full-time job and start my life. Maybe, just maybe, it will be with Roman as more than just a friend.

Today we have three final interview candidates coming in. We're cutting it close, but with all the guys being at the shop, I figured today was the perfect time. I managed to schedule two hours for lunch instead of their normal half hour. That's another reason it's taken me so long. Their schedules are packed. Luckily, we have someone rescheduled, making the extra time for today possible. They'll be able to eat in peace and then meet as a group with all three candidates. I loved all three of these candidates, and I hope that one of them will work because we are most definitely running out of time.

Grabbing the money from the kitchen island, I shove it into my purse and head out to my car. I have pastries to buy and the workday to get started. Oh, and my hot sexy... Roman. I don't know what we are or if we *are* anything, but I get to see him. I don't want to push my luck by asking him to label whatever this is. All I know is that I want more kisses. Lots and lots of kisses.

It's just after nine by the time I make it to the shop. The first appointment isn't until nine thirty, so there is still plenty of time for the guys to scarf down the pastries I picked up, compliments of my brother.

"Breakfast is here!" I call as I make my way to the break room. I didn't need to, though, because all five of them are sitting around the long table sipping their morning drinks of choice. "Aren't you a lively bunch." I grin. I move around the room and stand next to Roman. I place the bags full of goodies on the table and begin to unload.

"I could kiss you," Lachlan says as he reaches for a muffin.

"No kissing my sister," Forrest grumbles, reaching for one of the cinnamon rolls.

"This deserves some kind of reward, Forrest," Maddox chimes in. He opens the box of donuts and pulls out a chocolate-dipped one with sprinkles. He takes a huge bite, shoving half of it into his mouth and moans.

"That's his orgasm sound," Legend announces. "Must be good." He reaches into the same box, and he, too, chooses a chocolate-dipped donut with sprinkles. "I was craving this. I just didn't know it," Legend says, making us all laugh.

"Rome? What are you craving this morning?" I ask him. My voice is light and teasing, but I can feel a slight blush coat my cheeks. Luckily I wore my hair down today, so I dip my head and pretend to be arranging food to hide it.

I jump just a little, not enough that I think anyone will notice when I feel his hand on the back of my bare thigh. "Surprise me." He quickly drops his hand and I shake out of my trance, choosing what I know to be his favorite. A glazed cruller. He likes them glazed or with cinnamon sugar. I got one of each, but I know he prefers the glazed.

"Here you go," I say, placing it on a napkin and handing it to him.

"Thanks, Em." His green eyes sparkle and his heated gaze, although brief, tells me he's thinking about our kisses last night too.

"So, interviews today," I tell them, grabbing my own glazed donut and taking a seat next to Roman. "We have three candidates. Cleo, Lyra, and Drake. All three of them would fit in well."

"Tell us about them," Lachlan says.

"Cleo is currently working at the Waffle House in Nashville. She's tired of the first, second, and third shift rotations and wants something with a steadier schedule so she can have a life. She's a few years older than me."

"The next is Lyra. She's currently working at a veterinarian's office, also in Nashville, but it's not her jam. Her words, not mine. She's a receptionist, and she's not exactly an animal lover." I can't help but laugh, remembering her confession in her interview.

"Then we have Drake. He's got a background in working at tattoo shops. He worked for a few years for Inked Expression for Blaise and

Asher Richards. He just recently moved to Ashby with his girlfriend, and would like something closer to home if possible. He's fluent in scheduling, and ink and piercing. Out of the three candidates, he's the most qualified. However, he's asking for more money than the position pays, but you get what you pay for." I shrug.

"Thanks for taking this on, kid," Forrest says. "None of us had the time or the willingness to do it ourselves."

"It was fun. Once I got this place organized, it gave me something to do. However, it took me a while to get all five of your schedules to align. I go back to school the week after next, so we need to make a decision today, unless one of you wants to take on training the new hire. All three can start immediately. Drake is no longer working, and the other two didn't seem to mind not giving two weeks' notice, which I don't agree with. That could be us one day on the other side of that situation."

"Who is your pick?" Roman asks.

"Drake." I don't hesitate. "He's chill, and I think he would fit in well."

"And we don't have to worry about male clients hitting on the other two like they did you."

I playfully roll my eyes at Roman. "That was nothing and you know it."

"What happened?" Forrest asks.

Roman goes on to tell him about the incident that's not really an incident three weeks ago. "So, yeah, I think a man might be a better fit."

"What?" I turn to look at him. "You do realize you have just as many female clients that also throw themselves at each of you. Double standard much?"

"You're right." Roman nods his agreement. "I want to preface this by stating that it's not meant to be offensive. However, a man with morals won't take any of them up on it. Especially if he's been in this position already and is in a committed relationship. We don't have to worry about him getting hurt or dragged out of here by someone much bigger and stronger than he is while we're in our rooms doing our jobs."

"So what you're saying is because we don't have a dick swinging between our legs, we're helpless."

He reaches under the table and places his hand on my leg. "That's not what I'm saying at all. I'm saying that as employers, it's our job to ensure safety."

"You're digging the hole deeper." Maddox laughs.

"Yeah, you should just stop," Lachlan agrees.

"I'm enjoying the show." Legend reaches for a muffin, peels back the paper, and takes a huge bite. "Please proceed."

"I can see where you're both coming from," Forrest speaks up. "Let's just interview all three candidates and we can discuss after."

"I closed the books at four today so that we could meet after everyone is finished and make a decision. I know it's impossible to have you all be finished at the same time, but at least we have a cutoff. The last appointments are at four, and they all seem like they'll be a couple of hours at most. Hopefully, by six thirty or so, you'll all be finished. I'll pick up lunch and dinner today to make this as easy as possible for each of you."

"Take cash out of the register," all five say at once.

"I know the drill." I laugh, because what else can I do? These five men all have hearts of gold. They mean well, even when they piss me off.

"Fine, get to work. I'm having lunch delivered from the deli down the street, and then I'll probably just order pizza for dinner."

A chorus of "Thank yous" and "You're the best" greet me as they each grab another pastry and head off to start their day.

"I'll help you clean up," Roman says.

"Kiss ass," Legend mutters, and raucous laughter from the guys filters down the hallway. They think he's making up for ruffling my feathers, and while helping me cleanup is nice. I'm hoping for another kind of make up.

I start combining what's left over into one box, to toss the others into the trash. That's when I feel his arm wrap around my waist, and his lips against my cheek. "Morning, baby girl," he whispers.

My body melts into his. "Morning, Rome."

"We don't have much time, but I need those lips before I can start my day." With that, he turns me in his arms and kisses me. It's over before it started and nothing close to what we shared last night, but it's enough. For now.

"How's your hip?" He brushes his thumb lightly where my tattoo is beneath my loose-fitting sundress.

"Good. I'm surprised that didn't come up this morning." I assumed the guys would all be talking about it.

"I didn't tell them, and Forrest didn't mention it. I'm sure he doesn't want to talk about the fact that I had to get you naked, or mostly naked, to ink you."

"I'm a big girl."

He winks. "I know." He kisses me again before he releases me and steps back. He gives me a wicked grin and points his index finger my way. "You, baby, are addicting. I need to get to work." He turns on his heel and disappears out of the room.

I stand staring after him with a huge grin on my face. He's like a different man now that he's decided not to fight this.

Today is definitely going to be a good day.

"So, how are we doing this?" Maddox asks. "Are we voting on paper? Raising our hands? How's this going down, fearless leader?" He directs the question to me.

"I did my part of the job. I picked three and got them here. The rest is up to you."

"I actually liked all three of them," Lachlan speaks up. "It's going to be hard to choose."

"You already know that if I get to pick, I choose Drake."

"Oh, is that because he's handsome?" Legend asks, and Roman stiffens in his chair next to me.

Yeah, I managed to snag this spot again this evening for this meeting of the minds. "He's practically engaged. Did you not hear him gushing about his girlfriend? He's the most qualified and would take the least amount of training. I go back to school the week after next."

Roman shifts in his seat, and I can't help but turn to look at him. He looks surprised. I don't know why. I told him I was leaving soon. Did he not realize how soon that date was approaching?

"They were all three good," Legend chimes in.

"Who's your second pick?" Roman asks me.

"Lyra. She has more of an outgoing, in-your-face kind of attitude. She can handle the clients who try to hit on her." I glare at Roman and he winks at me in return. "Can I make a suggestion?"

"You know you can," my brother answers.

"I think you should hire two people. I've been working the hours, and when I'm not here, you all do it for yourselves. Rarely do all five of you hold the same hours, and the shop is open six days a week. Your schedules are packed. You could benefit from having someone here all the time."

All eyes are on me, but no one speaks up, so I keep going.

"Drake will be easy to train. He's been in this exact position at a shop that has a great reputation. He can take over training Lyra, who, in my opinion, will pick up just as quickly. I say you hire them both, and split the hours. That way, there is always someone here during hours of operation to man the desk, answer the phone, and greet the groupies." I stick my tongue out, and they all laugh.

"That's actually a really good fucking idea," Lachlan agrees. "I admit having you here this summer has spoiled me. I don't want to have to go back to doing without. The times you're not here and I have to do it, well, it sucks hairy donkey balls if I'm being honest."

"What exactly does sucking hairy donkey balls taste like?" Maddox asks him, barely containing his laughter.

"It tastes like dealing with the public. I want to do my job, not deal with the register and phone calls where I'm answering a million questions. And think about how much more productive we'll be, and that's more time with the gun in our hands."

"The shop is doing well financially," Forrest adds. "We can afford to do this, and you're on to something with productivity. This is an expense that we didn't want when we first opened, but our books are several weeks out. We can handle it now."

"Of course you can. The five of you have built an empire. It's something to be proud of. This little town of Ashby, Tennessee, has gained attention worldwide from some of your higher profile clients. This may be a small town, but you're the big fish in this pond."

"How long did you practice that speech in the mirror this morning, kid?" Forrest asks.

I ball up my napkin and toss it at him. "Ass," I mutter.

"Okay, let's get serious," Roman speaks up. "All in favor of hiring two people, raise your hand."

All six of us raise our hands.

"Raise your hand for Cleo," I state. No one raises their hand. "Lyra?" All six of us cast our vote. "Drake?" Again, all six cast our vote. "It's settled. I'll call both candidates. Drake was asking for more, and I think with his experience, we should meet him in the middle." We go on to discuss salary and easily enough, everyone agrees.

"Perfect. I'm going to get on this now."

"You want me to stay?" Forrest asks.

"No. I'll be fine."

"I have a drawing I have to finish up for tomorrow. I'll stay until she's done," Rome offers.

"You're still pissed at him about this morning, aren't you?" Legend laughs. "Dude, buy her some chocolate. Chicks dig that."

"Stop." I laugh, pushing at Legend's shoulder. "I'm not mad. I don't need any of you to stay with me. I have pepper spray, and I'm a big girl. I can handle closing up and walking to my car without the five of you hovering."

"I'll stay." Roman's deep voice leaves no room for negotiation. Not that I want to, but I have to put up a fight, so I sigh and roll my eyes.

"Thanks for taking care of this, Emerson." Maddox comes up to me and wraps me in a hug.

"Stop hogging her." Lachlan pushes Maddox out of the way and lifts me in his arms and jumps, making us both laugh.

"Oh, my turn." Legend pulls me from Lachlan into his arms and dances me around the break room.

"Can I have my turn with my sister?" Forrest pretends to be annoyed, but he's laughing with the rest of them.

"So greedy." Legend grins, as he twirls me into my big brother's arms.

"Thanks, kid, you saved us a lot of work. You've saved our asses this summer. I'm not looking forward to you going back to school."

"One more year, and I'll be home for good."

"Yeah?" Forrest's eyes light up. "You're coming home to Ashby?"

I don't look at Roman, and that takes effort. "There is no other place I'd rather be."

"Love you, kid."

"Love you too, Forty. Now go on, all of you. I need quiet to develop a training schedule and call your new hires. Work must be done."

They filter out of the room. As does Roman. I clean up the break room, which really only consists of combining the leftover pizza into one box and placing it into the fridge. When I look up, Roman is standing in the doorway, his shoulder leaning against the frame. His arms are crossed over his chest, and he's watching me intently.

"Do you know how difficult it was to watch them manhandle you?"

"They were just showing their appreciation."

"Come here, baby girl."

I don't hesitate to walk toward him. Once I'm close enough, he lifts me into his arms, and I instinctively wrap my legs around his waist and my arms around his neck. He kisses me. With the hunger that I saw reflecting in his eyes, I expected it to be a primal kiss, much like last night, but it's tender and slow.

"Been wanting to do that all damn day," he says, when he finally releases my lips. He rests his forehead against mine, and I soak up every moment of being in his arms. "Are you really leaving the week after next?" he asks.

"Yeah. We go back a week from Monday."

"That's not even two weeks."

"I have to go back."

"I know."

"I'll be home for Thanksgiving and Christmas, then spring break, and then next summer I'll be home for good."

"I want to see you every day until then."

"Okay." My heart is so full at his admission it could burst wide open. "We'll figure it out."

"Yeah," he agrees. Slowly, he places me back on my feet. "Grab what you need and we can work together in my office. I need to make use of all the time I can get before you leave."

"All right." I go up on my tiptoes and kiss the corner of his mouth, before moving to make sure the front door is locked, which it is. I gather what I need to make a schedule, and all three résumés, since Cleo deserves a call as well. I settle at his desk while he's at his drafting table. Every so often, Roman rolls over to where I'm sitting and kisses me, but then gets right back to work. Together, we work in silence, but it's not uncomfortable. How could it be when we're together?

ROMAN 11

DAYS. I'M DOWN TO MERE days before she heads off to college. I was up all night last night thinking about the consequences of what I've done. I kissed my best friend's little sister. I didn't just kiss her; I claimed her mouth like it was my own. We agreed we're not kissing or fucking other people.

That's a big deal.

I tossed every scenario around in my head, and I kept coming back to the same conclusion. I'm too weak to stay away from her. She's right: she's an adult who can make her own choices, and all I can do is hope and pray that when Forrest finds out, because I'm certain he's going to find out, that he finds a way to be okay with whatever this is.

I don't see a time in which I'll be ready, willing, or able to let her go.

Now, here I am on a Friday night, pacing my living room floor. I walked her to her car, mindful of the parking lot cameras, and my hands twitched to touch her. To pull her into me and kiss her goodbye, even though I'd already done so in the shop.

Which reminds me...

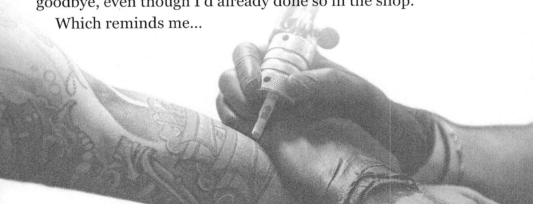

I pull up the shop cameras on my phone and erase the videos of me kissing her inside the shop. Thankfully, they are motion censored, and I tried to keep the PDA this time to my office. Well, outside of that kiss in the break room. I erase every trace of us together. Thankfully, it's not so much that the other guys will notice. Hell, they never look at the cameras. None of us do unless there is an issue. Either way, it's not a chance I'm willing to take.

I'm not ready for this to blow up yet.

Grabbing my phone, I quickly type out a text before I can change my mind.

> **Me:** Are you up?
>
> **Emerson:** Yes.
>
> **Me:** Can you get out of the house?
>
> **Emerson:** Where am I going to go?

My sassy girl. She wants me to say it, and I deserve that. After all the back and forth, I put us through. I should kick my own ass for holding off as long as I did. Now, I can count on my fingers how many days I have with her before she goes back to school. I could have had her all summer. I was certain that I could hold strong. I almost did, but she broke through the barrier of my stubbornness, and honestly, it's a relief to no longer fight what I'm feeling for her.

> **Me:** I can come and get you.
>
> **Emerson:** Like that won't be obvious.
>
> **Emerson:** Let me call Monroe. She can come and pick me up, and make it seem last minute, and she can drop me off to you.
>
> **Me:** Does she know?
>
> **Emerson:** Yes, and I trust her.
>
> **Me:** I trust you.

It's a gamble for anyone outside of the two of us knowing before we're ready for this to be more than what it is. But I do trust her.

> **Emerson:** Give me five.
>
> **Me:** Okay.

I toss my phone on the couch and continue to pace my living room floor. I keep glancing at my phone, so I pause to grab it and make sure the ringer is on. It's completely ridiculous, and there isn't another woman on this fucking planet who can have me checking my phone like a teenager other than Emerson.

I'm expecting a text so when my phone rings, I rush to answer it. "Everything okay?"

"It's more than okay. Monroe's driving home from her cousin's bridal shower that was in Nashville. She's going to swing by and pick me up. I told Forrest that we need to catch up. I have not spent any time with her this week."

"Oh, uh." I scratch the back of my head. "Would you rather do that?"

Fuck, please let her say no.

"I want to see you."

I exhale a sigh of relief. "Okay." How can I sound so fucking pussy-whipped already?

"I live with Monroe at college. I'll get to see lots of her. You, I'm going to miss." Her confession is softly spoken, and my heart squeezes in my chest.

"So, you're coming here?"

"I am."

"Are you staying?"

"Do you want me to?"

"Yes." I don't hesitate with my answer. "I want you here. We don't have much time left."

"All right. I have to work in the morning."

"I do too."

"I'm going to have Monroe pick me up and drop me back off at the house. That way, we don't have to worry about hiding my car."

"I hate sneaking around."

"Do you not want me to come over?"

"I want you here. I meant that, but I hate hiding you like a dirty little secret."

"Let's just give this some time, Rome. I promise everything will all work out in the end."

"Shouldn't I be the one reassuring you?"

"Meh, we both have a lot to lose potentially. I think we're both going to be doing some reassuring."

She's right, there are relationships on the line that can't be replaced. "You still think it's worth the risk?"

"I think you are worth it. Monroe just pulled in. I'll see you soon." She ends the call before I have a chance to tell her to be safe, so I type out a text because not telling her seems wrong. What has this woman done to me?

Me: Be safe, baby girl.

Emerson: Always.

I glance around my small house. This won't be the first time she's been here, but this will be the first time that she's here as mine. That's a big fucking deal. I don't have women here.

Not ever.

Emerson is different. We're barely started, and I know she's more.

I'm sitting on the front porch with my phone clasped tightly in my hand when Monroe's car pulls into the driveway. I told myself I would stay sitting, but I can't. I step off the porch, make my way to the passenger side door, and tug it open before Emerson gets the chance. She steps out of the car, and I pull her into my arms, pressing a kiss to her forehead. For the first time since I watched her drive away from the shop earlier, I feel my shoulders relax.

Bending, I peer into the car. "Thank you."

Monroe nods. "Take care of our girl."

Monroe is one of those people who loves life. She's carefree and easygoing and never takes herself too seriously. For her to be stone-faced as she issues that demand speaks volumes of how close they are.

"No other option," I tell her. Because there isn't.

I'd never let anything happen to her, and Monroe's unspoken words hit me hard. I'll never pressure her for more than she's willing to give me. I know that I'm a decade older than she is, but when I'm kissing her, when she's in my arms, it doesn't even feel like days separate us. We are one, and that's some heavy shit that I'm not going to let myself think about right now.

With a nod and a wave, Monroe backs out of the driveway. "Let's get you inside." With my arm around her waist, I lead her into the house. "Can I get you anything? Food? Something to drink?"

"We had dinner at the shop," she reminds me.

"Right. Thirsty?"

"Not right now. Thank you, though."

I nod. I'm nervous. I'm never fucking nervous.

"Uh... want to watch a movie?" When did I become the guy with no game? It's as if I've never talked to a woman before. Never talked to Emerson before.

"Sure."

"Good. Movie. Right." I nod toward the couch, and she kicks off her flip-flops and takes a seat. I turn off the lights, bathing the room in darkness with nothing but the muted TV for light. "What do you want to watch?"

"Anything. Whatever you were watching is fine."

"I wasn't actually watching it. It was on, then I muted it because it was annoying me, then all I could think about was seeing you, and the thought of watching TV slipped my mind."

"I'm glad you texted me." Her soft smile calms something inside of me.

"I'm glad you're here." I take a seat next to her and lift my arm. She snuggles up next to me. This is what I needed. What I was missing. Time with her where I don't have to think about being caught. I can just be me. The man that knows what he's doing is wrong, but is moving full steam ahead, anyway.

I pull up my streaming app and scroll through our options. "Tell me if something catches your eye."

"Honestly, Roman, I don't care what we watch. I'm just happy to be here, sitting on your couch next to you."

There's that squeezing sensation in my chest again. "Baby girl, you can't say things like that."

"Why not?" She turns so that she can look me in the eye.

"Because it makes it even more difficult for me to keep my hands to myself, and that's not why I asked you here. Not to maul at you. I just wanted to spend time with you."

She moves so fast to straddle my hips, it takes me by surprise.

"I don't know," she muses. "The mauling idea has its potential."

"Emerson," I warn.

"Roman," she fires back. "Do you not want me?"

Unable to take it a second longer, I grip her hips and thrust up. "Does that feel like I don't want you?"

"It's just us here. You still want me to stay, right?"

"Yes." I nod, because just saying the word isn't enough. I need her to know that, without a doubt, I want her here.

"Did you lock the door?"

"Yes."

"So no one can come in and see us."

"The guys all have keys."

"Hmm." She leans down and kisses my jaw, kissing all the way to my ear. "Then you better take me to your bed in case they decide to stop in."

"They won't."

At least I don't think that they will. We all have access to each other's homes and none of us bring women back to our places, so we don't have to worry about walking in on something we shouldn't. So even though I'm not expecting them, there is always a chance they could show up.

"But just in case." I stand with her in my arms, and she laughs. The sound winds its way around my heart, and my steps falter. I manage to steady us and carry her down the hall to my room. I place her gently on the bed, then go back to my bedroom door to shut and lock it for good measure. "Just in case." I make my way back to the bed in the dark and turn on the bedside lamp.

"They don't have a key to your room?"

"No."

"Perfect." She lifts her tank top over her head and tosses it to the floor.

I swallow thickly. "What are you doing?"

"Undressing."

"I can see that." My voice cracks. "Why?"

"I want to feel your skin against mine."

"Fuck," I mutter, as I run my fingers through my hair. "Emerson... we can't, I mean—shit, we can't sleep together."

"You want me to sleep on the couch?" She looks up at me with those innocent green eyes.

"No. I want you in my bed. In my arms, but this is too much. Too fast." I never in my life thought I would ever utter those words, especially not to the woman I crave more than anything else in my life. Yet, here we are. I'm trying to give in to this desire I have for her, but still be the voice of reason. It's too fast. Too soon. We need time to... fuck, I don't know... see where this goes. I don't know what the outcome will be, but tonight, we are not doing *that*.

"I happen to agree with you."

I nod. "Good. Okay."

"When I give that piece of myself to you, I want to know that you're in this as much as I am."

"I'm in this."

She tilts her head to the side and studies me. "When we get to that point, Rome, and in my heart, I know we will, you'll have a piece of me that no other man will ever get."

I let her words spin around in my head. She's not saying...? Is she trying to tell me she's a virgin?

"Spell it out for me, baby girl."

"I want you to be my first. In case that's not clear enough for you, I'm a virgin."

"Virgin?"

"With my brother and all of you around all the time, did you expect me not to be?"

"You've been away at college for two years."

"I have," she agrees. "But something inside me, the girl who's always crushed on her older brother's best friend, hoped it would be you. I was ready to give up that dream and get past it. Then you walked into my room the day before I left to go back to school on spring break, and you shattered my will to move on. In my heart and in my mind, I've always wanted it to be you."

I'm standing before her in a matter of seconds and dropping to my knees. We're eye to eye, and I take her face in the palm of my hands. "I don't deserve you. I'm too old for you, and we have so many twisted connections with your brother and the rest of the guys that this is going to get messy."

I want to tell her I would be honored to be her first, but the truth of the matter is that it scares the hell out of me. I know me. I know how I feel about her. I know the battle I've fought with her and with myself to stop us from being here. It's dangerous for me to know that I could be the first and only man to ever be inside her.

Something primal flows through my veins. I've never felt this kind of yearning before in my entire life.

"Then be messy with me, Rome."

"Baby girl, there is no one on this earth I'd rather be messy with."

I can't fight her. I can't fight what I feel for her, and when she turns those beautiful green eyes on me and bats those long eyelashes, I'm done.

"No sex. Not tonight." There isn't an ounce of insecurity in her tone. "But I need to feel your skin against mine. I've wondered how it would feel so many times. Please, Rome?"

I never stood a chance at denying her. "Okay." I kiss her quickly, then stand and take a step back before pulling my shirt over my head, tossing it to the floor. We both start getting naked. My eyes take over every inch of her, committing this moment to memory.

"You're beautiful."

"I—I've never been naked, not all the way in front of a man before."

I can't help it. I smile. "Just me?"

"Just you."

"Good." I snake an arm around her waist and pull her close as I softly kiss her. I want to fucking devour her, but I'm taking this slowly. She deserves to be cherished, and I want to be the man to make her feel that way.

Her tits press against my chest, and she shudders at the contact. I'm certain it's the contact and not the cool of the air-conditioning.

Either way, I pull out of the kiss and grab the cover, holding it up for her. "Climb in."

She does so with ease. I drop the cover over her.

"I need to get the lights and turn off the TV. If the guys drive by and see it on, they might stop, and nothing is keeping me from holding you all night." I kiss her temple and stride out of the room. I don't bother with clothes. The house is dark, except for the slight glow of the TV. I don't plan to be away from her for long. I double check that the door is locked, turn off the TV, and find my way in the dark back to my room. Again, I close and lock the door, and then turn off the bedside lamp and crawl into bed beside her.

"Come here, baby girl." I hold open my arms, and she nestles into me, resting her head on my chest. I wrap my arms around her as she exhales.

"It's better than I imagined it would be." Her hands roam over my abs. She slowly makes her way toward my cock.

I place my hand over hers, stopping her. "What are you doing?"

"Am I not allowed to touch you?"

I huff out a laugh. "Is it your life's mission to torture me?"

"No, but I've never touched another man, and... I thought we could, you know... explore."

"Never?"

"Never."

She's so open and honest with me. It's only fair I give her some honesty of my own. "I don't know that you can touch me and me not make a mess of us."

"Just from my touch?"

"*Your* touch."

"Can we do that? I want to watch you."

"Fuck."

"Please? Just like that night in my room, only this time I get to help, and so do you."

"Are you sure this is what you want, baby girl?" I want this, want her more than my next fucking breath, but I need clear consent from her. It's important with the way this is happening between us that I have at least that.

"I want you. I want this. I want us. I'm sober, and I'm of sound mind and body." She chuckles. "If you are anything, Roman, be certain that you are what I want."

"I want you."

That's all the encouragement she needs. She grips my cock and strokes me gently.

"Does it hurt?"

"No, baby."

"The piercing? Does it hurt?"

"No. It's meant for pleasure. Mine and yours."

I feel her body shiver.

"We'll work our way up to that."

She's fucking killing me with her innocence. It's a stark reminder of our age difference. She's going to be twenty next week, and an adult, but still ten years my junior. That should make me want to stop, but I don't feel that gap between us. I haven't for a while now.

"Where are you going?" I ask when she releases me from her grip and moves away.

"I need the light. I don't want to miss this."

All I can do is shake my head and smile, because this woman is impossible to say no to. "I'm all yours, baby girl."

She grins. It's one of triumph and mischief, and she scoots down the bed and grips my cock. She strokes me a few times before tentatively leaning forward and swiping her tongue across the tip.

I fist the sheets at my sides, because the alternative is to grip her hair in my fist, and she's not there yet. She's learning and exploring, and I'm the lucky bastard who gets to be the test subject.

"It really doesn't hurt?"

"No." I take my hand and place it over hers, showing her she can grip me harder. Pump me faster. "It doesn't hurt."

"Why is that so hot?" she asks, watching our joined hands.

I don't bother answering, because I don't have an answer. Normally, that would turn me on, but not to the point where I feel like I'm ready to explode. It's Emerson and her effect on me. There is no other explanation.

"I'm close." The words are gritty, like sandpaper on my tongue.

"Oh, I guess I should do this then." She pushes my hand away, leans over, and takes me into her mouth.

To the back of her throat.

My back arches off the bed, and I tear at the sheets from how fucking good her mouth feels wrapped around my cock. She releases me with an audible pop, and green eyes stare up at me.

"Am I doing it right?"

"Baby girl," I say huskily. "There is nothing you can do to me that's wrong. Do what feels right to you. Just be ready for me to push you away. I'm close."

"Already?"

"That's what you do to me."

She grins. "Don't push me away."

"What?" I croak.

"You heard me. I want to taste you on my tongue." With that, she lowers her head and takes me back into her mouth.

I fight my eyes rolling to the back of my head. I refuse to miss a moment of this. Not a minute later, I'm calling out to her. "Em... baby. I'm cl—close."

She hums around my cock, and I lose it. I spill down her throat. She laps at me as if I'm the best thing she's ever had in her mouth. I'm licked clean before she releases me.

"On your back." I'm panting, and my cock is still hard. "My turn."

The smile she gives me is one I will never forget. There are so many emotions, but she's happy. She's truly happy to be here with me like this. She wants me, and this growing, living thing between us. I make a silent vow to make her smile like this every damn day.

Once she's settled on her back, I move between her thighs. "Is this okay?"

"Stop asking. I want this with you, Roman." She reaches out and runs her fingers through my hair. "I want all of my firsts with you."

And your last. "Grip my hair, pull, do whatever you have to do. Lock your legs around my head. I don't care. Just hold on and enjoy the ride."

"I don't want to hurt you."

"Baby girl, there is nothing in this moment you could do that would hurt me. The harder you tug, the tighter your thighs grip my head, the more I know you're enjoying what I'm doing. If I do something you don't like, you tell me. I'll stop."

"Do we need a word or something?"

"No, baby. The word is *stop*. No questions. You say stop, and that's what we do."

"I'm not going to want you to stop."

I smirk. "Hands in my hair." I settle further between her thighs, lifting one leg, then the other over my shoulders.

"Oh."

With one hand, I hold her perfect pink pussy open, and the other slides up and rolls her nipple between my index finger and thumb, while my mouth gently sucks her clit.

"Oh. My. G—" She doesn't finish her sentence, because she can't.

I work at her like a starving man. To be honest, I am starving for her. It's been months of back and forth. Months of fighting when we could have been enjoying each other this entire time.

At least I can honestly say that I tried my hardest to prevent being here with her like this. Not because I didn't want to be. Fuck, I've thought of this moment more times than I care to admit.

The hand that's tweaking her nipple slides back down to get on the action, and I gently push one long digit inside her.

"Holy shit," she calls out.

I smile and gently pump in and out of her, all while exploring her with my tongue. Her hands tug on my hair, and her legs are locked tightly around me. Her body starts to tremble, and it's almost too much to pull my finger out and push back inside her. Her pussy is gripping me like a vise.

"R—Rome. What's— Fuck!" she shouts, and I drink in everything her body is willing to give me.

Every. Last. Drop.

When she releases her hold on my hair and her legs relax, I crawl up the bed and kiss her. She doesn't seem to mind her taste on my tongue. Reaching over, I turn off the light. She pulls me into another kiss, and I let her.

I don't know how late we stay up kissing and letting our hands roam over each other's bodies getting to know one another intimately, but hands down this is the best night of my life.

EMERSON 12

THE PAST FEW DAYS HAVE been nothing short of incredible. I've spent every single night in Roman's bed. Forrest thinks I've been sleeping at Monroe's. It's not uncommon for us to do that; however, I am missing my best friend and my brother. It's Wednesday. Monroe and I leave to go back to school on Monday, and I don't want to go. Sure, I want to finish my degree, and start my life and my career, but leaving him when I just got him feels like a special kind of hell that I'm not enjoying.

"Where are you headed?" Forrest asks.

"To Monroe's." That's been my go-to immediate answer the past several days. I do have a touch of guilt for lying, but I feel as though it's important for Roman and me to make sure we're in this. I mean, we both say that we are, but I'm concerned about how we will handle the separation once I go back to school.

"Can she not come here? I miss you, kid. You leave Monday. I feel like the last week or so I've barely seen you."

"I know, I'm sorry. We made plans for tonight, but we'll stay here tomorrow night."

"You know, if there is something you want to tell me about the two of you, I'm here to listen."

I freeze. "What?"

He looks uncomfortable. "I just mean if you're into her, and you two are, you know, a thing, that's okay. You don't have to hide that from me."

"Forrest." I wait until he and his pink-tinted cheeks look me in the eye. "Monroe is my best friend. That's all. Not that there is anything wrong with same-sex action, that's just... not my jam, if you know what I mean." He blinks rapidly. "I'm into men, Forty. I'm a penis girl," I say, and cringe.

He holds up his hands. "Stop."

"You started it," I sass, crossing my arms over my chest, and glare at him.

"I miss you. You don't usually stay at her place this many days in a row. I was trying to be supportive."

I move to the couch and sit next to him. "So if I told you that vagina was my choice, you'd approve?"

"Yes."

"What if I said I was dating a guy twenty years older than me?"

His face pales. "Please tell me you're not."

I grin. "I'm not. What about a guy ten years older than me?" I'm sure I'm going to get the same reaction, but maybe this will plant a seed, and he can see that choosing Roman isn't the worst that I could have done as far as our ages are concerned.

"That's better than twenty," he mutters.

"Forrest, I love you. You've done so much for me, and you've always been the rock I can count on. My anchor." I smile at him. "But you have to let me be me. I'm an adult now. You don't have to worry so much. I'm me because of the man you are. You helped shape me into the woman I am. Have faith that I'm making the right choices for me in my life." I pause. "That includes penis."

"Stop. For fuck's sake just stop." He rubs his hands over his face, and I grin.

That's what he gets. I appreciate his support, and I would do the same for him. You love who you love, but for me, that's definitely the male anatomy. One male in particular.

"Love you, Forty." I cackle as I stand from the couch.

"I love you too, kid. I miss you."

"I miss you too. I promise I'll stay home tomorrow night, and then Saturday is my party, that I told you I don't need to have."

"Everyone needs a birthday party, no matter how old you are." He grins widely. "The big 2-0!"

"It's just another day. We really don't have to have a party."

"We do. We're closing the shop down early and everything."

"Forrest! Don't do that. There will be more birthdays." How he managed to slip that onto the schedule without me knowing is beyond me.

"Consider it a going-away and birthday bash all in one. Besides, you know we celebrate all our birthdays. It's not just you, kid."

"I know, but I hate the attention."

"It's still happening. Love you. Be safe."

"Love you too," I say, making my way toward the front door.

I pick up my overnight bag and head out to my car. The plan is that Roman will pick me up at Monroe's. Her parents are out of town for a few days, some kind of work thing for her dad that her mom tagged along for. It means we don't need to worry about them asking why my car is there, but I'm not.

I pull into Monroe's driveway an hour early. We definitely need time to catch up. Climbing out of the car, I rush up the front steps and knock on the door. A few seconds later, she pulls it open, smiling widely.

"What are you doing here?"

"I missed you." I pull her into a hug, and she laughs.

"Come on in." She steps back so that I can enter the house. "Tell me all the things."

"You tell me about you first. Anything new going on? I don't want this to be all about me."

"Em, I'm living vicariously through you. No action for me this summer, just hanging out with the parents, mostly. Is your birthday bash still on for Saturday?"

"Yes. I tried to talk Forrest out of it before I left to come here. No dice."

"He loves you. And it's not like they only celebrate your birthday. It's all five of them. Hell, they even celebrate my birthday." She smiles.

"I know. I just hate the attention. I just want to hang out."

"And we will. With cake and singing."

"You're just as bad as Forrest."

"You understand why this is important to him, right?"

"I do. We didn't have birthday parties growing up, and he wants to make up for that."

"Not just for you, but for himself too. He's still that little boy inside who missed out just like you did. He didn't have a big sister to take him away from it all."

Her words hit me in the chest like a wrecking ball.

My brother has always been invincible to me, taking me to his place on weekends, and moving me out as soon as I turned eighteen. There was no way my parents would have let it happen before then, and we both agreed getting authorities involved wasn't the right way to go. They didn't abuse me, but they were more interested in their alcohol than their kids. I got pushed around a little, but they never actually hurt me. I was never physically injured, just my heart got bruised. I don't know why, but I never considered what Forrest went through.

I'm an asshole.

"No, you're not," Monroe soothes.

"I guess I said that out loud, huh?"

"You did. Forrest knows you love him. Just keep in mind sometimes his motivations might be just as much for him as it is for others."

Reaching into my back pocket, I pull out my phone and dial Forrest. I have a sudden urge to tell my brother that I love him.

"Em? Everything okay?"

"I love you." My voice cracks. "I'm sorry for giving you such a hard time about the birthday parties. I know you mean well, and it's coming from a good place."

He's quiet for a few seconds. "We didn't get them."

"I know."

"We can change that. For us, for our future children."

"You plan on making me an aunt?" I tease, to lighten the mood.

"Maybe one day."

"Love you, Forty."

"Love you too, kid."

"I'll see you tomorrow at the shop."

"See you," he says, ending the call.

"Feel better?" Monroe asks.

"Not yet." I toss my phone on the couch and stand. I move to where she's sitting on the love seat, and bend over, hugging her tight. "I love you, bestie. Thank you for being there for me with all of this Roman stuff, and helping be my voice of reason with Forrest. I don't know what I would do without you."

"You'll never have to find out. Now, tell me about Rome."

"I really like him, Roe. He's so sweet to me, and although we've messed around, he's still saying we should wait to actually have sex."

"Why?"

"He's still worried that Forrest is going to disown me or something crazy like that. Sure, he's probably going to be upset, but I know my brother. He'll get over it with time."

"I think you're right. I do think he'll be pissed, and even more so to find out this has been going on behind his back."

"That's on me. I convinced Rome to hold off to make sure he doesn't get tired of me. We don't know how this separation is going to work when I go back to school, and I think we just need time without outside influence."

"I can see both sides. You have to do what you feel is best. Forrest loves you. He loves Rome. It will all work out like it's supposed to. It might be bumpy, but you have to live for you."

"That's what I keep telling myself. I can't thank you enough for covering for me. I wouldn't be able to have this time with him without you."

"I got you, bestie. Besides, when the two of you are happily married, you can name your firstborn after me. I've earned that right." She winks.

"Have you been drinking?" I ask, blowing off the fact that the thought of marrying Roman has my heart fluttering in my chest.

"Nah, just an outsider looking in," she says as there's a knock at the door. She climbs from her seat and moves to answer it. "Hey, Rome. Come on in."

"Hey, Monroe. Thank you," he says, his tone serious. "This means a lot to both of us."

"Who am I to stand in the way of true love?" she replies, and I bite my cheek to keep from scolding her.

Their footsteps grow closer. "Hey, baby girl. You ready to go?"

"Yes. We were just catching up." I walk toward my best friend and hug her tightly. "I love you. Thank you for being the amazing human that you are."

"I love you too." Monroe smiles at both of us. "Now, you two kids have fun."

With that, Roman laces his fingers through mine and leads me outside. We stop at my car to get my overnight bag, and then we're on the road.

"Where are we going?" I ask, when he passes the turn that will take us to his place.

His hand is resting on my thigh, and he gives it a soft squeeze. "I'm taking you on a date."

"A date?"

"Yeah, this is more than just keeping you naked in my bed, baby girl."

"We can't be seen out together."

"I know. Trust me."

"Do I get a hint?"

"No, baby. No hints. Just sit there and look like your sexy self. We'll be there soon."

Fifteen minutes later, we're pulling down an old country road. "What is this place?"

"It's the backside of my grandparents' place."

"So, we're not going to be arrested for trespassing?"

He laughs. "No, baby girl. We're not going to be arrested."

"Hey, it was a legitimate question. What are we doing here?" I doubt he'll tell me, but it's worth a shot.

"I know we can't be seen out together, but I wanted to take you out anyway. I know you're leaving in a few days, and I don't know, Em. I guess I wanted you to have this memory to take with you. The distance is going to be tough. We're hiding this, which I hate, but I didn't want you leaving thinking that you're just a secret to me. I need you to understand that I know what I'm risking. I know the risk that you're taking to be with me, and I guess I just wanted us to do something a normal couple might do."

"Roman Bailey, are you a closet romantic?" I tease, to ease the seriousness of the conversation. I have to because when you have a man like Roman spilling his heart out to you, you either lighten the mood or cry, and I can already feel hot tears prick my eyes.

"I wouldn't go that far. Besides, I've never cared enough until now, so it's not that I'm a closet romantic. I'm an Emerson romantic." He flashes me a cheesy grin. "It's all you, baby girl." He taps his chest, right over his heart. "I feel you here, and I don't know what to do with that. I hate that you're leaving when we're just starting to figure us out, and I want you to know that I'm in this with you. There is no one else for me, and there won't be as long as we're...." His voice trails off.

"What are we, Roman?"

"We're just us, Em. I don't want to label it and add pressure when we're both already under enough for hiding this from our friends and family. We can't hide this forever, but you need to concentrate on school and graduation."

"You think we'll still be us at my graduation?" I feel insecure asking the question, but I'm also not one to back down from facing the hard times. The only way I'm going to know where his head is at is to ask him.

"I'd like to think so. I know that hiding what I feel for you for that long seems almost impossible. All we can do is take this one day at a time."

"This might be our last night together before I leave."

"What? Why?"

"Forrest asked me earlier why I keep staying at Monroe's when we usually split our time. He misses me."

There is just enough light from the dash of his truck for me to see his throat bob as he swallows hard.

"Then we need to make this the best night." He leans over the console and kisses me softly. "Stay put. The grass is tall. I'll come around to get you, but I need a few minutes."

"Okay." There isn't a single thing this man could ask of me that I would deny him.

A few minutes later, he's pulling open my door. "I'm going to carry you."

"I can walk."

"Work with me here, baby girl."

I nod, and he lifts me from the truck and into his arms. He manages to push the door shut with his hip. When we turn, I gasp. "What is this?"

"It's date night under the stars." He carries me to an area where a couple of lanterns are lit. "So, I thought about doing this in the back of my truck, but even with lots of covers, I couldn't imagine that would be comfortable for us. Then I thought I'd use an air mattress, but that would be a tight fit, so this is the end result."

He stops and lowers me to a small concrete pad. There is a huge air mattress that sits in the center, piled with blankets and pillows. There are two milk crates tipped upside down, holding lanterns on either side of the mattress. At the top of the concrete pad, there are two lawn chairs, a small folding table, and two coolers sitting beneath it.

"You did all of this?" I ask.

"Yeah, I wanted to take you on a date."

"This is..." I walk, turn to him, and wrap my arms around him. "Incredible, Rome. This is better than any other date you could have thought of. It's perfect."

He pulls me into his arms and trails kisses up my neck. The way he's holding me and the exhale as he buries his face in my neck, says more than words ever could. He wanted to do this, be here with me, and make it a special memory for us. "Are you hungry?" he asks softly.

"A little. What are we having?"

He moves to one of the coolers and pulls it open. "Chicken strips, mashed potatoes and gravy, mac and cheese, and biscuits."

"Perfect."

"Drinks and dessert are in the other cooler. I have beer, a bottle of wine, and water."

"Just water for now."

He nods and reaches into the other cooler and pulls out two bottles of water.

"I don't know how hot the food is. I hope the cooler at least kept it warm."

"Doesn't matter," I say, taking a seat in one of the lawn chairs. "It's perfect."

We fill our plates and talk about the new hires at the shop, college, and the time we're going to be apart. Everything feels natural with Roman.

"I'm so full. That was delicious."

"So, I thought we could spend the night out here. We don't have to. We can just stay a while and look up at the stars. I know there's no bathroom, but I came prepared." He points to a small tote. "Small bags for toilet paper, and wipes, just in case."

"You thought of everything." I swallow back the emotion clogging my throat. This man, he's been in my life for years, and when I started to see him as more than just Forrest's best friend, I never thought I'd be with him like this. Never in my wildest imagination did I see him taking such care with me. For me.

"I tried to."

"How about we stay for a while and see how it goes?"

"Deal. Come on." He stands, reaches for my hand, and leads me to the air mattress. We both kick off our shoes and climb under the covers.

"Did you buy this for tonight?" I ask, as I rub my hand over the plush dark-gray blanket.

"Kind of, but not really. I know we're always taking the blanket from my bed when we're watching movies, so I thought I'd buy us one for the living room."

"Rome." My tone is wistful, because this man, he melts my heart. Looking at him you would never know that he's the sweetest teddy bear, at least when it comes to me.

"I'm not used to having a woman around the house, but I thought you might like it." He shrugs as if this incredibly thoughtful gesture is no big deal.

It's a big fucking deal.

The night is cooler, so this throw is perfect to ward off the cooler air. I snuggle under the throw, and up against him.

"Wow. The stars are so bright tonight." The sky is black, but the millions of tiny stars look like sparkling diamonds shining down on us. It's a magical scene, the night is clear, and I can't think of anything more romantic than lying beneath a dark sky filled with diamonds with him.

"They are. I used to love coming out here as a kid. I used to camp with my grandpa."

"Why'd you stop?"

"His health declined, and I got older. Life just has a way of changing like that, I guess."

"It's so peaceful."

"I wanted to share this place with you."

I turn on my side and slide my hand up under his shirt. "Thank you."

He sits up and tears his shirt off, tossing it next to us. I lie down on his chest and relish the feel of his skin against my cheek.

"Thank you for this too."

"I know you like it when there is nothing between us." I feel him press a kiss on the top of my head, and the moment is so surreal it brings tears to my eyes.

I'm here with Roman.

We're together in a way I thought would always just be a fantasy of mine, and it kills me I have to leave. Lifting my head, I study him. He holds my gaze, and when it gets to be too much, I look away. I run my fingers over the ink on his chest. "You have an open spot here," I say, placing my hand over his heart.

"Yeah, it will probably always stay that way."

"Why?"

He shrugs. I don't pry, but it turns out I don't have to. "This is going to sound crazy, but I want that spot reserved for something or someone that I love."

I feel a pinch of sadness in my chest because I know I could fall in love with him. Hell, I'm already halfway there. More than halfway if I'm being honest with myself. I have to remind myself that we're new, and it took us months to get to where we are now. I can't help but wonder if maybe one day that spot might be mine?

Instead of giving him words, I place a tender kiss on his chest over his heart and lie back down, staring up at the night sky. "It's beautiful," I whisper.

"Yeah, you are," he says, holding me tighter against him.

We spend the next hour just gazing up at the moon and the stars. We don't talk much, and we keep our hands to ourselves for the most part. We do decide that since we both have to work the next day, to pack up everything and go back to his place. By the time we get there, we fall into bed, exhausted. When I close my eyes, I can still see the starlit sky. His arms are still wrapped around me, and his even breathing tickles my ear.

I hope I never forget the way I feel right now.

Happy.

Loved.

Safe.

ROMAN 13

"YOU TWO ARE COMING TONIGHT, right?" I hear Emerson ask Lyra and Drake. The three of them have been laughing and cutting up all week. She definitely chose well when it came to picking applicants for the position. They're both trained well enough that they'll be fine on their own.

"Forrest mentioned it, but I don't want to intrude," Lyra replies.

"The more the merrier. Besides, you're both a part of the Everlasting Ink family. And, Drake, you need to bring your girlfriend so we can all meet her."

"Lisa and I will be there," Drake tells her.

"Perfect. Why don't you two head out early? I'll stay and close up with Rome."

I smile. Her voice is full of innocence and sincerity, but I'm certain she's hoping to be able to steal a kiss or ten. My girl has been missing me as much as I missed her. Two nights without her lying next to me, and I feel as though I might lose my mind. How I'm going to handle her being away at school is beyond me. I've gone twenty-nine years sleeping alone, and a little over a week with Emerson, and I'm ruined.

"Are you sure? It's your birthday," Lyra points out.

"Positive. I'll see you all at the house tonight at seven. You have the address?"

"Yes," they reply at the same time.

"Perfect. You both are doing great. It was a pleasure getting to work with you. You both have my number. Call or text anytime. If I don't answer, I'm in class or clinicals, but I'll call you back as soon as I can. The guys are all great too, so don't be afraid to ask any of them."

"Everyone has been great," Drake says.

"Agreed," Lyra adds.

"I'm glad. All right, get out of here. I'll see you in a couple of hours." I hear their footsteps and then the quiet in the waiting area.

"Scott, you're good to go," I tell my client as I clean him up. The timing couldn't have been more perfect. I hand him a mirror, and he smiles and nods his approval before I wrap him up and go over the care instructions. Not that I need to. Scott is a frequent flyer.

"Thanks, man. How much do I owe you?"

"Emerson is out front. She'll get you taken care of." We shake hands, and he steps out of the room. I rush through getting my station cleaned up, and just as I'm stepping out of my room, Scott waves and walks out the door. I pull up my phone and pause the recording on the cameras in my office and the lobby area.

"What happened? He was on the books for another hour," Emerson asks. She has a look of concern on her face, and somehow that makes me fall for her just a little harder. She's worried about me.

"I know."

"Did he change his mind?" She steps toward me, just within reach.

"Nope." I snake my arms around her waist and kiss her.

"The cameras."

"I paused them."

She grins. "Smart man." She tilts her head back for another kiss. "Now, tell me how you finished so quickly."

"I knew this was going to be a brief visit. It was just a small piece, the name of his new baby boy. I blocked out more time than I needed, hoping that it would just be the two of us, and we could spend some time together."

"When did you do that?"

"Yesterday. I've spent too many sleepless nights without you, and I knew by today I'd need my hands on you. We have your party in a couple of hours, and this was the only way I could think to do it."

"I've barely slept," she says, resting her head on my chest.

"Something we're going to have to adjust to."

"I don't like it."

"Yeah," I agree. "Come on, let's go to my office. I'll lock the door, and unpause the cameras for this area. Leave the lobby music playing so they know we're still here."

"Do you think that they'll check?"

"Honestly, no, but we need to cover all our bases just in case."

She heads to my room, and I lock the door. Once we're both out of the lobby area, I unpause the cameras. It's overkill, but I still feel like it's important. I plop down on my chair and pat my lap. She comes willingly. Straddling me, she rests her arms on my shoulders, running her fingers through my hair.

Fuck, I never thought that was something I'd enjoy. I've had women play with my hair before when they were coming on to me, and I hated it. Hated their hands messing up my hair. When it comes to Emerson, I crave her touch, no matter where it is. I just crave her. It's that simple.

Wrapping my arms around her, I pull her close, burying my face in her neck. "I missed you, baby girl."

"Tell me this next year is going to go fast."

"Ten months. Not a year."

She laughs softly.

"Nine and a half months if we're getting technical."

"Are you counting down the days?"

"The seconds," I admit. "It's going to suck, but I'm so proud of you, Em. You're going to be graduating from college." I ignore the voice in my head, reminding me I'm too old for her.

"I'm excited. I'll still have my three months of clinicals to complete, but that's already set up at the surgery center here in town. I was lucky to apply early, and it helps that we're in a small town, and everyone knows everyone."

"So after graduation, you're home for good?"

"I'll be home for good."

"And I never have to sleep another night without you." We're almost a full year away from that happening and I shouldn't be insinuating that this will still be a thing, that *we* will still be together, but with the way I feel about her, I know we will be. At least I hope we will be. I fought tooth and nail against what I felt for her. Now I can't imagine a life where she's not mine.

"We can do this, right?"

"Of course we can. You'll be home to visit and when I can get away, I can come to see you."

She pulls back, and her eyes mist with tears. "You'll come to see me?"

"Yeah, it's not that far of a drive. Little over three hours, right?"

"Three and a half."

"Easy." I drop a kiss to her chin.

"I didn't think it would be this hard."

I don't ask her what "it" is, because I know she's talking about the separation between us. While I'm not ready for her to leave, never in my wildest imagination did I think I'd miss her as much as I do when I'm lying in my bed at night.

"We don't have much time before we need to head to your place."

She leans back, and that action has her grinding on my hard cock. "Then we better use it wisely." She's off my lap before I can stop her and dropping to her knees. She reaches for my button on my jeans, and I place my hand over hers.

"You don't have to do this."

"Do I look like a woman that's being forced?"

"No, baby girl, you look like you're mine." I didn't intend to say that, but that's been happening a lot around her. My mouth just blurts whatever's on my mind, as if I don't know what a filter is. I can't help but be straight with her. That's who I am.

We're lying to enough people, but I'll never lie to her.

"Yours." She nods as her lips curl into a smile. "Then I guess that means I can do this whenever I want."

She shakes off my hand that stopped her, and continues to unbutton my jeans, lower the zipper, and pull my cock out. She licks her lips, and I have to bite down on my cheek to keep from moaning like a fucking porn star when she takes me into her mouth.

I force myself to watch her instead of letting my eyes roll to the back of my head. Gently, with more tenderness that I would have thought I would be capable of right now, I gather her long brown hair in my fist to keep it out of her face. She might think it's a gracious gesture, but it's a purely selfish one.

I don't want to miss this.

She takes me deep, to the back of her throat, and my hips thrust forward. She gags, and I immediately pull back and try to push her off, but my stubborn girl shakes her head, and swats my hands away.

Again.

And keeps on going.

Her mouth bobs up and down on my cock like it's her job. She's taking control, and I'm gladly letting her. It's not long before I'm feeling that all too familiar tingling in the base of my spine. My balls tighten, and I know I'm not going to last long.

"Baby girl." I tap her shoulder with the hand that's not holding her hair. She doesn't stop. She just keeps right on going, like I didn't say a word. "Em, baby, you have to stop."

She doesn't stop.

This time I do close my eyes. Her hot wet mouth works me over, and when she takes me all the way to the back of her throat again, I can't hold it. I spill into her mouth in what feels like the most intense orgasm of my life. This isn't my first with her, but each one grows in intensity.

How the fuck am I going to live without her while she's at school?

When my cock falls from her mouth, I open my eyes in time to see her wipe her lips with the back of her hand. I don't know why, but that movement, along with the satisfied smile on her face, has me falling even more under her spell.

"Come here," I rasp.

She climbs back onto my lap, straddling my hips, and I waste no time pulling her into a kiss. I squeeze her ass as her tongue erotically slides against mine. In the back of my mind, I know we're running out of time, and no way am I getting off and she doesn't.

That doesn't work for me.

Standing with her in my arms, and my jeans falling down my thighs, I move her to sit on the table. I take a few seconds to pull up my jeans, grab my rolling chair, and get comfortable.

"Shorts off, baby girl."

"We need to get going," she tries to protest, but it's weak at best.

"You're right, we do, but, baby, we're not leaving this room until you're coming all over my face. Lose. The. Shorts." Her face turns a beautiful light shade of pink. She shimmies out of her shorts and places them next to her on the table. She discarded her panties, too, without having to be told.

"Good girl," I whisper thickly as I pull her to the edge of the table, brace her legs over my shoulders, and dive in to feast. Her taste explodes on my tongue. She digs her fingers into my hair and tugs when I insert one long digit inside her. She's tight and so fucking warm. I want to know what it feels like when her pussy is gripping my cock.

Slow your roll, Bailey.

I groan out loud, not able to hold it in when I think about the fact that I'm where no man has ever been. I'm the only one to taste this pussy, to feel her from the inside, and that's a heady feeling.

I always want it to be that way.

That's wrong of me, and I know it is, but I can't help how I feel. She's so much younger than me. She hasn't been able to explore and experiment the way I have. That's not fair to her, but the thought alone has fire coursing through my veins.

I'm the only man she needs.

Fuck the age difference.

Fuck it all. Everything except for the two of us. At this moment, that's all that matters.

Us.

"Rome." Her voice is raspy and so damn sexy.

I want her to come unglued. I want to drive her just as wild as she did me. I want her to feel, in every pore of her skin, that it's me making her feel this way. That I'm the man who owns her pleasure.

I add another finger, and she hisses as her hips arch up off the table.

My tongue traces her clit, and her legs clamp around my head. I smile before going back for more. She's close. Her pussy clamps down on my fingers, just as tight as her thighs, gripping my head like a vise.

"Come for me, Em. Give it all to me. It's mine. Your pleasure is mine," I tell her, before going back for more.

With one swipe of my tongue, she's shooting off like a rocket. She calls out my name, and I swear on all that I am, it's a sound I'll never in my life forget. I don't stop until her body relaxes.

Carefully, I remove her legs from my shoulders and stand. Leaning over her where she's still lying on the table, I kiss her softly. It's a complete contrast to the way my tongue was lapping at her pussy. I gave her the naughty part of me. Now I'm giving her the rest of me.

All of me.

The softer side. The man who thinks about her constantly. The man who's sleep deprived because after a handful of days with her next to me at night, wrapped in my arms, I feel lost without her.

"I didn't expect to fall this hard for you," I confess.

"Do you regret it?"

"No. Never, Emerson. You hear me? Whatever the outcome, I'll never regret a moment shared with you."

I kiss her once more, because I can't get enough of her, before helping her up, and assisting her with sliding back into her panties and shorts. I lift her off the table, placing her on her feet.

"Oh no."

"What?" My eyes scan her body, looking for something that might be amiss.

"We're going to have to erase the cameras."

"I paused the one in my room. Besides, it's pointed at the door for client confidentiality. There's a lot of ink you have to strip down for, and we don't record that. Just in-and-out activity of the room."

"I know, but I was loud, Rome. So loud."

I grin and drop a kiss on her temple. "I know."

She playfully swats at my chest. "I'm serious. Pull it up, and see if you can hear us."

I don't think she was that loud, but then again, I was so lost in her, so she could have been.

Grabbing my phone from the desk, I pull up the app and choose the hallway camera. I hit Play, and sure enough, you can hear her calling out my name. Part of me wants to save the video to my phone so I can listen to it repeatedly at night when I'm alone in my bed and missing her. However, I know I can't do that. If I want to hear her come for me, I'm just going to have to get creative.

"Shit. Shit. Shit. What if they were watching that?" There's panic in her voice.

I step in behind her and wrap my arms around her. She leans her back into my chest and instantly relaxes. Holding my phone in front of her, I erase all the video footage from today. That way, it won't look as suspicious. We can just say it was an outage with the company or something. Hell, I'm sure the guys will never notice, but she's right. It's a risk, and it's better if we do what we can to prevent them from finding out until she's ready.

I'm ready now. I know the outcome, and I'm willing to face the consequences.

I could lose my part of the business if the guys band together and ask to buy me out. I could also lose one if not all four of my best friends since kindergarten, but I'm still here. I'm still wracking my brain with ideas about stealing time with her before she leaves, and how often I can get to Lexington to see her while she's finishing her last year of college.

I was all in the minute my lips touched hers.

I still have this heaviness in my chest when I think about Emerson losing her brother over us, but she's assured me it won't come to that. I know she's younger than me, but as she's told me time and time again, she's a grown woman. I have to trust her instincts. I'll never forgive myself if they don't make it through this once Forrest finds out.

I should walk away.

I'm an asshole for not putting her first, but I tried already. I tried my hardest, and she wouldn't let me.

I'll just have to make sure he understands what this is.

It's not just for fun.

We're not just passing the time.

We're falling.

I'm falling.

And we're all in.

EMERSON 14

AFTER ALL MY INSISTENCE THAT I didn't need a birthday party, I've had a great time. Drake and his girlfriend, Lisa, and Lyra are perfect additions to our little family. The guys have been their crazy silly selves, and it's just been... nice.

The only thing that would make tonight better is if I didn't have to hide how I feel about Roman. We've done well staying away from one another. I've gone out of my way to engage Monroe and Lyra, and even Lisa, when she's not glued to Drake's side.

Not that I blame her. We're all unfamiliar faces, but as the night's worn on, she's relaxed more and more.

Roman and I have shared longing gazes when no one else was looking; at least I hope no one was looking. I also managed to snag a seat next to him when we were eating, but other than that, no contact. We're not counting his hand on my thigh under the table.

It's harder than I thought it would be. The closer we become, the more difficult it is to pretend like he's not more to me than just one of the guys. One of my brother's best friends.

"Em!" Lachlan calls out. "Get your ass over here and give me a hug. You're leaving in two days." He's more than a little tipsy, but I do as he says.

"You going to miss me, Lach?" I ask, wrapping my arms around his waist. I feel his lips press to the top of my head. Not unlike anything Forrest or any of the others have done in the past. They all treat me like their little sister. Well, not all of them.

Roman definitely did not treat me like his little sister earlier tonight in his room at the shop.

"Stop hogging her," Maddox calls out. "I need a hug too." He juts out his bottom lip and stumbles, so he sits his ass on one of the homemade benches around the fire. He's trying to make a sad puppy-dog face, but he's laughing, so it's not really working for him.

They're all wasted. Everyone is except for Lisa, Roman, and me. Lisa is the designated driver, and they're dropping Lyra off. As far as Roman and I, well, we both knew we'd slip up if we were wasted, so we've nursed our drinks all night, and as everyone around us grows more intoxicated, the more I feel my shoulders ease. If I stare a little too long, they'll be less likely to notice, and even if they do, they more than likely won't remember it.

"You two are ridiculous." I laugh, as I pull away from Lachlan and make my way to Maddox. He grins as I lean over and offer him a hug. He pulls me into him, and this time I'm the one who's stumbling. I laugh as I right myself, holding on to his shoulders before standing back to my full height.

"What the hell? Emerson, you better head this way, missy!" Legend hollers. He's standing on the other side of the fire with his arms wide open. "I need some birthday girl snuggles too."

"I'm her brother!" Forrest replies. "I should get all the birthday snuggles." He's sprawled out in a lawn chair, sitting off to the right on his own. He was feeling queasy, so we all decided to give him a wide berth.

"So are we," Legend counters.

"Yeah!" Lachlan and Maddox chime in.

"Rome, help us out here." Legend pulls Roman into the conversation. "Tell Forrest she's ours too."

My belly flops because I am Roman's, just not the way Legend thinks I am. I hate that we are lying to them, but it won't always be this way. If we can make it through me being away to finish my last year of college, and we still want this, then we'll tell them.

They're all going to be mad we kept it a secret, but I'd rather do that than Roman decide I'm too young, or he's just not feeling this relationship thing, and they all be pissed at him for breaking my heart. Because if that happens, my heart will indeed be shattered into a million tiny pieces with his name on them.

I tell myself not to look at him. However, I know that if I don't, it's going to be obvious. With Legend's arm still slung over my shoulders, I turn and lock eyes with the man who holds my heart.

Does he know? Does he even realize what he means to me?

His eyes sear into mine. I can feel the heat of his gaze all the way to my toes. His eyes flash to where Legend's arm is around my shoulders before settling back on my own.

A slow smile spreads across his face. "I'm gonna need me some of those birthday girl snuggles," he says, patting his lap.

My body instantly reacts to the sound of his voice, desire pooling between my thighs.

"My man!" Legend calls out.

He releases me, and on shaking legs, I make my way toward Roman. His eyes never leave mine, as I take cautious steps that carry me around the fire to where he's sitting.

He pats his lap again, and I dramatically roll my eyes, pretending like this entire scene is ridiculous.

That's what I want them to see. What I want them to think.

What they can't see is the way my heart pounds in my chest. They can't feel the way my palms grow sweaty. I manage to keep a steady gait regardless of how unstable my legs actually feel. They can't see how turned on I am just from his heated stare.

"Come on, birthday girl," he says. His voice is low and deep, slicing through me like a caress when we're lying together skin to skin.

I move to sit on his lap, and he immediately wraps his arms around me. It's not the blaze of the fire that warms me within, but his embrace. "Hey, baby girl," he rasps. His thumb slides beneath my shirt, and he traces my skin just above the waistline of my jean shorts.

"My sister," Forrest says again. "Why am I the last to get birthday snuggles?"

"It's okay, Forty," Monroe says from her chair next to Forrest. "She's saving the best for last."

"The real for last," he says, and I don't even have to look at him to know that he's smiling. I can hear it in his voice. Slow speech and all from all the adult beverages he's consumed. "Come here, kid. I'm feeling left out."

Roman tenses, but after one more gentle squeeze, his arms fall away, and I stand freely. I don't turn to glance at him over my shoulder. I won't be able to hide the longing I feel for him. I just want to stay on his lap, wrapped up in his arms.

"The birthday girl!" Forrest yells, entirely too loudly. He taps his lap, and I can't protest because I just did the same thing with Roman. I perch myself on his lap and he gives me one of his big-brother bear hugs. "How dare they steal my big brother thunder," he grumbles.

I pat him on the shoulder and chuckle. "You were the first," I tell him.

"Damn right. Hear that, boys? I was the first. I hold the big brother title." Forrest thrusts his hand in the air, the same hand that's holding his can of beer, and it spills all over both of us. "Oh, shit. Sorry, Em."

I laugh and shake my head. "It's fine, Forrest. Just a little beer. I'm going to run inside and change. Does anyone need anything?" I ask, standing from his lap.

"Can you bring me a hoodie or something?" Monroe asks.

"Sure, Lyra? Lisa?" I ask the other ladies.

"No, thank you," they reply in unison.

"There's a hoodie in my truck," Legend tells Monroe. "It's on the passenger seat."

"Do you mind?" she asks him.

"Nah. Come on. I'll go with you to get it." He holds his hand out for her, and waits for her to stand and join him. She takes his hand and, together, with a little bit of wobble in their steps, they head to his truck that's parked right next to the house to grab Monroe a hoodie.

In my room, I pull my soaked T-shirt off as I make my way to my en suite bathroom and toss it over the sink. Grabbing a washcloth, I run it under some warm water and wash the sticky beer from my skin. Luckily, it wasn't enough to soak my bra, but somehow it still smells like beer. Reaching behind my back, I unclasp it and leave it lying over the sink with my soiled T-shirt before turning off the light.

I gasp when I see Roman sitting on my bed. He has the sketchbook and the huge art set of pencils and markers that he and the guys gave me earlier for my birthday in his hands. I know the art set wasn't cheap, and they gave me three huge sketchbooks. They all know I love to doodle, and word finally spread about the lily tattoo Roman did for me.

"What are you doing in here?" My eyes flash to the door that's now securely closed.

"It's locked," he explains.

"What if they come looking for you?"

He shrugs. "Told them I had to shit. I shut the bathroom door and turned on the fan just in case." He grins as he stands and walks toward me. "I wanted a few minutes with you." He stops when we're toe to toe. He cups my breasts, one in each hand, as if he's testing their weight. His thumbs glide over my nipples that are already hardened peaks, longing for more of his touch.

"Rome."

His eyes that were locked on my chest snap to mine. "Hold on tight, baby girl." That's the notice I get before he bends, grabs the backs of my thighs, and lifts me into the air. I lock my legs around his waist, and my arms around his neck, trying to hold in my squeal of surprise and delight at being in his arms.

He walks until my back hits the wall. "I need you to scoot up."

"Scoot up?"

"Rest your back against the wall, and I'll take care of the rest. Hold on to my head or my shoulders whatever you need to do, but trust me, I got you."

I ask no more questions, because I do trust him. This is dangerous as hell, but also so fucking hot that he needed me enough to sneak into my room while everyone is still downstairs.

I rest my back firmly against the wall, and just as he said, he lifts me so that my breasts are eye level for him. I bury my hands in his hair, because it's one of my favorite things to do. I like the way it feels to be tethered to him.

He tilts his head back and smirks. I'm usually the one looking up, so it's weird for our roles to be reversed. "We don't have much time, and we're not leaving here until you come for me." He pulls a nipple into his mouth and nips gently before sucking hard, and I moan at the pleasure of it.

"Shh, baby girl, as much as I love to hear you, you're going to have to be quiet. Cover your mouth if you have to."

I nod and place one hand over my mouth, while the other grips the back of his neck, holding him to my breast, because I don't want him to stop.

"You're always so responsive for me." He moves to the other breast, doing much of the same, nipping softly and then sucking hard, all while he's rolling the opposite nipple between his thumb and forefinger. He has one hand draped under me, holding me up, and the other is working its magic on getting me off.

I don't reply, and I'm pretty sure he's not expecting an answer. Instead, I close my eyes and just feel. His mouth is fucking my breasts. I don't know of another way to describe it. His hand that's holding me up slides beneath my shorts, and one long thick digit slips inside me.

"Oh," I moan, but the sound is muffled because this time I was prepared, keeping my hand over my mouth.

"So wet for me, baby." His tone is raspy, and deep, and so fucking sexy. I hear laughter from outside, and I'm reminded of how dangerous this is. Instead of begging him to stop, I feel my body tighten.

He does this thing with his teeth, and then soothes it with his tongue, and it's as if my nipples are suddenly a button for pleasure. He glides his finger in and out, in short, languid strokes, due to the confine of my shorts and the position that we're in.

My legs tighten around him, and my back arches off the wall.

"There she is. Come for me, baby girl. Give it all to me," he demands.

My body coils like a tight spring and explodes. I'm breathing heavily, and so is he. He removes his finger and sucks it into his mouth. Once he's satisfied, he helps me slide down his body and wraps his arms around me tightly. He buries his face in my neck and breathes me in. We don't say a word as we hold one another. Finally, he pulls back and smiles sweetly.

"I'll let you get dressed." He carries me to the bed, sets me down, and kisses me so damn slowly, I'm melting into the mattress.

"What about you?" My hand brushes over his hard cock, hidden beneath his jeans.

"I'm okay," he says, kissing me chastely once more. "I wanted you to come undone for me. That's all I needed."

"I can be quick." I reach for him again, and he groans.

"We'll figure out a way to see one another before you leave." He runs the pad of his thumb over my bottom lip. "Maybe you can say you're leaving but come to my place first? You can park your car in the garage."

I nod as the details start to take shape in my mind. "I won't be able to stay long. Monroe and I always do a caravan thing. Safety in numbers and all that. We like to get back to school before it gets dark. We'll also need to go to the grocery store because our apartment has been empty all summer."

"What time does Forrest think you're heading back?"

"Noon."

He nods. "Come to my place. Tell Monroe you'll leave by one thirty. That should still get you back to Lexington with plenty of daylight." He pauses. "I'll call and reschedule my appointment to later in the day. I'll need a distraction knowing that you're driving away from me, anyway."

My heart squeezes in my chest. "Done."

He leans in and kisses me. "I needed to remind myself and you that you're mine," he whispers. "I didn't like their hands on you. When my hands were itching to touch you, to hold you, to claim you as mine."

"So you were jealous?" I ask, barely containing my smile.

I should be pissed that this little rendezvous was about jealousy, but let me tell you, when a man like Roman Bailey gets jealous and possessive over you, you embrace it, not fight with him about it.

His hands cradle my cheeks. "I was jealous." His lips descend on mine. More laughter floats in from outside, and he pulls away. "I'm going to head down the hall to the bathroom. You get dressed. I'll see you back out there." He kisses my forehead and steps away from me. He walks toward the door and turns to look at me over my shoulder. I don't know what I'm expecting, but a wink and his hand to his lips to blow me a kiss is not it.

He reaches for the handle, but I call out for him. "Rome." He stops and glances at me over his shoulder. It's on the tip of my tongue to tell him I've fallen in love with him, but I chicken out. "Thank you for—" I feel my face heat. "You know."

"Never thank me for pleasuring you, baby girl. Your pleasure is a gift to me. I should be the one thanking you." He releases his hold on the handle, turns on his heel, and in a few long strides is leaning over me on the bed, his arms braced on either side of me. "It's a pleasure to know that I'm going back down there with your taste on my tongue and your scent on my hand. They can hug you and joke around with you, but you're mine. I know it. You know it. Eventually, they'll know too." He kisses me quickly and stands. "Get dressed, baby girl. We've both been gone far too long." With that, he strides back to the door, releases the lock, checks the hallway, and slips out.

I stare after him, wishing that things were different. I wish I could see the future. He's in this now, into me, but we're about to spend a lot of time apart. That can put a strain on the most in-tune couples. I know waiting is the right thing to do. Why rile everyone up if this doesn't have lasting power?

Shaking out of my thoughts, I grab a sports bra and a T-shirt, and count to one hundred before heading back downstairs.

"What took you so long?" Lachlan asks. "Did you have the shits too?" He cackles.

"I had to change clothes and give myself a bitch bath, so I wasn't all sticky with beer." I glance at where my brother is sitting with his chin to his chest, arms crossed, and eyes closed.

"They're dropping like flies," Lisa jokes, pointing to where Maddox is lying on the ground.

"Do you need help getting them inside?" Lisa asks.

"No. Wait, where are Monroe and Legend?"

"Legend's passed out in his truck, and Monroe said she was going inside to crash."

"Okay. Thank you. Are you good to get everyone home okay?"

"We're all set. Thank you for having us." She leans in for a hug. "It was nice to meet everyone."

"You're Everlasting Ink family," I remind her. "This will be your new normal."

Her smile is huge. "Looking forward to it."

She manages to wrangle Drake and Lyra, and lead them to their car.

"I'll start getting these guys to bed," Roman tells me.

"I can help."

"Just check on Monroe, and maybe Legend. I'll help your brother and Maddox and then come and get him too. Sleeping in the truck is never fun."

"And you? Where are you sleeping?"

He leans in and presses a kiss to my temple. "I'll hold you until you fall asleep, but then I'm going to take the couch or one of the extra beds. Wherever is open."

"You're staying?" I ask, surprise evident in my tone.

"Baby girl, you're here, and I can get away with it without it being obvious. Of course, I'm staying."

Together we start getting everyone to bed, putting out the fire, and locking up the house. Just as he promised, Roman slips into my room and slides into bed next to me. He wraps me in his arms, and we both sigh, content. "Sleep, baby girl." I feel his lips on my shoulder and close my eyes.

I wish he'd be next to me when I wake up, but at least he'll be here. I'll get to see him. Maybe I can convince all the guys to stick around and hang out since it's my last day. Anything to spend more time with him.

"JUST NOT FEELING WELL," I tell Forrest on the other end of the phone. "I'm going to sleep it off. Hopefully I'll be fine with my afternoon clients. If not, I'll reschedule them."

"You need anything? Em and Monroe are heading out of town. I can have them drop something off."

I close my eyes, because I know that I'm going to hell for this. "Yeah, maybe ask Em if she minds stopping by and dropping off some headache medicine. I took the last of mine in the middle of the night."

It's not a complete lie. I did take the last of mine last night before bed. I've done nothing but obsess over the fact that she's leaving today and won't be home until Thanksgiving. The lie is that I need them now. What's one more when my lie of omission—that I'm falling for his little sister, the one that's ten years younger than me—is already out there in the universe?

"Sure, I think Em is getting ready to leave. They're meeting at Monroe's and will follow each other back to school like they always do."

"Thanks, man. I'll give her some money when she gets here."

"Don't worry about it. I got you covered. I'll call later to check in." He ends the call, and I drop my cell phone to the couch. Guilt sits heavy on my chest, but dammit, I need to see her, and this is just one more fail-safe that we're not going to get busted. I won't see her again until the end of November unless I can manage to get time away to sneak up there to visit her.

My phone rings and I groan until I check the screen and see the image of her smiling face. "Hello."

"Are you okay? Forrest said you weren't feeling well. I can stay another day and drive back to school tomorrow. What do you need?"

"I'm fine, baby girl. I had to make something up when Forrest realized I changed my schedule."

"So you're okay?"

The concern in her voice touches a place deep in my soul. A place I didn't know existed until I let her into my life as more than just my best friend's little sister. "I'm good. But now we're good if someone sees you here."

"I still can't stay long."

"I know. We'll make every minute count."

"I'm on my way there now. I just picked up some headache medicine."

"I am out, so that's not a complete lie, and I have a feeling I'm going to need it watching you drive away from me."

She's quiet for several seconds.

"I'm really going to miss you, Rome. I'll be there in five."

The line clicks off, and I know she's trying her hardest not to cry. Just the thought of her being upset crushes me.

I stand and walk toward the front door, and then pace back to the couch. I need to get a handle on my emotions. If she's dreading this separation as much as I am, I know her chest is aching, and her fingers itch to hold on to me as tightly as she can. I have to be the one to act as though this is going to be a piece of cake when we both know it's going to be hell.

I never thought I'd ever be in a position that being away from someone would cause me physical pain, yet here I am. I run my fist over my chest, because although you can't see it, the ache of already missing her is real.

I hear her car pull into the driveway, and I don't bother lifting the door to the garage like we originally planned. I bought us an alibi for the brief hour that she'll be here with me. I look over at the corner of the room where her gift sits, making sure everything is ready.

Taking a deep breath, I tug open the door, and she's standing there. Her bottom lip trembles and I'm certain the guys can hear my heart cracking all the way at the shop.

"Baby girl." I open my arms, and she rushes into them, allowing me to wrap my arms around her. "Let me shut the door," I whisper, my lips next to her ear. I don't want to let her go any more than she wants to release me, but I also need to remember that it's my job to save us from prying eyes.

For now.

Emerson takes a few steps back, allowing me to shut the door. I lock it for good measure. At least we will hear someone unlocking it before they can take us by surprise. I don't anticipate company. All the guys are at the shop today, but I'm constantly thinking about ways to keep her safe. To keep this secret between the two of us, because that's how she wants it. I'll give her until graduation.

Without a word, I entwine her fingers with mine and lead her to the couch. I start to sit, but she shakes her head.

"Can we go lie down?"

"Anything you want, baby girl." I change directions and lead her down the hall to my room. The bed is wrinkled and unmade, and the evidence of my tossing and turning last night stares back at me. "I didn't sleep well."

"Me either."

Knowing that she loves lying next to me, skin to skin, I tug off my T-shirt and climb into bed, patting the spot next to me. She does the same, stripping out of her T-shirt and bra before joining me. I curl my arm around her, bringing her to my chest.

The blinds are pulled shut, so my room is dark, regardless of the sun shining high in the sky today. Running my fingers through her hair, I try to memorize this moment. You'd think I was losing her forever, by the heavy beat of my heart in my chest. I've never had anxiety, but this ache, that has to be it.

It's not heartbreak, right? I'm not losing her. She's just going back to school. In less than a year, we'll be right back here.

Permanently.

At least I hope that's the case. I'm giving her this last year to finish school, but when she comes home, I want her to come home to me.

"How do you feel about taking a year off to move to Lexington?" she asks. Her voice is thick, and although I hear a bit of humor, her tone is still laced with sadness.

"I would if you needed me, but you don't."

She lifts her head. "I do need you."

"That's not what I meant, baby girl. You're fierce and determined, and I'd just be in your way. I know this is your last year, and you need to focus on that. You're there getting an education to obtain the career of your dreams, and I'll be here living mine, keeping this spot right here next to me warm for you."

"Just me?"

"Of course just you. Is that what has you so upset? You're afraid I'm going to replace you? You're the first woman to be in this bed, and you'll be the last." I know it's a big declaration, but the words tumbled out before I could stop them.

Not that I wanted to.

I'm telling her the truth. I can't even imagine anyone else owning this spot next to me other than her.

"It took me all summer to wear you down. I'll be gone longer than that."

I pick up her hand that's resting on my chest and bring it to my lips. "Just you. Always you." No matter what happens between us, whatever the outcome, I know without an ounce of doubt that no one will ever love her like I do. The other side of that is that I'll never love anyone else, not like I love her.

Oh, fuck!

I'm in love with her.

My arms hold her a little tighter. I knew I was falling harder every day, but it's the first time I've actually thought the words. Do I tell her before she leaves? Do I wait to see what this first separation does to us? Fuck, why are love and relationships so complicated?

"What are you thinking about?"

"You."

"You tensed up."

I turn to my side, and she does the same, facing me. "I've been open with you throughout all of this. I never once denied that I wanted you. I know we're lying to everyone else, but, baby girl, I've never lied to you."

She nods. "I know. And I hate that we're lying too, but between my age and my brother, we have enough against us without adding the pressure of me going back to school."

"When you come home, after you graduate, we'll tell them."

Even through the sadness, I can see the sparkle in her emerald eyes. She likes the idea, which takes some of the weight off my shoulders. She's in this. I'm in this.

Resting my hand on her cheek, I stare into her eyes, and I know this moment is one I'll always remember. Every moment with her is one that I've captured in my mind and hope to never forget.

"That's a good plan. That way, you won't be here to deal with the aftermath all on your own."

"It's not too late to change your mind. We have some time."

"I think we need that time, Rome, but not because I don't think that this is going to work out. No, we need the time to grow closer. The distance is going to be tough, and we don't need all the other added pressures."

"My girl is beautiful and smart."

She laughs just as I intended for her to. Her hand travels down my abs, and I know what she's after. My cock is rock solid for her, but we're not going there.

"Not today," I tell her.

"I want to."

"I know, baby girl, and trust me, I love your hands on me. I crave it, but we don't have much time left, and I'm not sending you back to college unsatisfied. Besides, what we have growing between us is more than the physical. Just let me hold you because it's going to be far too long before I can do this again."

"It's going to be a long time for this too." She tries again to palm my cock, but I stop her, bringing her hand to my lips.

"I can live with that. I need to memorize what you feel like just like this," I say, hugging her tightly. Her bare breasts press against my chest, and she sighs.

"I love the feel of your skin against mine."

"I know you do."

"When I come home, after I graduate, we have to agree to sleep naked every night."

"What if the house catches on fire, or there's a break-in?" I ask, my amusement clear in the tone of my voice.

"It's worth it." She grins, and I kiss her.

I intend for it to be a quick peck, but once my lips touch hers, I can't pull away. Instead, I take my time tasting her while letting my hands roam all over her body.

"I think it would be worth the three-and-a-half-hour drive for a kiss like that," she says, once we both come up for air.

"I think you might be right." I kiss the end of her nose. "Come on, get dressed. You need to meet Monroe, and I have something for you."

Her eyes light up, and I vow to make that happen as much as I can. When she smiles like she is right now, her green eyes look like sparkling emeralds.

Knowing that if I don't climb out of bed, and force us to get moving, we might not at all, I toss back the covers, and do just that. I grab my discarded T-shirt and slip back into it, while she quickly gets dressed as well.

"Come." I hold my hand out for her and she takes it. I lead her to the living room and grab the gift bag from the corner. "This is for you."

"You already got me something for my birthday. The sketchpads and art set, that was from all four of you, right?" she asks, making sure that she's correct that Lachlan, Legend, Maddox, and I all went in to get her a gift.

"Yeah, that was from all of us, but this is just from me. It's not much, but no way could I not get you your own gift."

"What is it?" she asks.

"Open it and find out." I move to sit on the arm of the couch and pull her with me. She's standing between my legs as she reaches into the gift bag. "Card first," I tell her.

She nods, removes the card from the bag, and slides her finger beneath the flap. She reads the card, and the brief note I wrote, and grins when she holds up a gift card for the café she talks about that's just down from their apartment.

"You didn't have to do that." She leans in for a kiss.

"I wanted to. There's five hundred dollars on there, so you should be set for a while."

"Roman!" she scolds. "That's too much."

"Baby girl, if you were going to be here, it would be more than that. You know you don't pay when you're with me." I raise my eyebrows, and she shakes her head, but there's a small smile tugging at her lips.

"You're impossible."

I shrug, because she's right. When it comes to her and taking care of her, I am impossible, and she hasn't seen anything yet. When I can take her out, and we don't have to hide this, my girl's going to be spoiled.

"Open the rest."

My heart races as she reaches into the bag and pulls out the throw blanket I bought for our night under the stars, and for her to use here when she's at my place.

"This is just like the one we used that night under the stars," she says. She peers around me to see if she can find the exact replica laying over the back of the couch.

She won't find it.

She's holding it.

"That's the same blanket."

She has a confused look on her face, which I expected.

"Rome, you bought that to keep here. I'll need it when I come home to visit." She holds the blanket out for me.

"Then bring it with you." I take the blanket from her, unfold it, and wrap it around her shoulders. "I'm not going to be there to hold you. I won't be able to hug you after a bad day, or even a good one. I want you to take this blanket with you, and when you need me, you wrap yourself up just like this and pretend I'm there."

Tears immediately well in her eyes. "Roman Bailey." She doesn't say more, instead she kisses me. It's soft and sweet, just like her. "This is... incredible."

"It's not much, but it's the best I could come up with."

She pulls the blanket to her face and inhales. "It smells like you."

I wasn't sure if she'd notice. I nod. "Yeah, I might have slept with it since that night. It used to smell like you."

Her hands move to my face, cupping my cheeks, and the blanket falls to the floor. I don't bother to reach for it. She has my full attention.

"You are everything I've ever wanted. I've dreamed of you being mine. I'm going to miss you." She leans in and kisses me. She eventually pulls back, just enough so that we can make eye contact. "I'll sleep with you wrapped around me every night."

"And you'll call and text. I don't care when or what time. I'll do my best to answer. If I can't, leave a message. If it's urgent, keep calling and I'll know that you need me."

"I don't want to disrupt your life."

"Baby girl, you are my life. If you need me, you keep calling and I'll know. Deal?"

"Deal."

"Good. Now kiss me. It's time for you to go. I don't want you arriving after dark."

I slide my hand behind her neck and kiss her like it very well could be our last time. My heart cracks just a little, and it makes me feel like a pussy. I can handle a little separation. We aren't the first to deal with it.

"Be safe. I want updates when you stop, and call me when you get there."

"You sound like my brother." She playfully rolls her eyes.

"Not your brother, baby girl. I'm just yours."

"Mine."

One more swift kiss, and I help her put her blanket back into the bag and walk her to the door. "Be safe, Em."

"I will. I'll see you soon."

"I'll see you soon." I open the door for her and watch her walk to her car. I wish I could walk with her, but it's the light of day, and that would blow our cover should someone drive by. So for now, I stand here in my doorway and wave as I watch my heart drive away.

November can't get here fast enough.

I force myself to go into the shop for my two clients at the end of the day. I'm quiet, but the guys don't call me out on it. They think I'm still not feeling well, and I'm not.

My heart hurts.

Emerson left my place just after one. It's five thirty now, and I haven't heard from her. She texted me around three and said they were stopping for food and were going to fill their cars up while they were stopped. I feel better that they are traveling with one another. At least she's not alone. However, she should have arrived back in Lexington by now, if my calculations are correct.

"You're all set, Matt," I tell my client. He stands and stretches. "Drake is at the front desk. He'll get you taken care of and go over aftercare." That's a perk of hiring Drake. He really does know his stuff. I walk Matt to the door. "Drake, can you talk Matt through aftercare?"

"You got it." He nods, and I walk back into my room and shut the door. As I'm reaching for my phone, it rings.

Fucking finally.

"Hey, baby girl," I say softy, not wanting the guys to hear me.

"We made it. We're going to order pizza and get groceries tomorrow. We're both exhausted."

"I just finished with a client and have one more. I'll call you when I get home."

"Perfect. I'm going to start unpacking."

"Talk soon, baby." I end the call and place my phone back on my desk. Relief washes over me knowing she made it back to college safe and sound. I miss her already, but we've got this.

Less than a year and I never have to be away from her again.

EMERSON 16

"DID YOU TRACK IT?" MONROE asks, as she settles next to me on the couch with a large bowl of popcorn.

"Yeah, says it was delivered today."

"Have you heard from him?"

"Not for a couple of hours, but he was working on a back piece, so that's to be expected."

She grins. "I have no doubt as soon as he opens it, he's going to call."

"I'm having regrets," I tell her.

"What? Why? The man is a total badass until it comes to you. You soften him in a way I've never seen before. He's going to love it, and probably going to play the five-finger shuffle more than a few times." She winks.

"Where do you come up with this stuff?" I laugh.

"Fine." She playfully rolls her eyes. "He's going to stroke his cock until he comes thinking of you."

"All because I mailed him a blanket."

"Your blanket, Em. He gave you one, and you gave him one. Did you write the note the way we discussed?"

"Yes, and it's corny as hell, and he's going to wonder what the hell he's doing dating or whatever this is, a woman who's ten years younger than him."

"Photo evidence or it didn't happen." She holds her hand out for my phone.

I know my best friend, and I knew she would ask, and part of me wanted her opinion on how corny it was, so I did indeed take a picture. I swipe through my images, pulling up the one in question, and hand her my phone.

Monroe dramatically clears her throat. "'Rome, I thought it was only fair that I be there to hold you when you need me too. Counting down the days, XO Emerson.'" She hands me back my phone with a proud smile on her face.

"You did good, Em. It's short and to the point. Not over-the-top corny. Not at all." She pops a handful of popcorn in her mouth, and chews. I can tell from the look in her eyes she has something to say. "Do you want to know what I think?"

"What?" I steal a handful of popcorn.

"I think that you're going to bring that man to his knees. Hell, he's halfway there."

"I don't want to bring him to his knees. I just want to be with him."

Monroe reaches over and places her hand over mine. "I see the way he looks at you. Everything is going to work out. I can feel it."

"Enough about me. What about you? It seems like ages since you've been on a date."

"Yeah." She sighs. "I see the way Roman looks at you, and I want that, you know? I'm not going to settle for subpar when I get to witness epic." She winks. "Besides, the guys who have been interested lately are out for one thing, and you and I both know I'm holding out for love."

"Yeah."

"You love him, Em. It's okay to take things to the next level."

"Right." I laugh. "Try telling him that. He's all 'we can wait, blah, blah, blah.'"

"I get it, though. He's worried as hell about your relationship with your brother. Maybe he thinks that if this one thing stays unchecked, that it will make a difference."

"Maybe," I reply as my phone rings. I smile when I see his name pop up. "Hey, you. How was your day?" I answer.

"Baby girl," he rasps, and my heart skips a beat. "It's been over two weeks since I've tasted your lips, and I'm feeling that. I'm feeling the loss of you here with me, like missing a fucking limb. I'm not sleeping at night because my arms ache to hold you. I'm bone-ass tired. I rushed home from the shop tonight because all I want to do is talk to you. I know you have an early class tomorrow, and we can't stay up late, so I blew off the guys and told them I wasn't feeling a beer." He pauses. He's breathing heavily, but I don't dare say a word. "I get home and there's a package on my front porch. I didn't order anything, but I carry it inside, kick off my shoes, and give it a better look. It's from my girl, so I'm anxious to tear it open."

"Did you?" I finally ask him. I'm hanging on his every word. My eyes glance at Monroe, and she's munching on popcorn with a grin on her face. She gives me a thumbs-up and I shrug. I'm not sure yet if my gift was a good thing or a bad thing.

"Yeah, Em, I opened it." Another long pause. "It smells like you." His voice is soft, almost reverent.

"Yeah, I slept with it, with both of them, for a few nights. I know it's lame that I stole your idea—" I start, but he cuts me off.

"Not lame, baby girl. Fucking incredible. We're going on three weeks of me missing you, and this—it's everything I needed today. The only thing that could be better was if you somehow managed to tuck yourself into this box with it."

I chuckle. "Pretty sure I'd need a bigger box." My heart soars knowing that he loves his gift, even if I stole his idea.

"What are you doing right now?"

"Just sitting on the couch chatting with Monroe, stealing her popcorn."

"Hi, Rome!" Monroe calls out.

"I'm sure you heard that, but Roe says hi."

"Tell her I said hello."

"Rome says hello."

"Emerson?"

I sit up straighter at him calling me by my full name. "Tell Monroe goodnight and go to your room. You might want to lock the door and turn on some music if you don't want her to hear you."

"Hear me?" I ask, and Monroe grins wider.

"I'm gonna take this to my room and watch a movie. With headphones. You know those noise-canceling ones my mom bought me so that I could concentrate on studying. Yeah, I'm going to use those." She winks as she stands with her half-eaten bowl of popcorn, her phone, and a bottle of water in her arms. "Night, Em. Love you."

"Night. Love you too," I tell her. "She just went to bed."

"Lock up, baby."

"Okay. Do you want me to call you back?"

"No. Fuck, no. I miss the hell out of you, and I'm not losing any more time. Take me with you to lock up."

I do as he says, making sure the apartment door is locked, and I turn off the lights. When I make it to my room, I don't bother with the overhead light. Instead, turning on the small bedside lamp. Just as he instructed, I close and lock my bedroom door.

"I'm in my room."

"Good girl," he husks, and heat pools between my thighs. "Em?"

"Yeah?"

"I'm going to hang up and call you back with a video call. I need to see you."

"Okay." The call ends abruptly but rings in with a video call not seconds later. "Hey." I smile at him.

"Damn, seeing your smile is all it takes to brighten my day."

"I miss you."

"I miss you too. Can you do something for me?"

"Anything."

"Strip. I need you naked."

"Only if you do too."

"Done." The phone jostles and then all I see is the ceiling of his bedroom. "You stripping for me, baby girl?" His voice is deep and gruff, and so incredibly sexy. I can't see him, but I can hear his clothes rustling.

I clear my throat and start to strip. "I am now."

"Fuck yes, you are," he says, and I can't help but smile.

Once I'm rid of all my clothes, I climb on the bed and lift my phone so he can only see my face.

"Don't hide from me, Em."

"I feel weird," I confess, and I close my eyes because that's just another reminder to him about how inexperienced I am. Another glaring sign that says he's ten years older than me.

"We don't do anything you're not comfortable with."

"I want to, Rome. I just don't know how to."

"There is no right or wrong way, baby girl. You do what feels right. You don't have to show me if that makes you feel uncomfortable."

"Are you going to show me?"

"Is that what you want? You want to see me stroke my cock while I think about you?"

"I do now," I say with a nervous laugh. He laughs too, and that seems to break some of the tension coiling inside me. "What do you want to see?"

"Anything. Everything."

The camera pans down his abs until he reaches his cock. His fist is gripping it tight, his piercing shining like a beacon in the night.

"This is how much I miss you," he says, his fist tightening as he strokes himself from root to tip.

"Damn," I mutter.

"Are you wet for me?"

I nod. Then ask, "Do you want to see?"

"Only if you want to show me."

"That's not what I asked you." I find my voice. This is Roman. I've known him my entire life and I know he's not recording me or doing anything malicious on his end. I let my nerves get the better of me, but now, seeing him, I'm more turned on than I ever thought possible in a situation like this.

We miss each other, and if this is what he needs to get through our separation, who am I to deny him? Besides, I've spent a few nights with my vibrator since I've been back at college, and it's just not the same. Not after experiencing orgasms from the hands and the mouth of the man on the other end of the line.

"Yes. I want to see your pussy."

A rush of heat pools between my thighs and I know exactly what he's going to see when I show him. Because I am going to show him. We're in this together, and we have to deal with this separation the best way that we know how.

Taking a deep breath, I spread my legs and point the phone to the juncture of my thighs. I'm breathing heavily, and when I hear his groan of pleasure, I tilt the screen so I can see, and his fist is pumping faster over his cock.

"I need you to touch yourself, Em."

I think about the logistics of how that's going to work and get an idea. I grab the extra pillows and place them between my legs to prop up my phone.

"Oh, fuck me," he says, and I grin.

Lying back, I pretend like it's just me here in the room, that Roman can't see me as I slide my fingers over my clit. I rub gently, and my belly quivers.

"I need you to hold those lips open for me, baby girl. I need to see all of you."

Doing as he asks, I use one hand to hold myself open for him, while the other explores. "Like this?" I ask softly. I hate I need his direction and bringing notice to that, but I also want this to be good for him. I'm learning as we go, and from the rapid stroke of his hand on his cock, I'd say Roman doesn't give a fuck that I need direction. He's enjoying the show.

"Slip a finger inside. Nice and slow."

I do, and the sensation has me moaning, "Rome." His name is a whisper on my lips.

"Don't stop," he rasps. "Your pussy's crying for me. Fuck me, I wish I was there to devour you. I would take every drop you have to give."

His words send sparks of desire rolling through my veins like a summer storm. "I'm close."

"Come for me, baby girl. Come. Now," he grits, and I do. It's as if his words have a direct line to my orgasm as wave after wave of pleasure flows through me. I faintly hear him grunting his approval, and shouting, "Oh fuck," but I'm too lost in my own release, the one I've been chasing since coming back to college.

All I needed was Roman.

"I needed you too, baby," he answers, and I realize I said the words out loud. "I need to clean up, but don't hang up, okay? Just... wait for me." His voice is almost pleading, and it's not what I'm used to when it comes to Roman.

"I'll do the same."

I climb off the bed and slip into my robe before darting across the hall to the bathroom. I clean up as quickly as possible, wash my hands, and as I'm reaching for the towel, I catch a glimpse of my reflection in the mirror. My face is flushed. My pupils are blown, and my eyes are glassy, but I'm smiling.

This must be what being in love looks like.

Turning off the light, I dart back to my room, closing the door, but leaving it unlocked this time. I climb under the covers, curl up with the blanket he gave me in my arms, and pick up my phone.

He's there, lying in the same fashion, snuggled with the blanket I sent him. "It's a poor substitute," he says softly. "But it smells like you, and that's exactly what I needed today."

"Tell me about your day."

"Nothing extraordinary happened. I got up, went to the gym, and went to work. I had a back piece I was working on. It's a new client, and he's going to need a few more sessions, but it's going to be badass."

"Of course it is. You're doing it."

He chuckles. "How about you? Tell me about your day."

"Good. Nothing eventful here either. Classes, and came home to study. Monroe and I made pasta for dinner, and then we were just sitting on the couch talking when you called."

He yawns, and I know we should probably hang up.

"I can let you go so that you can get some rest."

"I haven't been sleeping."

"It took me some time to get used to it too. I still wake up and reach for you."

"I knew this would be hard, Em, but damn, I didn't know I'd still be struggling weeks into this separation."

"Do you regret it? Me? I mean, waiting for me?"

"No. Never. Just get that thought right out of your head. I can never, and will never, regret you, baby girl. Ever."

I pull the blanket he gave me closer to my face and snuggle into it. His familiar scent is fading, but the meaning of the blanket is still here. I sleep with it every night. It's even wrapped around me when I study. I might have even turned down the thermostat because I was hot when we first got back to school. I have no shame.

"Tell me something, baby."

"Like what?"

"Everything. Tell me everything."

"I'm excited and a little nervous about graduating," I confess. "I know this job is going to be stressful at times, but I really love all of my classes. They're kicking my ass, but nothing worth having comes easy, right?"

"Like us."

"It's effortless with you."

"That's not what I meant. It's the outlying issues, like the fact that we're hiding this relationship. Even when you're not here, I fall harder for you every day. It's difficult to be lying to all four of them. Hell, I haven't even told my parents."

"Do you want to? Tell your parents, I mean?"

"Yeah, baby girl. I want to tell them. The moment I kissed you, I was in this, Emerson. I'm torn because I want you. I crave time with you, but that worry for you is still there. I'm not worried about me. I accepted my fate when I lost my willpower to resist you. However, I still fear you losing Forrest over this, and, baby girl, he's your family. He's the one who's stood by you, and made a home for you. I've been through it all, and it tears me up inside thinking that you could lose that because of me."

"Not because of you, Rome. If that's the choice he makes, then that's the choice that Forrest is going to have to live with. I will forever be grateful for all that he's done for me, but I'm a big girl now. I don't need him to handle my life anymore. He got me out and helped me get to where I am, but he has to let me make my own choices." I pause, listening to him breathe. "I choose you, Roman."

"Maybe he'll be mad, but just learn to accept this. Accept us?" There's hope in his voice.

"He'll have to if he wants to be a part of my life."

"I hate this for you."

"Not for you?" I ask.

"He's one of my best friends. I love him like a brother, but it's your name tattooed on my heart."

"I like this softer side of you."

He laughs softly. "I'm just me, Em."

"I know. You've always been nice to me, good to me even. All of you have. I was the annoying little sister." I cringe at the mention of our age difference, hoping he doesn't latch on to that next. "But you're different with me now. Softer is the best way I know how to describe it."

"I guess that's what happens to a man when he gets his dream girl."

My mouth falls open, and he chuckles.

Fucking video call.

He yawns again.

"You should try to get some rest," I say to change the subject. He really does look wrecked.

"I think with this gift I got today, I might actually be able to." He gives me a sleepy smile. "Sweet dreams, baby."

"Night, Rome. Sweet dreams." I blow a kiss at the screen, and he does the same before we end the video call. Plugging my phone in, I turn off the bedside lamp and close my eyes. I drift off to sleep with my heart full, and my body relaxed.

ROMAN 17

"THERE HE IS, THE BIRTHDAY boy!" Forrest calls out as I walk into the shop.

"My birthday isn't until Sunday," I remind him.

"It's your birthday week." He shrugs. "We're grilling at my place, Sunday, right?"

"Yeah." I nod. There's no point in trying to get out of it. This is his thing, and we all accept that. Forrest and Emerson didn't have the best childhood. Forrest's was worse than Emerson's because he got her out of that house as much as possible.

"So what's the plan?" Lachlan asks.

"I was thinking we could head into Nashville Saturday night, hit a few bars, listen to some music," Maddox suggests.

"Nah." I'm quick to shut that shit down. "Just not feeling it. Why don't we just order some pizzas and pick up a couple of twelve packs of beer? There's a fight on Saturday night, right? Let's Pay Per View that and just chill."

"You sure?" Forrest asks.

"Yeah, low-key is the name of the game, my friend."

"Low-key, my ass. You're dirty thirty, brother." He holds his fist out for me to bump into his. "The last of us to leave our twenties. We need to do it up big."

"Splurge on a bottle of Crown other than just beer."

"That's what you call doing it up big?" Legend asks.

I shrug. I can't tell them that I miss Emerson like a fucking limb, and that in no way do I want to go to bars and have women hitting on me all night. Not because she can't trust me, but because it will be obvious to them, I'm not into it. Then they're going to start asking questions. Ones I can't answer.

Hell, they're already suspicious.

I did break down a few weeks ago and went to Get Hammered, the bar down the street, for beers after work. It's not that I don't want to hang out with them, but Emerson only gets so much free time from studying, and I can't talk to her when they're around. Since we all work together, they are always around. I just like going home and ending my day with her.

"Thirty is the new twenty, man," Maddox says adamantly.

"Just not feeling it this year."

"Fine," Forrest grumbles. "But we're getting Peach Crown this time." He stalks off to his room to get ready for his day.

"What are you doing here, anyway?" Lachlan asks. "I thought you were off today and tomorrow because you're helping your dad with the deck?"

"Yeah, I am, but I needed to come in and pick up my Bluetooth speaker. I'm going to need some tunes while we work."

"At least it's a nice day. It's supposed to be cooler this weekend."

"It's the third week of October. It's supposed to be cold."

"Yeah, but at least it's in the fifties today, so you won't be freezing your balls off. You might want to reproduce one day."

Instantly, a vision of Emerson carrying my baby pops into my head.

Fuck me, this girl has me twisted in a way I'll never unravel her from my heart.

"Not reproducing anytime soon," I counter, moving toward my room to grab my speaker. Emerson just turned twenty this summer. She's not ready for kids; at least I don't think she is. Hell, that's not something we've talked about. We need to get through telling everyone we're together, and then we can cross that bridge. In the meantime, I'll leave those thoughts for when I'm alone and missing her, and can't stop thinking about when she comes home for good after graduation.

I grab my small speaker and the charging cord just in case, wave to Lyra, who's manning the desk, and head out.

We try to take at least one day off during the week, but we also have paid vacation time. We hardly ever use it, but I did take tomorrow as a day so that I can help my dad finish up the back deck that he started on their house. He started it last weekend, but I worked late Saturday. I helped on Sunday, but it's still not finished. I'm hoping we can wrap it up today, and tomorrow I can just chill and wait for Emerson to get out of class. I chuckle as I drive toward my parents' when I realize I'm a thirty-year-old man waiting for his secret twenty-year-old girlfriend to get out of her college classes so I can talk to her.

I should be ashamed, but my heart won't let me. We're both adults, and I can be honest with myself at least when I say that I love the hell out of that girl.

After parking my truck in the driveway of my parents' place, I head into the house, calling out for them.

"In the kitchen," Dad calls back.

"Something smells good," I say, kissing Mom on the cheek and giving Dad a pat on the shoulder before taking a seat at the table beside him.

"Your mom made her homemade cinnamon rolls."

"I'm making lunch too. Chicken and dumplings. One of your favorites."

"You spoil me, woman," I tell her.

"Leave her be. She misses having you home, and she enjoys it," Dad says.

"Dad, I haven't lived at home for a decade."

He nods. "I know, but you are still our son, and we miss you."

"Well, I'm here for you to put me to work for the next two days. Today is my day off, and I took tomorrow as well. We're going to wrap this deck up so that it's done and off your plate."

"Thanks, Rome. I only have one side of the railing that needs to be finished. Joe and Larry came over yesterday and we got a lot of it done."

"That was nice of them."

"Your aunts bribed them." Dad laughs.

I hold my hands up. "You can stop there. I don't need the details."

"Mind straight to the gutter." Mom shakes her head, but she's smiling.

"This isn't my first rodeo," I tell them as my phone alerts me to a message. I quickly dig into my pocket, hoping it's from Emerson. I smile when I see her name.

Emerson: Well, I didn't plan on wearing my coffee this morning, but here I am.

It's followed by a picture of her light-colored jeans covered in what I assume is her coffee.

Me: You okay? Did you burn yourself?

Emerson: I'm fine. It was lukewarm at best. I went to the library early to study and stopped to get it on my way, so yeah, it wasn't a huge loss, and the cup was only maybe a quarter of the way full. Thankfully.

Me: I hate that, baby girl, but I'm glad you didn't get burned. It could have been much worse.

Emerson: Facts. Missing you. Have a good day building that deck.

Me: Thanks. Text me later.

Emerson: Always.

I shove my phone back in my pocket and look up to find my parents staring at me. Dad is smirking and Mom has a grin from ear to ear lighting up her face.

"There he is," she announces.

"I've been here the whole time." I reach for a cinnamon roll and dive in.

"Oh, you were sitting here, but you were with whoever you were texting. Who is she?" Mom asks.

Fuck.

"Nosy." I point my finger at her and she grins.

"Fine. Don't tell me, but whoever she is, I like her already for putting that dopey, happy grin on your face."

"Mom," I groan, and they both laugh.

"Eat up," Dad says. "I hope to finish today so you can take tomorrow off and do nothing. Or... something." He winks, and my shoulders shake with laughter.

I love my parents. They're supportive and not pushy. I know it's killing my mom not to pry and beg to meet the mystery woman, but they're letting me take this at my own pace. She'd truly flip her lid if she knew that she already knows and adores the woman who has stolen my heart. I've never brought anyone home to meet them. I never wanted to.

Not until Emerson.

I finish scarfing down my cinnamon roll, thank Mom with a kiss on her cheek, and follow Dad out to the back deck to get to work.

I'm stepping out of the shower when my phone rings. I make a dash for the sink where I left it, not willing to miss a call or a text from Emerson. I'm aware of how whipped that makes me sound, and I'm okay with it. I miss her like fucking crazy. Those calls and text messages are our lifeline. I smile when I see it's a call.

"Hey, baby girl, how was your day?" I greet her.

"Meh," she says, and my protective instincts kick in.

"Emerson. What's wrong?"

"Nothing." She sniffs. "Everything. It's just been a shit kind of day."

"Tell me everything."

She sighs heavily, and I'm preparing myself to coax it out of her when she finally starts talking. "You know about the coffee. I bombed a big test, which sucks, but the entire class failed miserably, so we get to retake it. Then on the way home, I got a flat tire. Thankfully, one of the guys from class, Gabe, was behind me. He stopped to help me, not that I can't do it on my own, but it's raining, and I felt bad, so I stayed outside of the car to help him, and we both got drenched. I came home to shower and curl up in bed, and my blanket no longer smells like you, and I fucking miss you, Rome. I miss you so much that my chest physically aches, and I hate this. I hate being away from you, and today just fucking sucks."

"I'm sorry you've had such a bad day. I miss you too, Em, so much."

"I'm sorry I'm unloading on you. I know you're going to get annoyed that your much-younger girlfriend, or whatever I am to you, can't handle the pressure of being away from you and our adult—whatever this is, but a girl is only so strong, and everything piled up on me today, and then it's your birthday this weekend, and I won't be there to hug you or kiss you or wish you a happy birthday in person, and it just sucks."

"It's just another day, Emerson. How about when you're home for Thanksgiving, we do something special to celebrate? We'll pretend it's my birthday?" I'm scrambling for anything and everything I can think of that will make her feel better.

"Yeah," she says, but I can still hear the sadness in her voice.

"Don't cry, baby. I hate that you're upset and I'm not there."

"I'll be fine. Just hit me all at once and I wanted to hear your voice." I hear rustling. "I have a study group in an hour. Can I call you after?"

"You better. Are you sure you're okay?"

"I'll be fine. I'm sorry I dumped all of this on you."

"That's what I'm here for, baby girl. Let me carry some of this for you, and you're mine. I don't care what you label it or how you say it. What matters is that you're mine, I'm yours, and we'll get through this together. I hate that I'm not there, and I wish more than anything that I could hold you right now."

She sniffles, and fuck, I thought my words would ease some of her worry and make her feel better. "I need to get ready. My hair is still wet, and I need to stop crying so my face isn't all blotchy. If this study group wasn't for the class of the test we all bombed, I'd skip it."

"Call me when you get home. We'll watch a movie together."

"You sure?"

"Positive." It's on the tip of my tongue to tell her I love her, but I won't do that over the phone.

"Thanks, Rome. I'll call you later."

The call ends, but my racing heart is still thumping wildly in my chest. I hate that she's so upset, and her age has nothing to do with missing me. I miss her too.

I finish drying off, then slip into a pair of gray sweats and a long-sleeve T-shirt. I pace back and forth in my room, worried about her. Lifting my phone, my thumb hovers over Monroe's name, to text her and have her give me her own status report when an idea hits. I'm off work until Wednesday. The guys think I'm busy helping Dad. It's three o'clock, and she's three and a half hours away. I can be to her place by seven. Her study groups are always a couple of hours long.

Fuck it.

I grab some socks, slip my feet into a pair of tennis shoes, and lock up the house. I'm going to see my girl. It's been too fucking long.

It's six thirty when I pull up outside of her apartment. I even stopped for gas and to take a piss. My foot was heavy on the gas the entire way here, both from excitement and the need to be that person for her. The one to show up for her when she needs me.

Grabbing my keys, phone, and the bag of her favorite snacks I picked up at the gas station, I head inside. When I reach her apartment, I rap my knuckles against the door, and take a step back. My chest is tight, and my hands are clammy. I hope this is a good surprise. I'm well aware that just showing up at her place might not have been the best idea, but I have the time off tomorrow, and well, she needs me, and if I'm being honest. I need her too.

"I'll get it." I hear Monroe call out. When she pulls open the door, her mouth falls open in shock. "Hey, Em, it's for you."

"I'm not here," she calls back.

"For real, it's for you."

"I'm not expecting anyone. I have a phone call to make," she grumbles.

I can hear her footsteps as they grow near, and my chest does this funny squeezing thing when I hear her say she has a phone call to make. She's eager to call me. She appears in the doorway and blinks a few times before she bursts into tears and launches herself at me. I catch her easily, handing the bag of snacks to Monroe, and walking us both into the apartment. I move to the couch and sit with her in my arms. She's sobbing and her fingers dig into the back of my shirt as if she's worried I might disappear.

I hear the door close and footsteps carry down the hall, which I assume is Monroe going to her room to give us some time. I don't know how long we sit huddled together while her tears soak my shirt, but eventually, she lifts her head. Her eyes are red-rimmed, and tears are still flowing freely.

"What are you doing here?"

"Dad and I finished early, which you know, and I'm off tomorrow. When you called, I knew I had to get to you." I wipe her tears with my thumbs. "You needed me, baby girl. Where else would I be?"

"Where do they think that you are?"

"I didn't tell anyone I was leaving. The guys know I took off tomorrow to help Dad. They don't know we finished today because my uncles came over to help him yesterday. I'll think of something if it comes up."

"I can't believe you drove almost four hours on a whim just to see me."

"I hated that you were upset and had such a bad day and I wasn't here. I had the time away from work scheduled, and I can't think of a better way to utilize that time."

"So you're staying?"

"Is that okay? I can get a room," I offer.

"No. Please, no. I want you to stay." She leans in and I close the distance, kissing her softly.

"Have you had dinner?" she asks.

"Do snacks from the gas station count? Speaking of?" I glance over and see the bag sitting on the chair. "I brought you and Monroe some of your favorites."

"You know my best friend's favorite snacks?"

"Baby girl, we've known each other for years. I pay attention, and Monroe is always with you." I shrug.

"We just had dinner. I can warm you up some leftovers. Cheesy chicken and rice."

"I'm good for now."

"You promised me a movie."

"I did."

"Come on." She starts to climb off my lap, but I hold on to her. "Tell me where we're going, beautiful. I'm not ready to let you go just yet. In fact, be prepared for me to be glued to your side until I leave tomorrow."

"I like the sound of that." She kisses me again, before pulling back and telling me which room is hers.

We strip down, her in her panties and my T-shirt, and me in my boxer briefs, and climb under the covers. I pull her into my arms as we lie on our side and stare at her laptop screen. The movie is on maybe five minutes before she's sound asleep. Reaching over, I close her laptop and place it on the nightstand. Pulling her close, I snuggle into her, and close my eyes.

It's the best night's sleep I've had since she left.

"LACHLAN, YOU OUTDID YOURSELF WITH the turkey this year," I tell him. "Who knew a deep-fried bird would be so good?"

"I did, obviously," Lachlan replies with a wink.

"Obviously," I parrot back to him.

"I'm stuffed," Monroe says, shoving her plate away from her.

"We still have pie. Lots and lots of pie," I remind my best friend.

"I know. I helped make them, but I can't do it. Not right now, at least." She rubs her hands over her flat belly as if she can feel the difference after all the food we just consumed.

"Well, boys and girls, it's time for some football." Maddox pushes back from the table and heads toward the living room.

I smile as everyone files in after him.

Every year, as long as I can remember, we've been having our own Everlasting Ink family Thanksgiving on the Friday after the actual holiday. Forrest records the games from Thanksgiving Day, and we all pretend like this is the actual day. I once referred

to it as Friendsgiving and my brother about had a heart attack. He made it very clear that everyone around the table that day, which included the two of us, Monroe, and the other guys from Everlasting Ink, were family.

He's right. Everyone here today is family we chose, and I think we did a damn fine job. We invited Drake, Lisa, and Lyra, but they already had other plans. I made sure to tell them that if they could make it next year, to plan to be here. I also told them that if they hadn't made plans yet, to save Christmas evening for us as well.

On Thanksgiving Day, Forrest and I spend the day watching movies and catching up. We prep for the big meal the next day. Some years, we've gone to the guys' houses and have dinner with their families. They invite us every single year, and we used to go. However, when I turned eighteen and moved in with Forrest, I asked him if we could start our own tradition, and that's when our movie and prep day started. This was our third year in a row, and I love every second of it.

I can't tell you how many times I almost broached the subject of Roman and me. I even thought about just suggesting I'd met someone older, but I didn't want to ruin the day or my visit home. We're only here until Sunday. We have to drive back for a couple of weeks of exams before we come back home for Christmas break.

By the time I make it to the living room, everyone is sprawled out. Forrest is in his recliner, already looking like he's half asleep. Maddox is sprawled out on the love seat, while Lachlan and Legend are on one end of the sectional. Monroe and Roman are on the other end, and wouldn't you know there is just enough space between the two of them for me. I plop down and pull one of the throw blankets off the back of the couch, and snuggle up. I'm already wearing leggings and an oversized sweatshirt. Perfect napping attire.

"Oh, I want one." Monroe hops up and steals the blanket from the back of the love seat. Maddox doesn't even put up a fight when she takes it from the back. These guys know we're always cold. She takes her spot on the couch and snuggles deep.

"Give me some of that," Lachlan says, and pulls the cover over him as well.

"I'm going to fix this." Legend gets up and runs downstairs. He comes back with three blankets. He tosses one to Maddox, one to Forrest, and keeps the other for himself.

"What about me?" Roman asks, pretending to be hurt he was left out, but we all know he's just kidding from the tone of his voice.

"Sorry, only found three. Em, we taught you to share, right?" Lachlan says. He then proceeds to wrap himself up like a burrito on his end of the couch.

"Yeah, Em, share. If I have to, then so do you." Monroe taunts.

Have I mentioned that I love my best friend? "Fine." I act like I'm being put out. "But you better not be a cover hog." I already know he's not. He just holds me closer so that we're both snuggled up at night or on the couch. But here, we can't snuggle, not like we're used to, but this is better than I could have hoped for this cold Friday afternoon. Belly full, snuggled up with my man and all my favorite people. I'm calling that a win for today's festivities.

Roman settles the cover over him, making sure that I'm also covered, and his hand immediately finds mine beneath the covers. The room is quiet, with the recorded football game in the background. I'm warm and Roman's hand is wrapped tightly around mine. The last thing I remember is Forrest and Maddox, both snoring as I drift off to sleep.

My eyes flutter open, and the room is dark. The TV is on, but the volume is still down low. Once my eyes adjust to the lighting, I see Forrest still asleep in his chair, and the others are all asleep too. Even Roman, my human pillow. As bad as I hate to move away from him, I know I need to. I try to sit up and his arms wrap around me tighter. I lift my head just enough to see his eyes, and he's staring right at me. He bends his head and presses a kiss to my forehead, then sits back and closes his eyes. I glance to my right and see that Legend and Monroe have somehow changed places. She's curled up on him, just as he is her, and Lachlan has his head in Monroe's lap.

I smile because the five of us are like a twisted pretzel. Roman's hand is still locked tightly around mine, and his thumb traces over my knuckles. He's not ready to break this connection yet, and I know that if I pretend to still be asleep, I can lie here in his arms a little longer. Thankfully, Monroe and the guys have found themselves in a similar situation, which means there shouldn't be any question as to why I'm using Roman as my pillow.

Closing my eyes, I try to go back to sleep, but it's no use. Out of nowhere, I hear a thump, then "Motherfucker," and I can't help it. I start to laugh. Roman joins in and when I sit up, I see Maddox lying on the floor by the love seat.

"You okay, Mad?" I ask between giggles.

Roman slips his hand up the back of my sweatshirt and traces his fingers down my spine. I try like hell to pretend he's not touching me, but it's difficult.

"Too big for this fucking thing," Maddox grumbles.

"You want to come over here, and join our Monroe sandwich?" Lachlan asks.

"Hey," Monroe protests in her sleepy voice. Then we hear a grunt, and I'm sure she's either whacked him on the back of the head or dropped an elbow.

"Just kidding, Roe, but you are comfortable," Lachlan adds, trying to kiss up to her.

"Can you jokers not see I'm sleeping?" Forrest grumbles groggily.

We all laugh, and just like that, my solo time with Roman is gone. Slowly, we all sit up and stretch. Roman manages to touch me under the radar, his hand still on my thigh beneath the covers.

"Pie," Monroe announces. "I'm gonna need me some pie. Em?"

"Let's do it." Roman squeezes my thigh and moves his hand, and I toss back the cover, and stand, pulling Monroe to her feet. Linking my arm through hers, I lead her to the kitchen. We break out the pumpkin, apple, and pecan pies that we made and serve up a piece of each for the guys. She and I do the same, but our pieces are a fraction of the size of theirs.

It takes us a few trips, but we serve the guys dessert. They all offer to help, but we wave them off. No sense in all of us being up and in the kitchen.

"Oh, God," Maddox moans as he takes a bite. "You two made these?"

"Just like we do every year," I remind him.

"Marry me." He looks at me, then at Monroe. "The offer stands for both of you if I get pie like this more than just on holidays."

I feel Roman stiffen at my side, and I bump my leg into his. Maddox isn't being serious, but when I glance over at Roman, he's glaring at his plate. "Nah, you're not my type."

Maddox scoffs. "What? Sexy, artistic, good in bed, stable career, owns his own home, isn't your type?"

Everyone laughs, except for Roman. I don't know what to say to that, because he described himself and every other man in the room, including mine. They're all totally my type, but Roman is the only one I see that way. I start to panic, not sure how to get out of this when my bestie comes to my rescue.

"I'm mean, I'd take a go if you agree to be my sugar daddy," she quips, and this time Roman joins in with the laughter.

"Well, you can be my sweet momma, you know, because of the pies," Maddox tells her. "I think it's only fair I'm your sugar daddy." He winks at Monroe. "We could have some fun with that, Roe."

"Meh, we better not." She shoves an enormous piece of pie in her mouth.

"None of you asshats are marrying my sisters."

Roman stiffens again, and I want to scream in frustration. This day has been perfect, and this silly banter is not going to ruin it.

"Technically, Monroe isn't your sister," Lachlan points out.

Forrest glares at Lachlan. "Same as."

"Anyone want leftovers before I play Tetris to get them in the fridge?" I ask. I still have all three small slices of pie on my plate, but I'm desperate to change the subject.

"Is that a real question?" Roman asks.

I turn to look at him, and he gives me a soft smile. "Umm, yes?"

He tosses his head back in laughter. "Are you hungry?"

"Nope. I can't even eat this." I hold up my plate. My stomach swirls with anxiety. I don't need Roman getting scared about us again.

Roman takes my plate and places it on top of his. He makes a point of using my fork to cut off a big slice of pie.

"I'm in for leftovers," Forrest says. He stands and makes his way to the kitchen, with Maddox, Legend, and Lachlan on his heels. Monroe winks and heads that way as well.

"Where's my sugar daddy? I need a back rub," she calls out. The guys all erupt in laughter that floats to us in the living room.

"You good, baby girl?"

"Yeah, I'm good. I just… don't need him getting in your head," I say honestly.

"He's not," he assures me. "It was just an off-the-cuff statement. It's okay."

I nod. "I missed you."

"You have no idea, baby." He runs the pad of his thumb across my bottom lip. "You better go." He nods toward the kitchen. "I'll be right in once I finish this."

"So, what, three bites?" I tease him.

"Lately, you're the only meal I savor."

"Lately, you've not been savoring me either," I sass, and stand to go to the kitchen with everyone else.

Roman reaches out and catches my wrist. "Baby girl, you know that your sweet pussy is what I crave. When I came to see you, it just wasn't the right time. You were upset, and I didn't drive to see you for *that*."

"And before I left for college?"

"Can a man not just hold his girl anymore?" he asks. He's teasing, but there's also truth to his words. He just wanted to be with me, and I appreciate that, but I'm missing his touch.

I crave it.

"Before I leave on Sunday." I don't say more, because he nods. He knows what I mean.

"We'll figure it out, baby girl."

"See that you do." I wink, and he releases my wrist, and I join the others in the kitchen. All the guys have a plate, while Monroe sits on the counter by the sink, giving them shit about where they're putting it.

My brother and his four best friends are all good-looking guys. They're inked up and fit as hell. They all eat a ton, and we often tease them about where it's going. Not an ounce of fat on any of them. I can feel my thighs expand just thinking about a piece of cake. Men don't know how good they've got it.

Roman joins us a few minutes later. He pats his flat belly and places both of our plates into the dishwasher. "You assholes leave any for me?" he asks.

"You better hurry," Lachlan tells him. "The mac and cheese is getting low, and Maddox keeps eyeing it."

"Ticktock." Maddox grins, shoving turkey into his mouth.

Roman makes himself a plate while I hop up on the counter next to Monroe and watch the guys work their way through the leftovers. She leans her shoulder into mine and I mouth, "Thank you" to her for keeping the guys occupied while Roman and I talked. She nods, and I know without a doubt my bestie would have found a way to warn me if someone was headed our way.

"So, I'll see you in a few hours?" I ask Monroe.

"Yep. I'm going to my grandparents' for a few hours. You two kids have fun." She wags her eyebrows, and we both laugh.

"Thank you, Monroe. I hate asking you to lie for us, but I need to spend some time with him before we head back to school."

"I got you, bestie. Go be with your man. I'll be at the hotel to get you in a few hours. I'll text you when I leave my grandparents' place."

"I love you. Be safe."

"Love you too."

I open the front door and step out onto the porch just as Roman pulls into the driveway. I race down the drive to his truck and hop in so we can be on our way.

"You being chased?" Roman teases as he leans over and kisses me.

"No, but I'm ready to get out of town. I hate that you're wasting money on a hotel room that we're not even going to be spending the night in."

"I can afford to do it, and that's nothing compared to what I'd do to spend some time with you."

"You have better things to spend your money on," I counter.

"Agree to disagree. Now, tell me how school is going? Are you ready for that exam you were stressing about?"

I tell him about school, and he listens intently, all while holding my hand. We make it about an hour from home, and he pulls into the lot of the hotel. Monroe already has my bags in her car. She drove this time. I'll drive home for Christmas since they're brief trips.

"It's obvious what we're doing," I whisper to Roman, as we step into the lobby to check in.

"Baby girl, we're not doing anything wrong. If this makes you uncomfortable, we can go."

"No," I rush to answer. "I want to be here."

"I just want to spend some time with you where I don't have to sneak kisses or pretend like you're not all that I think about. No pressure."

"No way, buddy." I slip my arm through his. "You promised to make me your snack."

He freezes, bending to look at me. I smile widely, and he tosses his head back in laughter. "You're trouble," he mumbles as he presses a kiss to my temple.

Roman takes care of checking us in and leads me up to the room. "My lady," he says, holding the door open for me.

I step into the room and reach for my hoodie, pulling it over my head and dropping it to the floor. Next, I shimmy out of my leggings, realizing I forgot to kick off my shoes. I do that, and tear my leggings and socks off after letting them all land in a pile on the floor.

"Stop." He takes two long strides to reach me. "Let me do the rest." He runs his knuckle over my collarbone and down to my breasts. "I feel like Christmas came early." He smiles, and this smile it's different. Softer somehow.

"Well, you better start unwrapping."

He steps back, kicks off his shoes, and pulls his joggers off. He does that sexy thing that guys do and reaches behind his neck and pulls off his hoodie and the T-shirt underneath all in one go.

"Now we're even."

"I don't want us even, Rome. I want us naked."

He steps close again. "What my girl wants, my girl gets." He strips out of his boxer briefs, then takes his time removing my bra and panties. "Now what?"

"Touch me."

"Where?"

"Rome," I whine.

"Don't get shy on me, baby girl. You were just telling me you wanted us naked. Tell me what you want now."

"You."

"My hands, my tongue, my cock? What do you want, Emerson?"

"All of the above."

He laughs softly as he starts to kiss my neck. His attention moves to my nipples, tweaking both at the same time. I arch my back into him, and he drops his hands, wrapping them around my waist, and holding me close. His hard cock presses against my belly. Reaching out, I grip him and stroke, running my thumb over his piercing. He hisses out a breath.

"You first," he says, pulling my hand away from his cock.

"I thought it was whatever I wanted."

"You failed to voice what you wanted, but you need to remember that you're first, always."

"We'll see," I taunt.

"On the bed, baby."

I scramble to the bed, arms at my sides, legs spread open for him. I should feel embarrassed, but Rome is the only man to see me this way, fully naked and exposed. His heated stare makes me feel sexy and wanted. I don't have time to be self-conscious.

Roman follows me, holding himself up with his arms braced on the mattress by my head. He holds my stare, which causes my heart to race. He's looking so deep into my eyes, I swear he can see my soul.

"You're beautiful," he murmurs, dipping his head and sucking a hard nipple into his mouth. His tongue does this magical thing that has me reaching up to bury my hands in his hair. He takes his time, before moving onto the other breast.

His lips trail down my belly, and he shuffles down the mattress, careful not to crush me with his weight. He settles on the mattress between my thighs. "Legs up, baby girl."

Knowing the drill, I lift one leg, then the other over his shoulders, and he burrows deeper between my thighs.

"You say stop, and we stop."

I nod. "I trust you to drive me wild," I say with a saucy grin.

"That mouth." He smirks. "You better not hold back on me. I need to hear you."

"Yes, sir." I nod, and his green eyes flame with need.

"It's been too damn long, Em. Too long since I've tasted this sweet pussy. You better hold on, baby girl. I'm about to feast." That's the only warning I get before he sucks my clit into his mouth and unleashes on me.

His tongue, his fingers, he's everywhere all at once. The sensation is overwhelming.

I already feel my orgasm building. My vibrator, and even phone sex that we've resorted to, it's nothing like the real thing.

The feel of his calloused hands.

The warmth of his bare skin pressed to mine.

His hot breath.

The soft yet warm stroke of his tongue.

I'm on sensation overload.

My orgasm hits me out of nowhere. One minute I'm in a blissed-out state of just feeling, and the next I'm gripping his hair, spiraling out of control as the fire builds deep in my core and explodes. My heart sprints in my chest, as if trying to outrun the pleasure that burns through my veins. I think I call out his name, but I can't be sure. The one thing I am sure of is that was by far the most intense orgasm of my life.

Roman kisses up my belly and takes the time to savor my breasts again before he settles next to me on the bed. He rests his head on my shoulder, and his big hand on my belly that's still quivering.

"I fucking missed you," he says huskily.

His words empower me. I know we don't have much time, and no way am I leaving him without having him in my mouth. I want more. I want it all with him, but I want time for that. As in all night. I don't want my first time to be a rushed tryst in a random hotel room. Roman wouldn't agree to it, anyway. I know him well enough to know that when we finally get there, it's going to be more.

Everything.

With my sudden burst of need to give as good as I've gotten, I sit up and straddle his hips. His hard length slides against my pussy, and he groans. "W-What are you doing?"

"It's my turn to play."

"Baby girl." It's part plea, part scolding.

I smile because I love knowing I affect him just as much as he affects me.

"I'm just—" I rock my hips, and we both groan.

He lifts my hips, and I wiggle out of his hold, sliding down the bed. I didn't really think about my little tease because now I'll be tasting myself on him. I didn't think about it, but thinking about it has me turned on.

Tentatively, I peek my tongue out and taste us together. I flick at his piercing, and he jerks his hips. He gathers my hair in his hand, holding it off to one side.

"I'm not missing this," he rasps.

I grin and get to work.

I take him into my mouth a little at a time. I can't take all of him, but I take as much as I can, which causes tears to well in my eyes. Over and over, my head bobs, all the while he holds my hair.

"So good, baby girl. You take me so well," he praises, and heat pools between my thighs.

How is it possible that I just had the most epic of orgasms, and I already feel as though I could explode again?

"Fuck. Fuck. Fuck," he says, when my tongue plays with his piercing again, before taking him down my throat. "Baby, I'm going to come. You need to stop." His voice is gritty. "Emerson, pull off," he demands, but I refuse. "Fuck!" he roars as he spills down my throat.

I take it all, swallowing, enjoying that I can do this for him, that I'm the one making him lose control.

"Come here, beautiful." He releases my hair, and moves his hands under my arms, bringing me to him. I lie on his chest with his arms wrapped tightly around me.

We're both quiet while we catch our breaths. A quick glance at the clock tells me we have maybe an hour before Monroe is calling, and I'm perfectly content to lie right here until the last possible minute.

ROMAN 19

IT'S CHRISTMAS NIGHT. WE ALL got here around four to celebrate our Everlasting Ink family Christmas. It's closing in on midnight, and Monroe and I are the only two left other than Emerson and Forrest. I know I should leave, but I can't seem to make myself stand up and walk out the door.

Emerson and Monroe are in matching pajamas, and they're dancing around the living room, dancing to whatever latest hit is on the radio. Honestly, I'm not even listening, so I couldn't tell you what it is.

What I can tell you is my girl's long brown hair is flowing down her back in loose curls. Her green eyes are smiling as she bounces around and acts silly with her best friend. I can't take my eyes off her. Thankfully, Forrest seems to be watching them too.

Monroe does this silly hip thrust move, shaking her ass, and Emerson falls into a fit of hysterical laughter. My lips twitch, because seeing her this happy makes me happy. My dad always used to tell me that one day a woman would come into my life and her happiness would be my main priority. I always told him he was going crazy in his old age, but sitting here on this couch, watching her, I understand what he meant.

My girl is thriving, and I'm here to stand beside her to witness it. I get to walk next to her and stand proud while she accomplishes all of her goals. Well, kind of. She knows I'm there, but everyone else will find out soon enough.

The girls stumble to the kitchen laughing. I'm sure to make themselves another drink. They're not drunk, but they've had a few. We all have. I usually don't when I'm around her and the others at the same time, for fear that I might slip up, but tonight, I needed an excuse to stay.

Yeah, I know I said I can't make myself walk out the door. That's because I don't plan to. I'm going to sleep under the same roof as her. I might get lucky and sneak a kiss once everyone else is asleep, but it's enough to know we're here together.

I've lost my mind for this woman, and honestly, I wouldn't change it. I'd rather we not have to hide, but that's coming. We have a plan, and until then, well, I'll just have a few so I can't drive home.

"That's my gift," Forrest says.

"What?" I turn to look at my best friend. We've had a few drinks. Did he have more than I think he did?

"Seeing my little sister happy. Fuck, Rome, I want so much for her. The guilt I carry about leaving her in that house with them haunts me."

"She's here, and she's safe. She's healthy. She's happy." I'll make damn sure of all three.

"She was eight when I moved out. I knew they weren't hurting her, but I also knew she was neglected, and having to see them drunk all the time, laying in their own vomit, the fights she had to hear."

My chest tightens. I've heard this all before, but it hits a little differently when the person you're talking about owns your heart.

"I want so much for her, you know? I want her to have a successful career. Hell, as bad as I hate to say it, I'd be okay with her getting out of this sleepy little town of Ashby. They're leaving her alone, and I don't think they'll ever reach out to either of us. They know we won't give them money for their booze, not now that we're both adults, and they have no say in our lives. But to move away and forget those moments, I want that for her, even though I'll miss the fuck out of her."

"She seems to be well adjusted to me." I can't tell him I've spent hours and hours on the phone with her. She's talked about her parents, and how she thinks she needs to repay Forrest for all that he's done for her. Both feel a sense of owing the other. It's obvious the two of them need to sit down and talk about it.

"She is." He nods. "She's fucking thriving," he says, speaking my earlier thoughts out loud.

"She is," I agree.

"I want more for her than this little, small town, Rome. I want her to marry a doctor or some shit. Maybe she'll meet one once she starts her new job? I want her to have everything she missed out on. I want her to be spoiled and pampered. She didn't get that."

"You gave her that," I tell him. Internally I'm screaming at him, telling him that *I* am that man. I will bust my ass every fucking day to give her everything she ever dreamed of. The words are on the tip of my tongue.

"I tried, but she still lived without it for eighteen fucking years. Weekends with me, with us at that shop, weren't enough."

Panic rises in my chest. "She's happy, Forrest." My mouth feels as if I've been chewing on rocks. It's gritty and dry, as what he's saying takes root in my mind.

He's never going to approve of us together.

It doesn't matter how much I love her. I'll never be good enough for her.

He'll never forgive either of us.

"Doesn't matter. I want that for her. I'll encourage her to reach for better."

"Better than you?" I ask, feeling the walls starting to close in. "Better than the brother who loves her unconditionally and got her out as soon as he could? Better than the man who bought this big-ass house to give her the home she never had?"

"Yes." His reply is instant and without hesitation.

"Bullshit." I don't bother to try to mask my anger.

He turns to look at me. "She's my sister, Roman. You can call bullshit all you want. Until you walk in my shoes, you are in no place to judge me."

"She's happy. You did that, Forrest." Me too, but I keep that to myself. "You got her out of there, gave her a home, helped her get a car, helped her navigate college. She's well adjusted." I pause, collecting myself. This time when I speak, I'm calmer. "You can't dictate her life, man. That's not fair to her or to you. That's too much pressure. You got to live and make your own mistakes. She deserves that same right."

"She does." He nods. "However, I'm never going to stop pushing her toward the life she deserves."

My heart thunders in my chest like a field of wild horses. "What happens when she brings a guy home you don't approve of? What then? What happens when she falls in love with a man like you? The man who showed her what it feels like to love and protect your family?"

He shrugs. "I'll disapprove. No way will she be with someone I disagree with. Our bond is too tight for that. I'm not going to let some lowlife come in and her end up in a life that I got her out of. No way."

"What if he's not a doctor but still a good man? A man that loves her." I feel as though I just tore my heart out of my chest and handed it to him in the palm of my hand. I know what he's going to say, but I asked him anyway. I'm not the kind of man he wants for his sister.

"Honestly, Rome, I can't think of one person that I know that's good enough for my baby sister. I hope that never happens, but if it does, we'll have to navigate that land mine when we get there."

My heart stalls in my chest, and I suck in a deep breath.

She's going to lose her brother, and I can't let that happen. I fucking knew this was how it would turn out. My biggest fear is our reality. I can't ask her to pick me over her brother. She's young and still has so much ahead of her. Graduation and starting her career. It's going to hurt us both, but I can't be the reason she loses her only blood family. I have two loving parents and a handful of extended relatives.

She has her brother.

I knew that I loved her. However, it's not until this moment, knowing that I'm losing her, I realize how much.

I'll never love anyone the way that I love Emerson Huntley.

I opted to sleep in the basement tonight. I use the term sleep loosely. It's 3:00 a.m. and I'm still wide awake. I rub my chest over my heart, trying to soothe the ache. It doesn't help. I know nothing will take the pain away. How could it? I'm about to break the heart of the woman I love. Not because I don't love her. I crave her. She's in my blood, imprinted on my soul.

What is it that my father used to say? "The hard choice is usually the right choice." I hate that logic, but I fear he might be right.

This is the hardest decision I've ever had to make. I'm going to break both of us. She won't understand that I'm doing this for her, but I am. She needs him. She might think that what we have can convince him, but she didn't hear him tonight. He'll never approve of us.

It doesn't matter that I love her so completely I don't know who I am without her. It doesn't matter that there isn't a man on this earth who could love and cherish her the way that I could. All that matters is I'm not what he sees for her, and he'll fight for her to get the life he thinks she needs.

He doesn't seem to care that it might not be the life she wants.

The stairs creak, and I tense. I know it's her.

A minute later, she's sliding into bed next to me. I pull her close and breathe her in. My heart hurts. Am I having a heart attack? I'm only thirty, but this pain, it's more than I can bear.

"You're warm," she mumbles, snuggling closer.

"You cold, baby girl?" I whisper. My voice is thick with what I'm about to do.

"Not with your arms around me."

Fuck. I close my eyes and will myself to find the strength to do what I know needs to be done. It's more than just breaking our hearts. She's my best friend. I love the guys, and they will always be at the top of my list, but for me, my number one spot is Emerson. It will always be Emerson, and I don't know how to move past that.

How do I give up my heart and my best friend?

I hold her for a long time. We're both quiet, but neither of us is asleep. "I can feel the tension in your body," she finally whispers.

"I talked to your brother earlier."

"Yeah, it looked pretty intense. Monroe and I started to come back to the living room, but we decided whatever it was you were discussing needed to be aired."

"He's never going to accept this. Accept us."

"He has to."

"He won't, Em. He told me he would never let you settle for this small town, and any man in it. He flat out told me he didn't know a single man good enough for you."

"That's not his choice to make."

"I told him that. He said you would never be with someone he didn't approve of. Emerson, I can't be the reason the two of you have a divide."

"What does that mean for us?"

"You know what it means, baby girl." My voice quivers, and I swallow hard, fighting back the emotions threatening to overtake me.

"When?"

"The longer we stay together, the harder it's going to be."

It's already hard as fuck. Do I even know who I am without her?

"I go back to school on the second of January."

"I know."

"Can we wait until then?"

"Yes."

"I hate this, Roman. I hate he has this kind of control. I want to be with you. Forrest will have to learn to deal with that."

"And when he doesn't?"

She's quiet. I don't need her words because I know what that would do to her.

"He won't, Emerson. You should have heard him, baby. He's adamant that he didn't do enough for you. I think the two of you need to talk."

"No. He's taking you away from me."

"Baby, he doesn't know that he's doing that. He doesn't know we're together. We've been hiding this behind his back, something I'm sure will send his pissed-off meter to maximum levels if he were to find out."

"He's not my dad."

"He's not, but look at it from his side. He raised you as much as he could. Every weekend since you were eight years old, he had you staying with him. He bought this house to give you the home that the two of you never had. He may not be your father, but he feels responsible for you."

"He's not."

"I know." I press my lips to her hair. "There's also the fact that I'm ten years older than you."

"Do you feel it? The age difference when we're together?"

"No."

"Not even when we... you know, mess around?"

"Not even then. I know you're inexperienced, but you come alive for me, Em. I don't feel or see the difference. I know it's there, but when we're together, it's just me and my girl."

"I like being your girl."

"Yeah," I agree.

"Maybe we take a break?" she suggests. "I'll get through graduation, and when I move home, we can maybe try this again?"

"I want nothing more, baby, but he's not going to change his mind. Hell, he told me he'd rather see you move away and marry a doctor who will spoil you rotten."

"He doesn't know, Rome. You spoil me. You take care of me in ways I never knew I needed."

I hate I won't be the man to give her everything her heart desires.

"Didn't take long for me to realize there isn't anything I wouldn't do for you just to see you smile."

"You're really good at taking care of me. Mentally, physically, and emotionally. That's the hardest part. The connection we have, it's deep. So deep I don't know that I can ever get past it."

"I won't. Never, Emerson. There will never be anyone in my life who I care about as much as I care about you."

My breath shudders in my chest when I realize I never told her I'm in love with her. I thought we had time. I was going to make it special, but now, I can't see telling her, knowing that this isn't progressing. Telling her now would be selfish.

Loving Emerson will be a secret I'll hold in my heart until the day I die.

I'll never stop loving her.

"Maybe prolonging this will just make it harder."

"It doesn't matter when, baby girl. It's going to fucking suck."

"Can we still talk?"

"Every day."

"Promise?"

"Promise." It's going to kill me to take us back to just being friends, but I love her too much. The alternative is losing her only family, and I can't do it. I can't be the reason for that.

"So, tonight."

No. No. No.

I swallow back that reply and to say the right thing, even if the words taste like acid on my tongue. "Tonight."

"Set the alarm on your phone."

"What time?"

"Six, I guess. I don't want to risk him finding me down here."

I do as she says, setting the alarm, and pulling her back into my arms. "I hate this, Emerson."

"I hate it too, but we knew this was a possibility, right? I mean, you've been worried about this from the beginning, and while I think Forrest can go fuck himself where we are concerned, I get it. I hate it, but I get it."

"I don't know of another way."

"Yeah," she agrees. "If I'm being honest, I know you're right. He's stubborn where I'm concerned. He has this vision of what he thinks my life should look like. Maybe in another life."

"Then I might not have met you. I met you through your brother. So I'd like to keep this life and the memories of you being mine."

"I think I'll always be yours, Roman. I don't think my heart knows any other way."

"Our hearts are on the same page."

She's quiet and I think she's finally fallen asleep. "Rome?"

"Yeah, baby girl?"

"Don't let go, okay? Just for tonight. Don't let go."

I tighten my arms around her. "I'm right here."

I love you.

I stare at the clock and watch as every minute rolls into the next. I hold her, just as I promised. When my alarm goes off, I'm wide awake. I hate to wake her up. I don't want to leave this basement. This is the last time I'll ever have the love of my life in my arms.

Fuck.

I hate doing the right thing. It hurts so fucking much. Knowing I have to stay strong for her, I shake her awake gently. "Baby girl, it's time to go up to your room."

She nods and hugs me tightly. "Even with the distance, these have been the best moments of my life. The time that I was yours."

You're always going to be mine. In my heart, you're mine.

"Mine too," I say instead.

She sits up, and I follow her lead as she climbs out of bed. I lace her fingers with mine and walk her to the steps. The ache in my chest intensifies.

"We'll figure this out," she tells me. "A new normal for us, but we've got this. Right?"

"Yeah, baby girl. We've got this." I press a kiss to her temple and release her hand. My eyes follow her as she takes each step, walking away from me.

ROMAN KEPT HIS WORD. WE'VE talked every day. I still end my day talking to him. It hurts, but I've learned something about Roman Bailey during my short time as his girl, as he liked to call me. He's this tatted-up badass that feels deep in his soul. He loves me, my brother, and the rest of the guys. I also know that he cares for me; he might even love me. Sometimes I'm certain he does. However, love doesn't seem to be enough. The situation that we're in is difficult because of who I am to Forrest. I know that. We knew that going into this, but Roman, he's one of those guys who would rather suffer in silence if he knew that someone he cared about was spared the pain.

The problem is for us, the only one being spared any pain is my brother.

We're both hurting. We're struggling to navigate this new friends-only situation we've found ourselves in.

It's been a month since I've been back to school from Christmas break, and while we talk every day, the ache of knowing I'm no longer his, that he's not mine, is still a jagged beat in my chest. Its uneven rhythm is my new reality. One that I'm still learning how to live with.

There's a part of me that wants to call my brother and confess it all. I want to tell him I'm madly in love with one of his best friends. I want to scream at him for scaring Roman into thinking that he would never be good enough for me.

My phone rings. I reach for it expecting for it to be Roman, but it's Forrest. I hesitate before hitting Decline, sending the call to voice mail. I get an immediate text message.

> **Forrest:** Didn't need anything. Just wanted to check in with you. Haven't talked to you in far too long, kid.
>
> **Me:** I'm good. Just busy wrapping up getting geared up for graduation. Lots to do.
>
> **Forrest:** I'm so proud of you, Emerson. I see big things for you.

All I see for me is Roman, but I can't say that.

I send back a heart emoji and toss my phone onto my bed. I hate that I'm mad at him. He's guilty and doesn't even realize he's done anything wrong. That's wrong of me, and I need to do better.

Pushing my brother and Roman out of my mind, I need to focus on myself. That's all I can do. I gotta do me, and what I have to do is graduate. That means I must make my study group that starts in half an hour at the café just down the street from campus.

Climbing off my bed, I gather everything I need in my backpack and head out.

"There she is," Sally says when I walk into the café. "We thought maybe you were standing us up."

"Nope. I need to pass this class."

"Don't we all," Gabe says, setting a cup in front of Sally and nodding toward the counter. "Want anything?"

"Not right now. Thanks, though."

"All right, ladies and gents, let's do this," Allen says. He rubs his hands together before flipping open his textbook.

The four of us get busy. Surgical anatomy is going to be the death of me. We spend the next hour quizzing each other and coming up with different ways and silly sayings to remember the material.

"I need caffeine." I push back from the table. "Anyone need anything?" I ask, grabbing my wallet out of my backpack.

"Me." Adam hands me some cash. "Large black, extra strong," he mutters.

"Got it. Hot lava coming up."

I make my way to the counter and order Adam's large black and a hot vanilla latte for me. I hand over Adam's money for his and then pay for mine with the gift card that Roman got me. He keeps adding money to it, even when I tell him not to. I'm no longer his to spoil, but that doesn't seem to be stopping him.

When I get back to the table, Gabe hands me my phone. "Sorry, Em, I thought it was mine. It's for you." He grins.

"Hello."

"Baby girl. Who was that?" Roman asks.

I hold up my finger to the group, letting them know I'll be right back. With my latte in hand, I step outside in the freezing cold to talk to my "friend."

"That was Gabe. I'm at study group. I was getting a latte that you paid for, by the way. Thanks for that, but, Roman, you have to stop."

"I can't, Em. I can't stop. I don't know how." He sounds pained, and I feel that hurt in the center of my chest. "Is he the one who helped you fix your flat tire?"

"Good memory."

"I don't like it."

"Don't like what?"

"That this guy is getting so close to you."

I roll my eyes even though he can't see me. "He's not getting close to me. He's a classmate. We're on the same graduation track for surgical tech. He lives in Nashville. We have geography in common as well as our major."

"And he's your age. I'm sure Forrest would approve," he grumbles.

"Guess what, Rome? Neither one of you gets a say in what I do. I'm an adult. I'm single the last time I checked." I toss that out in anger, and I hate that I do, but I can't take the words back. "My life. My choices."

He's quiet on the other end. I can hear him breathing, but he's not saying a word. Finally, he whispers, "You're right."

"I hate that I am, Roman. I hate that I can't get over you."

"Get over me? It's been a handful of weeks."

"It's been a month, Rome."

"Feels like a lifetime."

There is so much that I could say. That he didn't want to fight for us, for me, but that's not exactly the truth. Roman would throw down for me. He wouldn't hesitate. He thinks that keeping us apart *is* fighting for me. Not us, for *me*. He's doing this for me, and I need to keep reminding myself of that. This is what he thinks is best.

Maybe once I graduate, we can figure this out, but right now, I can't get wrapped up in should we or shouldn't we. I have to focus on school and graduating.

Maybe we'll find our way back to one another, and maybe we'll both move on. Either way, there will be a huge piece of me that will always be his.

"I should get back inside. We have a big exam next week."

"Call me when you get home?"

"I'll text you."

"Em—" he starts, then clears his throat. "Okay, baby girl. Be safe."

"You too." I end the call, take a long pull from my latte, and head back inside.

"Girl, it's freezing out there," Sally scolds.

"I know." I place my phone on the table, take another long pull of my latte, and get back to work.

After two additional hours, our brains are fried. We agree to meet up again on Sunday afternoon. The exam is Monday, so that's one final push before we meet our fates. I drive home, replaying my conversation with Roman. He's struggling just as much as I am, but the choice has been made. He's holding on with both hands, and I love him even more for it. He's kept his promise to call me every day. His voice is the last I hear every night before bed, but where does that end?

We can't just live the rest of our lives attached at the hip as best friends and nothing more. I know I made him promise me, but now that I've had some time to think about it, it's not fair to him.

It's not fair to either of us.

We both need to move forward.

"How was study group?" Monroe asks as I step into our apartment.

"Ugh," I groan, and she laughs.

"If it makes you feel any better, mine sucked ass too. We're almost there, Em."

"I know. To make matters worse, Rome called. Gabe answered, and he was all 'who was that.'" I roll my eyes.

"Told you. He's lost in you."

"He's not supposed to be. He made the choice."

"Hold up." She raises her hands in the air. "The way you explained it to me, you didn't fight him. In fact, you said that you agreed with him."

"I did, but I fucking hate this, Roe. I don't know how not to love him."

Her face softens, and I hate the look of sympathy she's giving me. "As an outsider looking in, maybe this is what you need."

"How could tearing both of our hearts out be what we need? Well, my heart. I know he cares about me, but, Roe, I love him. This is not some schoolgirl crush on my brother's best friend. This is he owns my heart, my soul, my mind, hell, my body too."

"Four months, Emerson. You'll be away from him for four more months by the time we graduate and move back to Ashby. If in four months you're both still feeling this... longing for each other, you need to reassess. I believe with everything inside of me that Rome is doing what he feels like is the right thing for you. He's not worried about him, but he loves you, Emerson. You can't see it. You're too close to what's going on, but I see the way he looks at you. I've heard the reverence in his voice when he calls you at night."

"So, what? We hold out for the four months, and when we graduate and move back, we see where things go?"

"Something like that." She grins. "I have a feeling that it's all going to work out. Roman isn't a man to give up so easily. The only reason he's attempting to do so now is because he's built it up in his mind that it's the right thing to do."

"What do you mean, attempt? We're over."

"Are you? He calls you every night before bed. He texts you multiple times a day. He refilled your prepaid card and sent you a card via snail mail to tell you. And what about that package of gas station snacks that arrived last week?"

"He's just being nice."

Monroe shakes her head. "He's just taking care of the woman he loves, the only way he thinks that he's allowed to."

"Why, Roe? Why is this so hard?"

"Because the two of you are making it harder than it needs to be."

I stick my tongue out at her, and she laughs at the same time as my phone rings. "It's Roman. I was supposed to call him when I got home."

"He's worried about you."

"I can take care of myself."

"I agree. But when you love someone, their ability doesn't matter. You still worry. Answer it."

"I need to start separating, right?"

"You already are. Don't leave him hanging. I can see him now, pacing back and forth in his living room, running his hands through his hair. Debating on whether he needs to get into his truck and head this way."

"Oh, shit." My phone stops ringing. I immediately call him back. "Hey."

"Baby girl, is everything okay?"

"Yeah, I'm fine. I got home and started talking to Monroe and forgot to call you."

He exhales loudly. "That's good," he says. I know he wants to say more, but my comment that he doesn't have the right earlier is more than likely stopping him.

"I'm home safe and sound."

"How was your day, Em?"

"Lots of studying. My head hurts from information overload." Not just from studying, but constantly replaying our relationship, and everything Monroe and I just talked about. "Yours?" I ask.

"Just another day."

"Something had to have happened?"

"I missed you. Just like the day before, and the day before."

"Rome."

"I know. I know I'm not supposed to say that anymore, but I've never lied to you, Emerson, and I'm not going to start now. I miss you."

I can feel Monroe's eyes on me. "Maybe we should rethink this talking every day. I was holding on to you the only way that I knew how. It wasn't fair of me to ask that of you."

"You don't want me to call you?"

"You can. You just don't have to. I know you're busy, and now that you're not tied down, you can go out with the guys again. I heard them giving you a hard time when I was home at Christmas."

"I have no desire to go out. Being with you, Emerson, it changed me. I'm fine with staying in at night and talking to you about anything and everything."

"That's what couples who are trying to overcome the distance do, Rome. That's not us anymore."

"Baby girl." His voice is raspy, and I feel the pain through the line. "I don't know if I can stop."

"We have to try, Roman."

"I'm not giving you up, Em. You're my best friend. I know we said we can't date, but dammit, I can't just fucking cut you out of my life. I can't do it. I won't."

"You don't have to, but maybe we should cut back on the everyday calls."

"I'll try, baby. I'll try for you, but I don't know if I can do it."

"Maybe we just text on the days we don't call."

"How many days before I hear your voice?"

"Let's start with every other."

"So tomorrow, I don't get to talk to you?"

"We can text."

"I don't like it."

"Yeah," I agree. "I don't much care for it either."

"I'll try for you. I'm not promising you. I never want to break a promise to you, Emerson, and I feel as though this is one that I would break."

"That's all we can do is try."

Every day, I wake up and I try to forget what it felt like to be his. I would constantly count down the days until I was in his arms again. Now, I try to forget what it felt like to be wrapped up in him. I even tried to not sleep with the blanket he gave me last night. I lasted an hour before I was reaching for it, and holding it so tightly in my arms, I could feel the strain in my muscles.

"I need to get to bed. I have to be up early for class."

He hesitates. "Okay. Have a good day. Sweet dreams, baby girl."

"Night." My voice cracks and I hit end before he can keep me on the phone any longer. My phone falls to my lap, and Monroe launches herself at me from where she's sitting on the other side of the couch. She wraps me in a hug while I lose my battle with my tears.

This has to get better, right? It's been a month and I still cry at least once a day. I miss him so damn much. I miss the plans we had. I miss knowing that I had someone in this world that was all mine.

I have my brother, and he's been my protector my entire life. I love him for it, but the love I have for Roman is different.

Then, there's Monroe. She and I met in pre-k, and we've been by each other's sides ever since. I love her like a sister, and she is my best friend, but my relationship with Rome as my best friend differs so much.

Maybe it's the intimacy. When you bare your heart and body to someone, it's impossible for them not to take a part of your soul. I opened myself up to him completely, and he did the same.

Sitting up, I wipe at my eyes with the back of my hand. "Give it the four months, right?" I ask Monroe.

"Yeah, babe. I think things are going to work out. The road is a little bumpy, but when you get to the end, it's going to be worth it."

"What about spring break? How do I go home and not see him?"

"Easy. We don't go home. It's only a week. We can use the excuse we're gearing up for graduation."

"Your parents will miss you."

"Meh, they'll more than likely come to us." She grins. "We'll stay here. When we move back home, if you're both still struggling like you are right now, then I think the two of you need to have a serious talk. I know he's worried about Forrest never forgiving each of you, and sure, that's a possibility, but this pain that you're both in might be the lesser of the two evils."

"I hate to think that might be the case. I love my brother. I love them both."

"Four months," she reminds me.

I nod. "I'm in. We get through this last stretch, get through graduation, and when the distance is no longer a factor, we'll see what happens."

"That sounds like a good plan to me."

"Thanks, Roe. I know I've been a buzzkill recently."

"I'm sure you'll get your turn to repay the favor."

"I doubt it. You're going to learn from my mistakes and not get involved in a twisted mess like me."

"We don't know the future, but I know where to find you when I need you."

I give her a hug, and we lock up and head to our rooms.

She's right. The saying "only time will tell" rings true.

I hope time is what we need, because if not, my brother might get his wish. I might leave Ashby. I don't know that I can see Roman every single day and him not be mine.

ROMAN 21

"FUCK ME," FORREST SAYS, TOSSING his phone down on the table in the break room, where we're all eating lunch. It's a rare day that all five of us are here at the same time and our schedules align for us to eat together.

"I'll pass," Maddox says, taking a bite of his sub.

"Not my type," Lachlan quips.

"Definitely not," Legend agrees.

"What's up?" I ask him. There is concern etched into his features. There isn't much that would make my best friend react that way. I can't help but wonder if something is up with her. Emerson has been really quiet this week. Hell, who am I kidding? She's been quiet since she insisted on that stupid-ass rule that we can't talk every day. I hate it, and if I thought I missed her before, it's worse now.

"Emerson."

My shoulders stiffen, and I try to keep the worry out of my tone. "Everything all right?" I hope that sounded casual, because on the inside, my stomach is in knots, coiled like a snake.

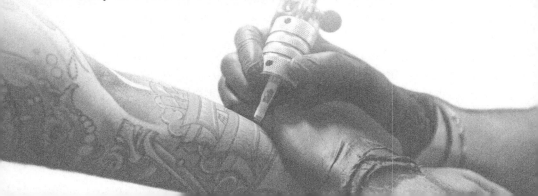

"She's fine, but she's not coming home."

"What?" Legend asks. "What do you mean, she's not coming home?"

"Ever?" Lachlan asks.

"Why?" Maddox asks.

He said she was fine. That doesn't keep me from pulling my phone out of my pocket and checking for a message from her. There's not one, but I'm not surprised.

At the end of January, she said we had to back off on the calls. It's now the beginning of April, and I feel her slipping further away from me every single day, and I don't know what to do with that. I know what it means for us to be together, but I can't seem to let go.

My heart won't let me.

So here I am going through the motions of life, while constantly thinking about her. If I'm lucky, I talk to her two to three times a week. That's it. I went from hearing her voice every night before falling asleep and often throughout the day to talking to her two to three times.

I hate it. I hate every fucking minute of it.

I've tried really hard not to take that anger out on Forrest. It's not his fault he wants what's best for her. He just doesn't know that what's best for her is me. I have to remind myself that we didn't tell him about us. I have to remind myself that *I* ended things to prevent a sibling war, which instead caused a raging out-of-hand war in my chest.

I fucking miss her.

With each day that passes, I realize that the decision I made, even though she agreed, was the wrong one. With everything inside me, I wanted to protect her from losing her only family, but what I failed to realize at that time, is that *I* am her family. The guys here at the shop, they're her family. Monroe is her family. The family who chose her. Not because of bloodlines, but because of love.

Knowing that I could have been the cause of their rift, that I would be the one to cause her unnecessary pain, guided me in the wrong direction. We had a plan. I deviated from that plan after talking to Forrest that night. Maybe if I would have just told him that I was the man that would love her and spoil her and treat her like she deserves to be treated, he would have been pissed, but we could have gotten through it.

"She's been distant," Forrest says. "Sending me to voice mail, not calling to check in as much." He looks up from his phone. "I was so desperate I called Monroe, and she assured me that she's fine. Just focusing on graduation." He points to his phone. "That's her excuse. Exams are coming up, and she wants to get a head start. She's been taking a class that's kicking her ass, I guess. Her study group went from meeting twice a week to three times."

She told me that too. At least if she's lying, her stories are consistent. She failed to mention that she wasn't coming home. That I won't be seeing her until graduation at the end of next month.

"Seems plausible to me," Maddox says.

"I'm sure she's just busy, man. She's an adult now, living her own life," Lachlan says gently.

"She's a smart girl, Forrest. If she needs you, she'll let you know," Legend adds.

I stay quiet. Not because I don't have anything to say, but for fear I'll blurt out that I'm in love with her, and lost her because I was afraid she would lose him if she chose me, so I keep my mouth shut.

"What about you? You going to give some unsolicited advice too?" Forrest asks.

I shrug. "I agree with them." I shove the rest of my sub into my mouth and stand from the table, gathering my trash. "I need to get ready for my next client." The words are barely out of my mouth when Lyra appears at the door to the break room.

"Hey, Roman, your first one for the afternoon is here."

"Thanks, Lyra. I'll be right there." I walk out of the break room and to my room. Immediately, I pull out my phone and send Emerson a text.

Me:	Forrest says you're not coming home.
Emerson:	Gotta prepare for exams and graduation.
Me:	I was looking forward to seeing you.
Emerson:	I'm doing the responsible thing.

Her words hit me like a knife in my chest. I know it's a dig at me. I truly thought with my entire being that I was doing what was best for her, but I think I was wrong. In fact, I know I was wrong.

I should have let her make that choice.

It wasn't my place to make it for her. I see that now. I understand where I fucked up. That I fucked up. The problem is I don't know how to fix it. I was hoping to get to see her while she was home for spring break, but that's not happening.

Part of me is tempted to cancel my schedule and go to her, but I know school has been tough for her this last semester, and a lot of that is the pressure and the sadness of what's going on between us. So I don't doubt for a minute that she truly will spend the week studying. That's the only thing that's keeping me from going to her.

> **Me:**   Have a good day, baby girl. I miss you.

I don't know what else to say. I created this mess. I didn't fight for us, because I was too busy fighting for her. It was a fight that wasn't mine to take on, and now I need to figure out how to fix it.

She graduates in seven weeks. Seven more weeks until I can see her again. Seven weeks to figure out how I'm going to fix this. If I've learned anything during the last few months, it's that I can't go on without her being mine.

Four hours later, I'm walking my client to the front desk. I smile at Lyra, and she nods, going into aftercare instructions and processing his payment. I turn to head to the break room and knock a pile of papers off the desk. When I bend to pick them up, I see a drawing that I know instantly is Emerson's. It's a moon and star design, and I'm immediately taken back to the night I held her under the stars. I can't help but wonder if that's what she was thinking of when she drew this.

I run my fingers over the design, and an idea hits me. Instead of going to the break room, I stop outside of Legend's door, knocking lightly on the frame.

"What's up?" He looks up from the design he's working on.

"What's on the books for you the rest of the day?"

"My last client canceled. His wife went into labor, so I'm just working on a design for next week unless we get a walk-in. You need something?"

"I do, actually. Some ink therapy."

"I'm in. Do you know what you want?"

"Yeah. Let me get it on some transfer paper and I'll be right back. Black and gray," I tell him, turning to stride down the hall with Emerson's sketch in my hand.

I'm aware that this is crazy, but I know this is her work, and right now, this is what I need. I need to feel as though I have a piece of her with me always. I've already made up my mind that I'm going to fight for us. I'll fight for her, and she can tap me in when she needs me.

I was trying to protect her.

I realize now, she didn't need me to protect her. All she needed was me to love her. I should have told her. Just another regret that I have where she's concerned.

She's trying to keep her distance, hoping that with time, we can both move on. I don't want to move on, and I can almost guarantee she doesn't want to move on either. She's doing what she thinks she has to do. I did what I thought I had to do, and we are both wrong.

We belong together.

I spend the next thirty minutes tracing every line of her drawing onto transfer paper. As soon as I'm done, I rush to Legend's office where he's still working on his piece for next week.

"Ready?" he asks.

"I'm ready." Reaching behind my head, I grab the neck of my T-shirt and pull it over my head, tossing it onto his desk. "Here." I hand him the drawing. His brow furrows, but he doesn't say a word about the design or why I'm getting a moon and stars tattooed on my chest. "Right here." I pat a blank area of skin over my heart.

"You sure?" he asks.

"I'm sure."

He nods. Once he has it placed, and I approve, he gets to work. We're quiet for several minutes, as I close my eyes and let him do his thing. "You good?" he asks.

I chuckle, peeling my eyes open to look at him. "Not my first time, man," I reply.

"Yeah, it kind of is. Does he know?"

"Does who know what? You lost me, man. I was zoned out." I must have missed something he said.

"Does Forrest know you're in love with her?"

My body instantly tenses. "What are you talking about?"

"Come on, Rome. This is Emerson's drawing. I saw her working on it."

I swallow hard. I don't know how much to tell him. "He doesn't know and neither does she." I decide to go with a version of the truth.

"You plan on telling either of them?"

"Yes."

"It's a slippery slope, brother," he says, going back to work.

"Fuck, Legend, I know, okay. I know it is, but I fucking love the hell out of her. I can't not tell her, and I'm scared as fuck we're both going to lose him over this."

"You prepared for that?"

"Yes."

"No hesitation?"

"None. I'm prepared to leave the business if that's what it comes down to."

"Whoa." He stops and looks up at me. "Those are big declarations."

"Did you miss the part where I admitted I was in love with her?"

He's still staring at me with his mouth hanging open.

"Years of hard work and sacrifice went into this business. A lifetime of friendship."

"Fuck me, I know all of that. I know what we went through to get where we are today. I know it's going to fuck up the dynamics if he wants me out. I hate it, but if I'm put in a position where I have to choose Everlasting Ink or her, I choose her. Every fucking day, all day long, I choose her."

"This isn't new, is it?"

I swallow hard. "No."

"Have you crossed a line with her?"

"Depends on which line you're talking about."

"You fucked her?"

"Don't." My tone is low and lethal. "Don't you dare talk about her like she's some woman we picked up at a bar. She's fucking everything to me. And if you want all the sordid details, no I didn't have sex with her, but we've... been together intimately."

Once I start talking, I can't shut up. I spill it all to him. I tell him how I resisted her, or tried to, and then just couldn't anymore. I tell him about our plan to wait until she graduated, and I tell him how I fucked it all up because the thought of her losing her brother, of her relationship with me causing her pain, was tearing me up inside.

"I had her. I lost her, and now I need her back. I'll do anything. I'd give up anything to make things right with her."

"Damn," Legend mutters. "Is she not coming home because of all of this?"

"She's had a class that's been kicking her ass, so I think it's a little bit of both."

"And her blowing Forrest off?"

"I think she's mad at him, or frustrated because of the speech he gave me, which, in turn, led to us breaking up."

"But you still talk?"

"Used to be every day, then she set this stupid fucking rule that it had to be at least every other day on the phone. But we text every day, yeah."

"And now you're getting ink over your heart that she drew?" It's more of a question than a statement.

"Yep."

He's quiet. I'm sure mulling all of this over in his mind. He finishes up my tattoo, cleans and covers it, before pulling off his gloves. "This means I'm an accomplice."

"What?"

"I know too much. He's going to be pissed."

"This conversation never happened. Look, man, I'm missing her like crazy, and she's going to be pissed as hell when I tell her that I told you, but you can't say anything. You have to let us work this out."

"You're going to tell her you told me?"

"Of course I am. I've never lied to her, and I won't start now. Fuck me, Legend. I'm trying to win her back, not fuck this up further."

He raises his hands in the air, letting me know he's backing off. "I won't say a word, but you need to fix this. You need to either grovel or let her go."

"I can't let her go."

"You might not have a choice." He voices my greatest fear.

"She loves me."

"Did she tell you that?"

"She didn't have to. I can feel it. I can't explain it. All I know is that until it happens to you, you won't understand it."

"You're really in love with our Em?"

"She's my Em, and yes, I'm in love with her."

"So possessive," he jokes.

"Again, until it happens to you, you won't understand, but I promise you there is nothing in this world I wouldn't give up for her. I'll do whatever it takes to prove that to her."

"You're talking forever, Rome."

"Won't be long enough."

"Holy fuck." He shakes his head.

"Just keep this between us. Please."

"Done. However, I'm not going to lie for you. That's not who we are."

"I know. I hate that we lied to you all, to him, but she wanted to wait, and when I tell you, there isn't anything I wouldn't do for her. I mean it. I let her call the shots. She has all the power."

"You're pussy-whipped without actually having the pussy."

"I warned you." My voice is low and gravelly.

"Retract the fangs, Rome. What I meant was, you've never slept with her, and she's got you under her spell. Once she gives in, I can't imagine how much worse it's going to be."

"I know she's younger than me. Those ten years were a big part of my hold-up, but when we're together, I don't feel them. However, I still knew they were there. I knew she was inexperienced, and I let her set the pace. I'll continue to do that. If she wants to wait until we're married, that's fine too. I don't care as long as at the end of the day, she's mine. I get to call her mine, and I don't have to hide that I fucking love her with everything I am." I'm breathing heavily by the time my little speech is finished, and I feel every word. Fuck the age difference. Fuck her brother if he can't see that she's my entire world.

I want to marry her. I want the rest of my life with her.

He slowly nods. I just dropped a big-ass heavy truth bomb on him, so there's a lot to process. "I hope it works out for both of you."

I nod, hold my fist out, and we bump knuckles. Grabbing my shirt, I slip it back over my head and go back to my space. I look around and all the hard work we put into building this business and our reputation stares back at me.

I'll miss it if it comes down to me giving it all up, but I'll do so without a single regret.

EMERSON 22

SITTING ON MY BED, I stare at the boxes surrounding me. This place, a home I've shared with my best friend for the last three years, holds so many memories. I know how incredibly fortunate I am that we both went to the same school. Different fields of study but both in healthcare. I'm grateful to my big brother for helping me make this happen. I owe him so much. I also owe him an apology.

To say the last four months have been difficult is a gross understatement. I had big plans for myself, and for my future. They all included Roman, and suddenly, I had to let them go. I'm still figuring out how to do that, but what I have figured out is that I haven't been fair to my brother.

He did nothing wrong. He loves me with everything he is, and I know he wants what's best for me. That's not a crime, and even if it were, he wouldn't know that he committed it. He had no idea that Roman and I were together, and that's on me. I chose to wait until I graduated. My fear held me back.

It wasn't fear of losing Forrest in my life. Our bond, much like our anchor tattoos, is grounded the way only two kids who grew up with neglectful parents could be. I knew he would be upset, but I also knew he would eventually come around. My fear was that Roman would lose interest. I feared that the newness of what we were together would wear off.

I was wrong on both counts.

Every damn day that man sends me a good-morning and good-night text. I get messages all throughout the day telling me about his day, or just telling me he missed me. Even when I left him on read, without fail, his messages never stopped coming.

He's coming today. They all are.

The guys of Everlasting Ink, my brother and his four best friends, have all been my biggest cheerleaders throughout life. Roman was always different for me. He became more, and today I see him face-to-face for the first time since I returned to school at the end of the Christmas break.

Four months should be enough time for a broken heart to heal, right?

My heart shouldn't race at the thought of seeing him. I shouldn't be hoping for a congratulations hug, just to hold him.

I tried. I truly tried to get over him. I even insisted we no longer talk every day on the phone, but he still called. Religiously, every other evening, my phone would ring, and like the lovesick fool I am for him, I answered. Sometimes I'd rush the conversation, and others I would pretend he was still mine.

That's really what it comes down to. I want him to be mine.

Four months isn't long enough for my heart to forget what it feels like to be his girl, and I'm almost certain, a lifetime won't be either.

"Em! We need to go or we're going to be late," Monroe calls out.

I stand, grabbing my purse and my phone, and make my way toward the living room. "It's hard to believe our lives are in these boxes."

"Right? It's going to be good to be home, though. We need to get started on looking for a place in Ashby. You know, moving back in with my parents is not my idea of a good time." She laughs.

"Your parents are awesome. It's not like they hover over you."

"I know, and I feel selfish even saying this, but once you're on your own, and you have to go back, it's just... different."

"You have nothing to feel selfish about. You're lucky to have them, and I know I'm lucky to have Forrest. I don't mind living with him, but the guys are always there, and some space is definitely going to be needed."

"Are you sure space is what you need?"

"You think it's not?"

"I think we've talked about this. When we move home, keep an open mind."

There's something she's not saying, but we don't have time to get into it right now. We're going to be late.

"Emerson!" Forrest shouts.

I smile as I make my way through the crowd to my brother. As I get closer, I start to move faster until I'm at a dead run. He opens his arms and braces his legs apart to catch me, just as I knew he would.

"I'm so fucking proud of you, kid," he whispers.

"Love you, Forty."

"I love you too." He holds me for a little longer before placing me on my feet.

"Come on over and share some of that love." Lachlan opens his arms, and I laugh, giving him an enormous hug as well.

"Come on now, don't hog her." Maddox tugs on my arm, tearing me from Lachlan. I pull away from Maddox, only to be lifted in the air by Legend. He spins me around, making us all laugh. He puts me back on my feet, hugging me quickly, and with his hand on the small of my back, hands me off to Roman.

Taking a deep breath, I lift my eyes to find his locked on me. Neither one of us says a word. However, when he opens his arms for me, I fall into his embrace. He turns us to hide the intimacy of the moment.

"I fucking missed you, baby girl," he says huskily. His hands have a slight tremble. As I pull away, I realize my legs are in a similar state.

I missed him too. However, I can't say that. Not here. So I take a step back, only to watch Monroe take her turn with all the guys, getting her hug of congratulations from each of them as well.

"Where are your parents?" I ask her.

"Oh, they just left to head to the restaurant. We're all having lunch together," she tells me.

"All of us?" I ask, looking at each of the guys. My gaze lasting a little longer on Roman than the others.

"Monroe's mom called yesterday, and I agreed," Forrest explains. "We're all here, so we might as well."

"Great." I plaster a smile onto my face. It's not that I don't want to eat with all of them. I'm just... honestly, I don't know what I am. Nervous to be around Roman. Nervous because I love him.

"Emerson!" I hear my name shouted. I barely have time to turn before Gabe is there, lifting me off my feet and spinning me around, much like Legend just did.

He places me on my feet and grins down at me, his arm still around my waist. "We did it, babe." He smiles proudly.

"We did." I return his smile because we worked our asses off this last semester. Between classes and clinicals, I wasn't sure I would make it to today.

"Who's this?" Forrest asks.

"Oh, right. Guys, this is Gabe. He was in the surgical tech program with me. Gabe, this is my brother, and his friends slash business partners, and you know Monroe."

"Nice to meet you." Gabe holds his hand out for my brother to shake, which he does.

"You too. So you two had class together?"

"Yeah," Gabe answers. "We were in study group, and I might have been this one's knight in shining armor at one point," he teases.

"Stop." I roll my eyes. "I had a flat a while back, and Gabe saw me pulled over on the side of the road and stopped to help me."

"Thanks, man," Forrest says with sincerity.

"We appreciate you looking after our girl." Maddox crosses his arms over his chest, which earns another eye roll from me.

"Anything for Em," Gabe says sweetly.

I hear a grunt, and I turn to see Roman glaring at Gabe. I ignore him. He doesn't have the right to be pissed off. Not that there is anything to be pissed about. Gabe and I are just friends.

"Is your family here?" Forrest asks Gabe.

"They are. We're heading out. I just needed to come and say hi before we left."

"It was nice to meet you," Forrest tells him again.

"You too." Gabe turns to me. "See you around?"

"You bet." I smile and wave. Gabe stops to give Monroe a hug and a kiss on the cheek.

"Is he why you didn't come home?" Lachlan asks, wagging his eyebrows.

"I thought we were going to eat?"

"We are. Let's go." Forrest wraps an arm around my shoulders. I hold my arm out for Monroe, and the three of us head to Forrest's truck.

"This place is fancy," Maddox says. "Thanks for graduating, Em. This gives us an excuse to try this place."

"You know, you could try dating. That's also a good excuse to try a place like this." Monroe laughs.

Maddox shudders. "Roe, let's not go talking crazy."

"You know, one of these days, all five of you are going to meet a woman who will change the way you think," Monroe muses.

"You trying to marry us off?" Lachlan asks.

"No." She giggles. "Just stating the obvious. You can't seriously want to be a bachelor your entire life."

"Not my entire life," Forrest speaks up. "It's going to take someone really fucking special to lock this down." He motions down his body and we all crack up laughing.

"Yeah? What are the qualifications?" Monroe asks.

"Are you submitting an application?" Lachlan asks. "If so, I can give you a list for myself." He winks at her.

Monroe points at him. "No." She shakes her head, smiling. "Forrest?"

"You're being serious?" he asks.

"Yep." Monroe takes a sip of her water. We're still waiting for her parents. Apparently, they got turned around and are stuck in traffic.

"She has to be family oriented. She needs to get along with Emerson, and respect that we're close. She needs to want to be with me for me, not for what I can give her. She needs to be someone who I know will always be in my corner, a true partner in life. She needs to understand that my job can have crazy hours to fit the schedules of my clients, and she needs to know that my Everlasting Ink family and our traditions are important to me."

"Is that all?"

Forrest shrugs. "Yeah."

"If you find her, hopefully, she has a sister," Lachlan tells him. "All the ladies I've met recently want the status that comes with being with the bad boy, or the fact that we're gaining national recognition for our ink."

"Same," Maddox agrees.

"What about someone who would give up everything for you?" Legend asks.

"What do you mean?" Forrest asks him.

"That's true love, right? What if you found someone who worked her ass off to build an empire, but to be with you, she'd have to walk away from that? What if she walked away from that for you?"

"Whoa." Forrest holds his hand in the air. "I wouldn't let her. Fuck that, she worked for it. We make it work." Forrest takes a drink of his water. "But yeah, I mean, that's pretty fucking intense if you think about it."

"That's a selfless love," Monroe adds softly.

I'm getting ready to tell them this is too heavy of a topic for a day that we're supposed to be celebrating. I can't sit here and talk about love and sacrifice when the man I love isn't willing to let me make my own choices to sacrifice my love for him. Sure, I agreed when he ended things, but it's hard to fight for someone who has already given up. Luckily, I don't have to talk about it anymore. Monroe's parents arrive, and small talk ensues as we order our meals.

"All the boxes go," I tell the guys. "They're spread out all over the place, and they're labeled, so maybe two trucks for Monroe's place and two to take back to Forrest's place?" I suggest.

"Got it." All five of them reply like the good moving soldiers they are. They loaded up Monroe's parents' SUV. They're headed back to Tennessee, and with these five guys, I'd say we won't be far behind them. As a graduation present, Monroe's parents hired cleaners so we don't have to worry about it. We can move everything to the trucks and be home in Ashby tonight.

"I'm going to check my room again. We're leaving all the furniture for the next person. Most of it is secondhand, anyway. I just want to make sure I didn't leave anything behind."

"Oh, me too," Monroe says.

We head down the hall. She turns right, and I turn left. I pull open each dresser drawer, making sure I didn't miss anything. I turn and yelp when I see Roman standing in my doorway. He steps into the room and closes the door. He studies me for a few erratic heartbeats before moving toward me. He doesn't stop until he's standing in front of me.

"What are you doing? You shouldn't be in here like this."

"Does he know you're mine?"

"What? Who are you talking about?" I hiss, my eyes flashing toward the door.

"Gabe. Does he know that you're mine?"

"I'm not yours, Rome. You ended things," I whisper hiss.

He ignores me and rests his palm against my cheek. "Does he know that your pussy cries for me?"

I swallow hard. "You should go."

"Does he know that you like to be kissed here?" He leans in and runs his lips over the column of my neck. "Does he know that I own this?" he asks, sliding his hand between my thighs. "That I was your first, and that you were mine?" He stands to his full height, and his eyes bore into mine, begging, pleading, but I'm not sure for what.

"That's not true," I scoff.

"It is, baby girl. You were the first one to ever matter." He bends his head and presses his lips to my forehead. I bite the inside of my cheek, trying like hell to keep the tears at bay. His lips are replaced with his own forehead. His hands move to grip my waist as we both stand as still as statues.

"Tell him to gear up for a fight," he whispers. "I fucked up, baby girl. I miss you, and I'm not afraid of a little competition."

Oh, damn. I know he thinks I'm with Gabe. I should tell him that we're not together. We've always been honest with one another, even when it's hard. However, before I can get the words out, there is a knock at my door.

"Em, you in there?" Monroe asks.

I take a step back from Roman. "Come in," I call out to her.

"Hey." She peeks her head in. "The guys were asking where Rome was."

"Just grabbing some boxes." He turns, lifts two into his arms, and strides out of the room.

"You okay?"

I nod but reply, "No."

Monroe chuckles. "Open mind, Emerson. Open mind."

"He says he's not afraid of a little competition. He thinks I'm with Gabe." Guilt sits heavily on my chest. I should have told him the truth.

"I figured with the hate glares he was tossing Gabe's way. I hope you set him straight."

"I was getting ready to when you knocked on the door."

"Yeah, probably best the two of you talk about this when there is less of a chance of getting caught."

"You're right."

"You will tell him, though, right?"

"Yes. I don't want to play games."

"For what it's worth, I saw the way he watched you today. The two of you, it's not over. I wouldn't be surprised if one of the other guys doesn't pick up on it soon. He's not even trying to hide the way he's looking at you."

"How's he looking at me?" I hate that I ask the question. I hate even more that I need the answer.

"Like you're his air, Emerson. That man is madly in love with you." She blows me a kiss and backs out of my room.

For the rest of the afternoon, I stay as far away from Roman as I can. It takes the guys no time to load up all five trucks. In fact, it was overkill, but I love them for it. By three, we're on the road. Forrest insists that Monroe and I be in the middle of them in some way as we drive in a caravan back to Ashby. If one of us stops, we all stop. It's completely ridiculous, and exactly the kind of thing I would expect from my brother.

He knows this is what Monroe and I do, and he's just trying to keep with the tradition, and be a part of it. Picking up my phone, I dial my brother before placing it back into the cupholder. His voice comes over the car's speakers.

"You good, Em?"

"I'm good, Forty. I just wanted to say that I'm sorry." I know I should be doing this in person, but I need to tell him now, and I'm not so sure if I did this face-to-face, I wouldn't spill the beans about being in love with his best friend.

"Sorry for what, kid?"

"Being distant the past few months. School and clinicals kicked my ass. I didn't mean to shut you out. Don't hate me."

"There is nothing you could do that I would ever hate you for. Nothing, little sister, you hear me? We're anchored," he says, referring to our tattoos.

"I love you, Forty."

"I love you too, kid. Now, who's going to convince this caravan we need ice cream?" he asks.

"Me obviously." I smile even though I know he can't see me. My heart feels a little lighter already. Now all I need to do is come clean to Roman. Toss out the truth and see where we land.

He laughs, and the sound makes my heart happy.

"I'll take full responsibility. Since you're leading, pull off two exits up. It's a small mom and pop shop that has the best ice cream I've ever eaten. I'll tell everyone I called in the stop."

"Got it, captain." He chuckles, and the line goes dead.

Forrest and I are going to be okay. His words replay over and over in my head. I know in my heart that I could tell him anything.

Our plan was perfect. Roman got cold feet, but it's hard to be mad at him when I know that his decision was made for me.

I think I need to apologize, but with Roman, it needs to be in person. Just like Monroe said, I'll go into the conversation with an open mind, and we'll just have to see how it goes.

ROMAN 23

I STARE THROUGH THE BLINDS of my bedroom window and watch the sunrise. I didn't sleep at all last night. Every time I closed my eyes, I saw Gabe with his arm around my girl, and my anger would spike.

Not at him. I know that he's innocent in all of this.

No, I fucked up, and now I'm paying for it.

I don't know what to do. On one hand, I think I should just let her go. Let her be happy with this guy. On the other hand, I know I can't do that. There has to be a way to fix this. There has to be a way to get her to pick me.

She did once. Surely, I can convince her to do it again.

Knowing I'm not getting any sleep, I toss the covers off and head to the shower. To make matters worse, today is my off day. I have nothing planned, so I'm going to spend the day trying to come up with a way to win her back. Maybe I can ask Legend to help me? He knows about us; he might have some insight. Maybe my parents? They've been married a long damn time. Surely, they have words of wisdom to pass on to me.

After a quick shower, I toss on shorts and a T-shirt and venture out to the living room. I don't feel like cooking, so cereal it is. Grabbing my laptop, I sit at the kitchen table, scarf down my bowl of cereal, and pull up a search engine. I can't believe I'm looking to the world wide web on ways to win my girl back, but I'm a desperate man.

With the notes app pulled up on my phone, I make lines and lines of notes. Even the ridiculous ideas like standing beneath her bedroom window with a boombox. It went on the list. It worked in the movies. Who's to say it won't work for me? I hope I don't get to that point of desperation, but I'm not passing anything up.

Three hours later, I'm overwhelmed. I stare down at my phone and the mile long list of ideas. "This is stupid," I mutter to myself. I just need to go see her. Forrest is at the shop today, so if she's home, we can talk just the two of us. That's what we need. Some face-to-face time to really talk and see where we both stand.

Until I know how serious she is with this guy, I can't really form a plan.

Ten minutes later, I'm in my truck and headed to their house. When I pull into the driveway, I exhale a sigh of relief that her car is here. Sure, she could be out with Monroe, but I'm hoping that things are falling in my favor. Rushing out of the truck, I race up the front steps and knock on the door. A few seconds later, the door opens, and she looks surprised to see me.

"Hey, baby girl." I smile. Fuck, it's good to see her.

"Rome. Hi. I wasn't expecting you."

"Is now a bad time?"

"Forrest isn't here."

"I know, baby. I came to see you."

She nods, stepping back, allowing me room to enter. "What's up?" she asks.

I turn to face her. "I miss you."

Her face softens. "I've missed you too, Rome."

"I fucked up. Emerson, I thought I was fighting for you, but in the midst of that battle, I forgot to fight for us."

"I know." There is sadness in her tone. "Maybe it just wasn't meant to be."

That hurts, but I don't react. "Does he know about us? Does he know that we still talk and text every day? Does he know that he's the competition?" I rattle off the questions.

"Roman."

"Does he know you're always going to be in my life? That I'm your brother's best friend? Does he know what he stands to lose?"

"He's not losing anything, Roman. This is ridiculous."

"You, baby girl. Does he know how precious you are? Does he love you the way you deserve to be loved?" My heart is racing as I ask the question. Surely, she can read through the lines and realize that I'm in love with her.

"Roman, you ended this." She waves her hand between us. "I'm not yours anymore, Roman. You gave me up."

"I did what I thought was best for you. The thought of being the reason you were at odds with your brother was eating me up inside. Baby girl, I never want to be the reason for your tears."

"But you are!" she yells. "Just say what this is really about, Roman. You don't want me, but you don't want anyone else to have me, either."

"Are you kidding me right now? I fucking love you!" I yell back. "It wasn't just your heart that I shattered that day." I lower my voice. My chest is rising rapidly with each breath, and I hate that I raised my voice at her. I'm fucking this up.

"I can't breathe. I can't think. I can't sleep. Not without you." She's standing frozen in the middle of the living room. I take a chance and make my way over to her. My hands rest against her cheeks, and I tilt her head up so that I can see her pretty green eyes. "I love you, Emerson. All of you. We can go tell your brother right now. I don't want to hide what you mean to me anymore."

"What about Forrest being pissed?"

"He's going to be." I nod. "I'm certain he's going to lose his mind. It hurts me to think that you're going to be fighting with him. I never want to be the reason for your tears, but I realized something these last several months."

"What's that?"

"I can't live without you being mine. My life is lackluster without you. Every fucking day I have something that happens that I need to share with you. At night, my arms physically ache to hold you. I realized that in trying to save you the heartache, I caused a new kind. It finally clicked with me that the heartache I caused separated us, and we were drowning in our sorrows alone. He's going to be pissed, and I know it's going to upset you, but something I didn't consider was that I'd still be there to dry your tears."

Her beautiful green eyes shimmer with tears.

"You needed me to be your partner, not your protector. I'll still always protect you, but I know there are some battles we need to fight together, and this is one of them."

"Rome." Her voice cracks.

"I've had a lot of time to think about this. I'm prepared to walk away from Everlasting Ink. If that's what he asks of me, then so be it."

"You can't do that."

"I can."

"You've worked so hard. You all have. You love that shop."

"I'll never love anyone or anything more than I love you, baby girl."

"We're not together."

Fuck. My shoulders fall. I thought I was getting through to her. How do I get her to understand she's everything? Every. Fucking. Thing.

"Gabe, I mean," she rushes to add, "we're not together. We never were. He's just a good friend that I shared classes and a study group with. He's engaged to his long-term girlfriend."

"You're not together?"

"No." Her hands rise to cover mine.

"I love you." I press my lips to her forehead, holding them there, just breathing her in. "Will you give me another chance? I know I fucked up, but I promise you, baby, I've learned my lesson. I know what life is like without you, and I can't do it."

"You want me?"

"More than anything."

"We're together?"

"In every way."

"How do I know you won't walk away again?"

"Let's go to the shop. Right now, we'll go tell him everything. I'll spend every day of our forever showing you that you're right here." I tap my hand over my chest.

"I don't know if I'm ready for that," she whispers.

"Baby girl, I don't want to hide how much I love you. You're not a dirty little secret."

"I need some time. If we're going to do this, I need to make sure that you're not going to leave me again."

"Never." I drop my hands and pull her into a hug. Her words finally register. I pull back and peer down at her in my arms. "You giving me another shot, baby?"

She nods. "I love you too, Roman."

My knees wobble. Somehow, I manage to move us to the couch, where I pull her onto my lap and kiss the hell out of her. My tongue explores her mouth as if it's the first time. She meets me stroke for stroke. I don't rush this. I savor every swipe of her tongue against mine. The way she grips my shoulders, and the feel of her ass beneath my palms, where I hold her on my lap.

I lose track of time, getting lost in my girl. When we finally break apart, I feel rejuvenated yet exhausted at the same time. "Can you do something for me?" I ask her.

"What's that?" Her lips are red and swollen, and my heart feels like it's too big for my chest.

"Can you come home with me? I didn't sleep at all last night. I need to sleep, but I need you close. I just got you back, and I'm not ready to let you go just yet."

"Forrest will be gone until six or so."

I nod. "I don't care if he knows, Emerson. I never did. My fear was for your relationship with him. I love the guy. He's my best friend, but there will never be anyone in my life who I'll put before you. Never. So, you lead us. You tell me when you're ready, and we do it. No backing out, no breaking up. It's me and you."

"Me and you." She nods.

I can tell that she's still uncertain. It's going to take time for me to prove to her that losing her is not something I'll ever do again.

Never.

"I can set an alarm. Can I park in your garage?"

"Yes."

She nods. "Okay."

"Okay." I kiss her again.

"Rome, you have to let me go if we're going to your place."

"Can you ride with me?"

"You know I can't."

I nod. I fucking hate it, but I agreed to let her lead us. "Fine. Let's go home." Her mouth falls open when I call my place home, but I pretend not to notice. She climbs off my lap and I stand. "I'll go ahead of you."

"Probably best," she agrees.

"Be safe, baby girl."

"You too." I kiss her cheek and force myself to walk out the door without her.

As soon as I get home, I pull my truck to the side of the driveway and open the garage door. My truck is too tall to fit inside, but it's perfect for her car. I pace back and forth until I see her car. I guide her in and quickly hit the button to close the garage door, before rushing over to open hers. I lace our fingers together and lead her inside. We don't stop until we get to my room. I close the blinds to block out the sun, and quickly strip down to my boxer briefs.

"You don't have to," I tell her when I see her chewing on her bottom lip. She's trying to decide whether she should strip too. I know skin-to-skin contact with me is her favorite.

"I want to."

I nod. I don't push her either way. This is her call. I just want her in my arms. She could wear a fucking parka for all I care. I just need to hold her.

Out of the corner of my eye, I can see her getting undressed. She leaves her panties on, moves to lock the bedroom door, and then comes back to the bed. I hold the covers up, and she climbs in next to me.

I don't hesitate to pull her into me, wrapping my arms around her. "Fuck, baby girl, I love you. Thank you for giving me this. I won't let you down. This second chance, it's everything. *You're* everything."

"I love you too." She rests her head on my chest, and just as soon as she does, she sits up in bed. Tentatively, she reaches out and rubs her hand over my new tattoo. "Wh—When did you get this?" she whispers.

"The day you were supposed to come home for spring break."

"Where did you find this?"

"It was in a pile of papers on the desk. I knocked them off by mistake and this is what I found. I knew I had to have it. It reminds me of our date under the stars."

"Because it is," she says. She looks at me with tears in her eyes.

"Don't cry, baby. I had to have a piece of you with me always." I reach down and rub her hip over her lily tattoo.

"I have a piece of you."

"You have all of me." I tap my chest, and she lies back down. "Promise me you'll be here when I wake up."

"I'll be here."

"Love you," I mumble, kissing the top of her head, and falling fast asleep.

I wake with a jolt, my heart racing. My arms tighten around Emerson as I exhale. She's here. It wasn't a dream. She's in my bed, and if I have any say, she'll always be here.

My body relaxes into the mattress, closing my eyes.

"You okay, Rome?"

My eyes pop open to see her peering at me. "Yeah, baby girl. I've never been better," I say, kissing the top of her head.

She moves to straddle my hips. I rest my hands on her thighs, feeling the silky softness of her skin. "You're beautiful."

She blushes and looks down. Her fingers roam over my chest until her palm is lying against my heart, over the tattoo that she drew. "I still can't believe you got this."

"You own what's beneath. It's only fair that I get some ink to symbolize that."

"Roman Bailey, a sweet talker." She smiles.

"Only with you."

Her hands continue to explore, but I leave mine on her thighs. The last thing I want to do is scare her away. I just got her back, and I'm not one-hundred-percent sure she's all in with me yet, so until then, this is her show.

Fuck me, who am I kidding? It's always been her show and it always will be.

Her hands glide over mine. She reaches between us and rubs gently over my cock that's screaming to be released from the confines of my boxer briefs.

"Is this for me?" She smirks.

"Are you teasing me, baby girl?"

She shrugs, her long brown hair falling over her shoulders. I move it back over her shoulder. I can't have those luscious locks blocking my view of her perfect tits. My mouth waters. I want the pebbled buds of her nipples in my mouth, but I hold myself back. I'm letting my girl drive.

"Can we take these off?" she asks. She doesn't wait for an answer. She moves off my lap, and I immediately lift my hips as she assists me with peeling my boxer briefs over my thighs.

I start to protest when she climbs off the bed. That's until I see her making quick work of her panties. When she climbs back on the bed, she straddles my hips again, and I moan when my cock comes in contact with her wet pussy.

My hands find their way to her tits as I roll her nipples between my thumbs and forefingers, showing them equal attention. She moans, tilting her head back. Her hair cascades down her back, and her slender neck calls to me.

Sitting up, I wrap my arms around her while my lips trail over her neck. I start at her collarbone and work my way up. When I reach her lips, I kiss her gently. On the inside, I'm raging. I want to pound against my chest and scream to the world that I got the girl, but on the outside, I'm taking my time. I need to show her that she's precious to me.

"I missed you, Roman," she murmurs against my lips.

I pull back and hold her head with my hands so that I have all her attention. "I love you, Emerson. I'm not me without you."

Tears pool in her eyes. "Show me."

"I will, baby girl. Every day I'll show you what you mean to me."

"Show me now."

My breath hitches. "Spell it out for me, baby. Tell me what you want."

I think I know, but with Emerson, there is zero room for miscommunication. I just got her back. I'm not losing her again because I'm thinking with my cock.

Her eyes look down at our laps.

"Eyes on me, baby."

She lifts her gaze.

"Tell me. There is nothing you can ask for that I won't give you."

"I just want you."

"You have me. All of me."

"I want this." She reaches between us and runs the pad of her thumb over my piercing.

"Words, Em, I need to hear you say it."

She squares her shoulders, and those big green eyes peer into my own. "I want you to make love to me."

My hands tremble at her words. She lifts hers to cover mine as they still cradle her cheeks. "We don't have to rush this." My heart thumps against my chest like a caged animal. My vision blurs briefly as the anticipation of what she's asking settles deep in my soul.

"I've always wanted it to be you, Rome."

"Baby." My voice cracks. I swallow hard and try again. "I'm yours for a lifetime. There're no rules or guidelines for this." It's important she understands. She's it for me, no matter what she decides. "I want you for forever, Emerson."

I drop my hands and wrap them around her waist, pulling her closer. I kiss her softly.

"I want to give you my last name. I want little girls who look just like her momma, and a little boy who will be momma's boy to tuck in at night. If you want to wait until that happens, until we're married, I'm okay with that too."

She opens and closes her mouth a few times. "You... want to marry me?"

I can't contain my smile. "Yes. I'm going to do it right, Em. I'm going to get down on one knee and ask you to be mine forever. You have some time to practice your yes." I wink at her, and she starts to laugh. The sound fills the room, and my heart.

"Make love to me."

I swallow hard. "I need to grab a condom."

I'm not going to argue with her. I want her. I gave her an out. She got to choose and I'm not going to try to talk her out of it. Instead, I reach between us and slide one long digit inside of her. She's soaking wet. I add another, and she rocks her hips against my hand. I lazily pump my fingers in and out of her, making sure she's more than ready for my cock.

"I'm on the pill. I did it while at school. After Thanksgiving, I thought— It doesn't matter. We're protected."

Right. Condom. I got lost in the feel of her pussy.

"You sure, baby?"

"It's just me and you, right?"

"Forever. It's been a long damn time since I've been with anyone. Long before spring break last year."

She nods. "Then we're good."

One hand slides behind her neck. I pull her into a kiss. "Grip my cock, baby," I mumble against her lips.

"What?"

"Take my cock in your hand and guide me into your pussy."

"Like this?"

"This way, you control the pace. You take what you can handle. You're in complete control."

"Rome, I don't know what I'm doing. It won't be good for you."

She tenses, and I can feel the insecurity rolling off her in waves.

My index finger covers her lips. "If you think for a second my cock being nestled into your tight, wet pussy won't be good for me, you've lost your mind, baby girl. There is no right or wrong way. It will be good for me because it's you." I feel her body relax. "It's just me, Em. The man who loves you more than life. We're in this together. Talk to me, and tell me what you need. I'm right here, baby."

"I'm nervous."

"We don't have to."

"I want to. Stop trying to talk me out of it." She gives me a hard look and I grin.

"There she is. There's my girl. Every piece of me is yours, Em. Just do what feels good, baby."

She nods and reaches between us, gripping my cock. She lifts up on her knees and positions my head at her entrance. She bites down on her bottom lip as she starts to sink down. She's already dripping all over my cock.

My hands are on her waist. My hold is firm, but I don't move. This is all her.

"You're so warm, baby." I've never been bareback before. "Your pussy feels like silk sliding over my cock."

She slides down a little further.

"Oh," she moans.

"You're doing great, baby girl."

"I need more, Rome."

"Take what you need. Your pussy will take everything you give it."

She slides down a little further.

"Feels so good." She smiles at me.

I kiss her. "You ready for more?"

"There's more?"

I chuckle. "I'm only halfway in, baby girl."

"I should just do it, right?"

Her green eyes look to me for answers.

"You do what feels right."

"It feels so good. I feel full, but it's not painful."

"It will be," I tell her.

"Can you lie back?" she asks.

I drop a kiss on her lips and fall back onto the pillows. She leans over and places her hands on my chest. She slides a little lower and digs her nails into my skin. "Am I hurting you?"

"Don't worry about me, Em. Claw the fuck out of me if you have to, baby."

"Ready?" she asks me.

I smile at her. "I'm ready for everything with you."

She nods and drops the rest of the way onto my cock. Her ass is resting on my thighs. She flinches, but other than that, she remains quiet. Her nails are sharp against my chest. Her breathing is labored, and her eyes are closed. Her head is tilted back.

Reaching up, I tweak her nipple, and she moans.

"Wow." Her eyes pop open. "That's making this better."

I nod. I keep playing with her tits, my hands gently massaging her nipples, and she starts to move. She rocks forward and then back a few times as she sets a rhythm. When she lifts up on her knees and falls back down on my cock, we both groan.

"Wow," she murmurs again.

"You like the way my cock feels, deep inside your pussy, baby girl?"

Her pussy pulses, and I have my answer. My girl likes it when I talk dirty to her.

"Your pussy's milking my cock."

"Rome." She breathes my name like a prayer.

"What do you need, baby girl?"

"Faster," she pants as she falls on my cock and grinds her hips. She's frantic with her thrusts as she chases her release. "There," she says, rocking faster.

My balls tighten and heat races down my spine. I'm not going to be able to last much longer. Sliding my hand between us, I thumb her clit, and she arches her back.

"That. Yes. Yes. Yes."

"I need you to come for me, Emerson. Your pussy feels too good, baby. I'm not going to last. I need you to—" I don't get to finish before she's calling out my name. Her pussy grips me like a warm, wet vise, and I release inside her.

She falls forward, resting against my chest. I wrap my arms around her as we both catch our breath. When she's finally recovered enough, she lifts her head and smiles. I feel that smile deep in my chest.

"When can we do that again?" she asks.

I laugh. "You're going to be sore," I tell her.

"Worth it." She moves to lie next to me and scrunches up her nose. "Messy."

"Worth it," I repeat her words, making her laugh.

I want to spend the rest of my life pulling that sound from this woman.

I WALK INTO EVERLASTING INK, carrying two enormous bags of takeout from Olive Garden. I was in Nashville today for a job interview and decided to grab the guys a special dinner. They refused to take any money for helping Monroe and me move home from college, so this is their thank you. I made sure to order lots of extra breadsticks because they fight over them like children.

Not that I blame them. Olive Garden breadsticks are the best.

My interview just happens to be on a day that all five of the guys are at the shop. It's been happening more often as they get busier. They're all working crazy hours as their popularity grows. They love every minute of it. I'm so proud of them. It's nice to be here to witness all of their hard work and dedication paying off.

Roman says he's prepared to walk away, but it won't come to that. I have faith that I can talk some sense into my brother. He might need some time to cool down once we tell him, but I'll fight, beg, and plead for him to see that this is what I want.

I want Roman.

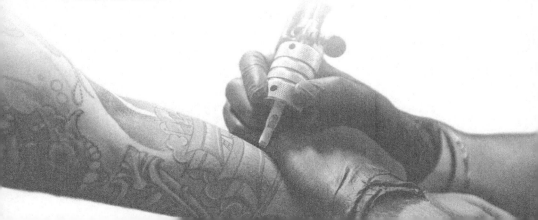

"Hey, Emerson. Let me help you." Lyra rushes around the counter and takes one of the bags from me. "What's all this?" she asks.

"A thank-you for the guys for helping Monroe and me move home. They wouldn't take money."

"You know they're going to try to pay you back for all of this too." She laughs.

"I've gotten good at dodging them over the years. I'll just make them feel guilty."

"Teach me your ways, ole wise one."

"Hey, I hear you're doing incredible. You and Drake have been great additions to the Everlasting Ink team."

"Em?"

I bite down on my cheek to keep from smiling at the sound of Roman's voice. Slowly, I turn. "Hey, Rome," I say sweetly.

His eyes roam lazily taking me in. I'm in a pencil skirt, a white flowing blouse, and heels. My hair is pulled up in a high ponytail, and by the way he's looking at me, you'd think he'd never seen a woman in a skirt before.

"How did it go?" he asks with a flare of desire in his eyes.

"Good. I think. I should hear something by the end of next week."

"This is the one you really wanted, right?" He's asking, but he already knows. He's trying to not make it obvious that he has personal insight to every facet of my life. I love him for the effort.

"Yes. I'm feeling good about it." I wink. He gives me a subtle nod, knowing I'll fill him in later.

"What's in the bags?" he asks. He steps close and places his hand on the small of my back, leaning over to peer into the bags. It's obvious that it's food. He's using his pretend curiosity as an excuse to touch me. Something I've noticed a lot in the last two weeks.

I can't believe it's only been two weeks since I moved home from college and we got back together. Roman has been attentive and sweet and goes out of his way to tell me every single day that he loves me.

He keeps asking me when we can talk to Forrest, and I know we need to, but I'm also enjoying just loving him without the prying eyes of my older brother. There's no doubt Forrest is going to be pissed. Is he going to disown me? No, he won't do that, but he might never talk to Roman again, and that scares me.

If I'm being honest with myself, I'm also a little worried he may change his mind again. He's done nothing since the moment he confessed his love for me but show me that love. He sends me messages, sneaks kisses, and cops a feel whenever he can. Even if it's just his hand on the small of my back to peer into an Olive Garden bag.

I still have this lingering worry, though. I know it's something I need to get past, and I'm working on it.

"Olive Garden," I finally answer. I turn to look at him over my shoulder and he kisses me. It's just a peck but I still freeze.

"She went to get the guys, baby girl. It's all good."

"You're taking a big risk, mister." I step forward, putting some distance between us.

"I'd risk it all for you, Em."

When he says things like that, it's really hard to even pretend to be upset with him. "Are you trying to make me melt here on the shop floor?" I ask. It's something I've been teasing him about the last two weeks. His words, they're sweet and loving, and they make me feel like I'm melting. Swoon city with this man.

"Is your pussy wet for me?" he asks.

"Please tell me you brought extra breadsticks?" Lachlan asks. He doesn't stop walking until he reaches me. He slings an arm around my shoulders and hugs me, kissing the top of my head. "Thanks for this, Em. How much do we owe you?"

"You're welcome. You don't owe me a thing. This is my thank-you for helping us move."

"That's what family's for," Maddox says, joining us. He kisses my cheek and grabs one of the bags.

"You all better hurry. We might eat it all."

"There are six orders of breadsticks," I tell Lachlan. "You each get your own order. No more." I point at him as if he's being scolded.

Lachlan grins. "Yes, dear." He winks and grabs the other bag before disappearing down the hall to the break room.

"Forrest and Legend are finishing up," Lyra tells me.

"Great. You go eat. I'll cover until their clients leave," I tell her.

"Oh, that's okay. You don't have to do that."

"I want to. Go, and make sure you take one of those orders of breadsticks for us to split. Guard them with your life," I say, making her laugh. It's funny until you're looking forward to a breadstick to realize the vultures ate them all.

Roman snakes an arm around my waist and pulls me into him. He kisses me soundly before resting his forehead against mine. "Do you have any idea how incredibly difficult it is for me to watch them hugging you and kissing you when you're mine?"

"It's brotherly."

He nods. "I know, baby girl, but they need to know you're mine."

"They're not going to stop," I tell him.

"Yeah, if anything they'll do it more to get under my skin, but at least they'll know they don't have a shot in hell with you."

"They don't want a shot," I remind him.

"I want you." He pulls me close, and his hard cock presses against my belly.

"Down boy," I tease. "You need to handle that."

"My office. I only need five minutes."

"Stop." I laugh, pushing him away. "Really. Get that under control." I point to his cock.

"You did this."

"Me? I didn't do anything."

"You're breathing, baby girl. That's all it takes where you're concerned."

"Sweet talker."

"Emerson lover." He smirks.

I shake my head, my smile so big I fear my face might crack. "Go."

"Fine." He leans in for another kiss, that I, of course, give him freely before he turns and heads down the hall. He turns off at the bathroom. He's going to need a minute.

I didn't think it was possible to fall more in love with him, but every day he does something as simple as ensuring I know what I mean to him, which makes me fall harder.

"What excuse did you use to get out of going to Get Hammered with the guys tonight?" I ask Roman.

He shrugs. "I told them I had a date with my girl."

"What?" I turn to look at him, well, as much as the seat belt in his truck will allow.

"I didn't tell them it was you, and I didn't tell them where we were going. But, yeah, I told them I had a girl that I was taking out to spoil her."

"Roman!"

He laughs and gives my thigh, where his big, tattooed hand is resting, a gentle squeeze. "Baby girl, we're going to tell them. At least this way, they won't be completely shocked that you've got me locked down."

"I don't have you locked down," I huff and sit back in my seat.

"You do have me on lockdown. You hold the key to my heart."

"Did you search the internet for sweet one-liners?" I ask him.

"No, but I did make a list of ways to win you back with the help of the world wide web."

"You did not."

He maneuvers his truck down the dirt path. He's taking us back to his grandparents' property, where we laid out under the stars on our first date. Once we stop, he picks his phone up from the cupholder, taps around on the screen, and hands it to me. "Did too." He sticks his tongue out at me, making me laugh.

I scroll through the list. Some of these are completely outrageous, and I can't see Roman using half of them. "When did you do this?" I ask, handing him his phone.

"The morning I showed up at your place. I was ready to do what I had to do to fight for us."

"Why haven't you deleted that?" I ask, laughing.

"Hey, this took hours of research. I'm sure I'm going to fuck up at some point over the next fifty-plus years. I might need to refer to it."

"Some of those, you might need to do some more homework," I joke.

He nods. "I'm willing to do the work." Leaning over the console, he kisses me softly. "I need a little time to get us set up."

"I can help."

"You can also sit your sexy ass in the truck and let me handle it." He winks and climbs out of the truck. He makes quick work of setting up the air mattress with a portable air compressor. Then he pulls the chairs and the small plastic table from the back of the truck.

Not being able to stand just sitting here watching him doing all the work, I hop out and grab the food that we picked up. This time we're having Mexican and it smells incredible.

"Baby girl, you're supposed to wait. You don't need to be walking through these high weeds."

"It's grass, Rome, and I'm perfectly capable."

"I know, but now I don't have an excuse to carry you."

"No, but the faster we finish setting up, we get to eat, and then comes dessert."

"Shit. I forgot dessert," he curses under his breath.

"Really? I thought we'd have each other for dessert." I try for innocence, but I can't hide my grin.

His head bobs. "You're right, baby, I could use your help." He winks and heat pools between my thighs.

"Get to work."

"Yes, ma'am."

We finish setting up and devour our meals as the sun sets.

"So, the interview was good?"

"I think so. I hit it off with the hiring manager. She's been a surgical tech for over twenty years. She oversees all the techs and reports to the nurse manager."

"You sure you want that drive?" he asks.

"It's only thirty minutes to Nashville, but I didn't tell you the best part. The hospital is opening a satellite outpatient clinic."

"Wait, is that the one that's going up at the edge of town?"

"Yes! So the position is going to be for Ashby."

"Damn," he mutters. "That's perfect, Em."

"I know. I feel really good about it."

He stands and offers me his hand, and together we lie down on the air mattress. "I'm so fucking proud of you, Emerson. You're following your dreams."

"I had excellent role models, you and the guys, and Forrest. You all helped guide me."

"I can guide you now too," he says, kissing me.

"You know, now that you mention it, I think I could use some guidance." I reach over and unbutton his cargo shorts, and slip my hand down his pants, then beneath the waistband of his boxer briefs. "Can you show me where this goes?" I ask innocently as I run the pad of my thumb over his piercing.

Roman rolls to his side and glides his hand beneath my gym shorts. "No panties, baby girl?" He tsks.

"I changed out of my interview outfit and decided there was no use adding another layer we were just going to take right back off."

He slides his fingers through my folds. "My cock," he rasps, sliding one long digit inside me. "Goes right here." He kisses my neck.

"You sure it will fit? I think we need to test out this theory," I mumble. His throaty laugh causes heat to radiate through my chest.

"I was made for you, baby girl. But if you need for me to show you, I will." He pulls his hand out of my shorts, and in no time, we're both naked and beneath the covers, under a blanket of stars highlighted by the moon.

He hovers over me, always mindful of his weight. I stare up at him with the night sky as a backdrop. I place one palm over his heart, over the tattoo of my art, and the other rests against his cheek.

"The road we traveled to get here was bumpy. I know that hiding isn't what you want, and I don't want to either. Let's plan to sit down with Forrest in a few weeks. I can't hide this much longer. You make me feel cherished, safe, and so loved. I'm swimming in all these incredible feelings, and it's hard to contain them." I can feel myself start to get choked up. I swallow hard, battling my emotions.

"You mean that? We can tell him?"

"We can, but, Roman, I don't want you to walk away from the shop. You put in just as much work, time, and money into that place as the rest of them did. You deserve to be there."

"It doesn't matter, Emerson. There is no choice to be made where you're concerned. I got a taste of life without you, and it's not something I ever want to live through again. I can work at any shop. There is only one Emerson Huntley. Soon to be Bailey." He winks.

"Let's get through telling my brother before we make plans to change my name."

"Before that, I think I was supposed to be showing you how well my cock fits inside you."

"Permission granted," I say, lifting my legs to lock them around his hips.

Reaching between us, he guides himself to where he needs to be, and slowly inches inside me. He stops to kiss me, and my body relaxes enough for him to push all the way in. We've had sex every day since our first day, and he's still a tight fit, but Roman always takes his time with me.

"So fucking good," he mumbles against my lips.

"You don't have to be easy with me, Rome. I won't break."

"You're precious to me."

"I know. That's why I want you to fuck me like you hate me."

His eyes widen in shock. He's been taking his time with me these past couple of weeks, and I appreciate that, but I want him wild and unhinged.

"What?" he croaks.

"You heard me. I want you to give me all of you." I use my legs, which are wrapped around his waist, to hold him inside me.

"Baby, it's too soon. You're still new at this."

"Am I safe with you?"

By the look on his face, you would have thought that I slapped him. "Of course you are. What kind of question is that?"

"A valid one. You would never intentionally hurt me, Roman. Babe, I'm not made of glass. We're in this together, and I know you're holding back. Don't. Not with me. Not anymore."

"You have to tell me if it's too much, Emerson. I mean it." He gives me a stern look.

"I promise."

It won't be too much.

Overwhelming? Possibly.

Intense? Most definitely.

Too much? Never.

"Slide your hands under my arms, and grip my back."

I do as he says as anticipation flows through my veins. My heart is pounding, and heat pools between my thighs.

"Your pussy is pulsing like crazy. You really want this?"

"I really want you. All of you."

"I'm yours." He pulls out slowly, and I can feel the delicious slide of his piercing against my inner walls. When he's almost all the way out, he slams back in.

And that sets the pace.

Fast, rough thrusts of his hips into mine, and all I can do is hold on. The night sky in the backdrop of the man I love, giving me everything he's got.

This is yet another moment when I fall even more in love with him.

"Touch yourself, baby girl. Play with my pussy, because I'm about to lose control, and you know the rule."

I do know the rule. I come first. He won't budge on this. Which is something else I've learned over the last couple of weeks. Moving my hands, I brace one on his bicep while the other slides between us.

As soon as I touch my clit, it's as if a jolt of electricity is injected into my veins. "Yes!"

"Good girl," he rasps between thrusts. "You gonna come for me, baby girl? Your pussy is trying to milk my cock, but not yet," he pants. "Not. Yet." He thrusts, and my orgasm tears through me. Wave after wave of intense pleasure rolls throughout my body. I arch my back, my nipples rubbing against his chest, only heightening the experience.

"My fucking girl!" Roman roars as he spills inside me.

His head is tilted back to the night sky, and I admire this man, *my* man. He's all I've ever wanted, and it's still sometimes hard to believe he's mine.

When he lowers his head to look at me, he has that dopey, joyful look on his face. "I love you."

"I love you."

He kisses me sweetly as he eases out of me. We clean up as best we can, with leftover napkins—not the best option, but it's what we have to work with. We get dressed, and he holds me in his arms.

"I wish you were coming home with me."

"I know. I couldn't think of a reason to stay with Monroe again. I've been using that excuse a lot lately. I promised Forrest I'd be home tonight and we could have breakfast together tomorrow and catch up."

"You should be waking up in my arms, and I should be making you breakfast before enjoying you as mine."

I laugh. I love that we can have fun together after such an intense moment. "One day."

"Soon. One day soon."

"Yeah," I agree. "Maybe, let's get through Forrest's Fourth of July bash, and then we'll sit down with him. I don't want everyone to be at odds when I know he's looking forward to this."

"Your brother loves any excuse to get us all together."

"He does," I agree. "He craves the family we never had. You and the guys are that for him."

"I hope he can see through the anger to know that I am his family. I'm going to be his brother for real."

"It might take some time, but he'll accept this. There is no other option. I'm in this, Rome. It's you and me, right?"

"Forever."

We lie out under the stars for another hour before we pack up and head back to town. He's sitting in the truck next to me, and I miss him already. Two weeks until the Fourth of July, and then we'll tell my brother.

I'm nervous and pulsing with excitement at the same time. Hiding my love for Roman grows more difficult every day.

"DO YOU KNOW WHO BOUGHT the Morgans' house?" Emerson asks Forrest.

"No. I didn't even see them have a showing. It must have been while we were gone."

"I love that house." Emerson juts out her bottom lip in a pout, and it's cute as hell. I wish I could kiss her pout away. I should get some kind of award for resisting my girl in that sexy emerald-green bikini she's wearing that makes her eyes pop.

"I know you do. Hopefully, they'll be easygoing neighbors."

"Could they not have waited to sell until I'd secured a job and been working for a while?" Emerson grumbles.

"You want to be my neighbor, kid?" Forrest asks her.

"In that house? Sure." She shrugs. "You would have just had to make sure you knock before entering and all that."

"You planning on running around naked?" he teases.

"Wait," Lachlan, who is in the pool a few feet away, holds his hand in the air. "Can I get an invite to this naked lounging? Will there be other ladies in attendance?"

My shoulders stiffen and I tell myself to relax. I know none of these guys want my girl, but I'll be damned if their teasing doesn't raise my protective instincts every damn time. I remind myself they don't know she's mine, but they will. Tomorrow, in fact. Today is the Fourth of July. Emerson and I agreed we're going to sit down with Forrest tomorrow and spill all. The guys will find out soon after.

I admit I'm nervous. Not for me, but for her. He can hate me if he wants to. He'll never understand how I'd be okay with that until he finds the love of his life. Me and the guys are tight. They are my brothers, but Emerson, she's... mine.

My everything.

I meant it when I told Emerson that she changed me.

"Stop." Emerson laughs, and the sound eases the tension inside me. "No invitations, but you know I might be with a man friend or something."

Monroe spits out her drink. "Man friend? What are you, eighty?" She's bending over in the chair she's sitting in, laughing.

"You know what I mean." Emerson is laughing too.

"Wait. Hold up." Forrest leans forward. "Are you seeing someone?"

"What if I am?" Emerson asks. She's still smiling and laughing. I have my sunglasses on, but my eyes are trained on her. If she wants to tell her brother now, I'm game. I don't think that's what she's doing. If I had to guess, I'd say she's warming him up to tomorrow's conversation that he doesn't know is coming.

"I need to meet him. Why isn't he here? What kind of man won't come to hang out with his girl's family?" Forrest grumbles.

"Maybe it's new?" Maddox says, and I bite down on the inside of my cheek to keep from laughing when Forrest glares at him. I shouldn't be laughing. That glare is soon going to be pointed in my direction.

Forrest loves his sister, that's not a fault, but he needs to realize she's her own person.

"It's not new," Emerson says. There is an air of confidence in her voice, and that has my chest expanding with love for her. She knows that we're in this together. Whatever the outcome, it's always going to be the two of us against whatever situation we're faced with. She's confident and secure in the love that we share, and it shines through her like a beacon in the night.

"How long?" Forrest asks.

Emerson shrugs. "A while."

"Who?" Forrest's tone is filled with disbelief. He's stunned that his sister is dating, and he didn't know about it.

"When I'm ready for you to know, I'll tell you." She holds his stare.

"Emerson," he growls, and I sit up straighter in my seat. I don't see this getting out of hand, but I won't let him start yelling at her.

"Forrest, I'm an adult. Do I drill you on every random girl you take out? Do I ask you who you're sleeping with? We're both adults. When I'm ready to share him with you, I will."

"It's my job to look out for you," he tells her.

"Not anymore, Forty," she says softly. "It's your job to support me. Be there when I need you."

"I want to meet him."

She nods. "Fine. I'll invite him over tomorrow." She doesn't dare look my way, but I can feel my mouth lifting in a smile.

She did this on purpose to set up our meeting tomorrow. I just assumed I'd show up, and we'd blurt it out. My girl set him up. She's just given her brother a heads-up that the conversation is going to happen, and he can stew on it so he's not caught off guard.

"So no naked lounging?" Lachlan asks, and we all laugh. The tension is officially broken.

The next few hours are filled with lots of laughter, fun, and food. The sun is brutal today, but that hasn't stopped us from enjoying ourselves. We're all going into town later to watch the fireworks. I hate that I won't be able to hold her while we watch them. I feel like any activity that involves staring up at the night sky, even if it's bright with colorful lights, is ours.

"Anyone need anything from inside?" I call out.

Maddox and Lachlan are in the pool. Forrest and Legend are playing a game of war, and Emerson and Monroe are standing next to the pool. They've been in and out all day. Drake and his girlfriend, Lisa, are out of town visiting their family, and Lyra is as well. So we're missing the newest members of our Everlasting Ink family.

Everyone waves me off, so I head inside to use the restroom and grab a bottle of water from the fridge. I'm not drinking today. I don't trust myself to stay away from Emerson, even the slightest bit inebriated, and I don't want a hangover tomorrow. I need to be in top shape when I tell my life-long best friend that his sister is the love of my life.

Opening the patio door to walk outside, it's barely shut when I hear Monroe yell out Emerson's name. My eyes scan the yard for where I last saw them. They're not there. I see them at the edge of the pool. Emerson is lying on the concrete with everyone standing around her.

My heart pounds as I run to her. I skid to a stop and take in the situation. Forrest and Monroe are kneeling next to her, while Lachlan, Maddox, and Legend stare down at them.

"What happened?" I ask. My voice is gruff and shaking, and I don't give a single fuck if my feelings for her are outed because of it.

"She fainted," Legend tells me. He places his hand on my shoulder, and I appreciate the effort to keep me calm. He knows what she means to me.

I kneel. Her hair is in her eyes. I push it behind her ear and there's a cut on her temple. "You're bleeding, baby girl," I whisper.

"She hit her head," Monroe tells me. "We were going to swim, and she just fainted."

"How do you feel, Em?"

"Okay. Just weak, I guess. I don't know what happened. I was really hot and got dizzy. That's all I remember."

"We need to call an ambulance," Forrest says. His eyes are wild and full of panic.

I ignore him. "Can you stand?" I ask.

"Yeah, I think so. I'm not dizzy anymore."

"Let me help you." I stand and offer her my hands. She's wobbly but manages to stand. She sways, and I pull her into my arms. "I've got you," I whisper.

"Emerson, I'm going to call the squad," Forrest says. "We have to get you checked just to be safe."

"No. I'm fine, just a bump on the head." She gives me a pleading look, one she knows I can't say no to. Fine, we can compromise.

"No ambulance," I concede. "But we're taking you to get checked out."

"Rome, I'm fine. Really. I just got too hot. We've been out in the sun all day. I overheated, that's all. I just happened to be on the concrete and bumped my head."

"Probably, but we're not risking it. You need that cut looked at too." I nod at the cut on her temple.

"You guys are overreacting."

My hand tightens around her. I'm holding her up. She's weak. I'm glad Forrest isn't fighting me, trying to take her from my arms, because it's not happening. "I'll take you, baby girl. Everyone else can stay here."

"Fuck that," Forrest says. "I'm going with you."

At least he doesn't call me out for my endearment for her, or that I'm holding her like she might disappear if I let go.

"What he said," Lachlan says. I look up and Legend, Maddox, and Monroe are all nodding.

I smile down at Emerson. "Looks like you have an entourage, baby girl."

She slumps in my arms. "Fine. But this is crazy. I'm fine."

"I'm sure you are, but let's let the professionals tell us for sure. We're not risking you." What I really want to say is I'm not risking you. I want to tell her that seeing her on the ground with blood at her temple took ten years off my life. I want to tell her she promised to love me for a lifetime, and that we'll do whatever we have to do to take care of her.

"I'll drive," Legend says.

"Keys are in my truck." I bend and lift Emerson into my arms, bridal style.

"We'll be right behind you," Forrest says.

I nod and carry Emerson to my truck. I'm glad Forrest is not insisting on riding with us. I'm holding on to my worry, but I need a minute. Just a minute to not wear this mask of staying strong.

Legend opens the back-passenger door for me. I set Emerson on the seat, and then climb in next to her, pulling her into my arms. Before I can get the door shut, Monroe is jumping into the passenger seat, with what looks like her purse and Emerson's in her hands, and some clothes.

Just as we're backing out of the driveway, Forrest comes rushing out of the house with his keys in his hands. I see Maddox take them from him before I turn my attention back to Emerson.

"How you feeling, baby girl?" I smooth her hair back out of her eyes.

"I'm fine."

"Probably," I agree. "It's not a risk I'm willing to take. There's usually a reason for someone fainting out of the blue."

"It's called overheating."

"I love you." I hug her a little tighter. "Just humor me, okay?"

"Okay," she concedes. I meet Legend's eyes in the rearview mirror, and he nods.

"Thanks, Legend," I tell him. "I appreciate you helping me."

"We're all worried about her," he replies, keeping his eyes on the road.

"Yeah, but other than Monroe, you're the only one that knows about us. You knew I needed to be the one to take her, to hold her just to feel that she's safe. So, thank you, brother," I tell him.

Emerson gives me a questioning glance.

"He did my ink." She nods. Those four words are enough for her to know I spilled the beans to Legend.

He nods. And we're quiet for the rest of the drive toward the hospital. I hold Emerson close, and my heart rate starts to slow the closer we get to the hospital. I'm sure she overheated, and if it were anyone other than my girl, I might have said keep a close eye on them and follow up with their doctor. But not with Emerson.

"Hey, Em, I grabbed our cover-ups. I thought you might want to have a little something more on when going into the hospital," Monroe says once we pull up outside the emergency room.

"Thank you."

Monroe hands me the cover-up, and I help Emerson slip it over her head. Pushing open the door, she slides across the seat, and I lift her out of the truck. "You okay?"

"I'm fine."

With my hand on the small of her back, we make our way inside. Her legs are steady, and she really does seem fine. Relief washes over me. We stop at the desk, and she explains what happened.

"You can have one person go back with you."

"Yeah, that's not going to work." Monroe laughs. "There are five of them." She points to me and Legend. "Her brothers," she adds, and I cringe at being referred to as her brother, but desperate times call for desperate measures. "Very protective. Can we please just all go back with her? The other three will be here any minute."

Just then, the door whooshes open. Forrest, Lachlan, and Maddox come stalking into the emergency room, and over to where we're standing at the desk.

"Told you." Monroe laughs.

"I really shouldn't, but it's slow today, and Dr. Jacobs is on and he's pretty easygoing. Here's the deal. I'll let you all back, but you need to stay out of our way as we take care of the patient, and if anyone asks who gave you permission, you didn't get it from me." The young woman gives each of us guys a pointed stare, and we all nod our agreement. "Good. Meet me at those double doors. Quietly," she adds.

We do as she says. Monroe slides her arm around Emerson's waist, and the rest of us follow along behind silently like we were told. We're led into an exam room and are told someone will be in soon.

"How are you feeling, kid?" Forrest asks.

"Honestly, I feel fine. I know you all care about me, and I love you for it, but this is embarrassing. I got too hot and fainted. We're wasting time and money when we should be enjoying the day."

"That's good," Forrest says, ignoring everything she said.

"Ugh." Emerson rolls her eyes and crosses her arms over her chest. "Overbearing Neanderthals," she mutters.

Monroe, who is sitting on the edge of the bed, chuckles, which makes Emerson laugh too. My shoulders relax. She really appears to be doing better. My girl is going to be mad at me for making her do this, but I'll make it up to her. Nothing a few orgasms can't fix.

"Knock knock." The door pushes open and a nurse walks in. "Well, I wasn't expecting an audience." She walks over to Emerson. "Are we okay to proceed with everyone present?" she asks.

Emerson nods.

"Let's get some vitals then, shall we?"

"Sorry about them," Emerson says. "They're a little protective."

"Girl, nothing wrong with that. That's what family is for." She begins to check the cut and clean it, declaring that she doesn't need stitches, just a butterfly bandage. Apparently head wounds bleed, making them appear worse than they are.

"See," Forrest taunts his sister, and laughs when she groans in frustration.

That simple act between brother and sister has everyone relaxing. For me, it's the time I got with her on the way here when I was holding her that I finally relaxed a little. Otherwise, it's hard to tell how I'd be reacting right now.

The nurse taking Emerson's vitals talks to her about what happened. "I'm going to draw some blood just so we can rule out a few things."

"Like what?" Monroe asks.

"Dehydration, and a few others. We'll have the results soon." She smiles at Monroe, and then at Emerson. The nurse, whose name is Tabitha, is quick and efficient and is out of the room in no time after drawing some blood and hooking Emerson up to IV fluids.

"You all should go. Monroe can stay. I'll be home later."

"Not happening, little sister," Forrest says, crossing his arms over his chest.

I'm glad he declined, because I'm not leaving.

The room is full of whispered chatter, as we're all afraid of being too loud and getting kicked out. Emerson laughs at something Maddox says, and she looks so carefree and happy. I relax even more. The stress of the afternoon is still there, but seeing her like this helps ease some of the worry.

After thirty minutes, there's another knock at the door, and an older gentleman steps in. "Well, it looks like I'm late to the party."

He smiles. He walks to the bed and holds his hand out for Emerson. "I'm Dr. Jacobs."

"Nice to meet you. Emerson Huntley, but you already knew that." She chuckles.

"I did. Are we okay to speak freely in front of your guests?" he asks her.

"My family, and yes."

Dr. Jacobs nods. "Tabitha filled me in, but why don't you tell me too? Just so we're sure to cover all of our bases here."

Emerson goes on to tell him how she was hot, then dizzy, and she fainted. Dr. Jacobs slips on some gloves while he listens. Once she's finished, he listens to her heart, checks her pulse, and smiles warmly at her. "I have your bloodwork results, and we've concluded a diagnosis. Are you comfortable with receiving those results, or should we clear the room?" he asks her.

I stand up tall from where I was leaning against the wall. I notice the rest of the guys do the same. Monroe, who is sitting in a chair next to the bed, sits up straighter. Dr. Jacobs has our rapt attention.

"They'd just stand at the door and listen." Emerson laughs. "It's fine. They're my people."

Dr. Jacobs nods. "Very well. Emerson, I believe you fainted because you're pregnant."

Emerson's mouth falls open, and I take a step toward the bed and stop. Blood whooshes in my ears. "Did you just say pregnant?"

"Yes," the doctor confirms.

I don't think. I act.

I rush to the side of the bed and drop to my knees. I take her hands in mine. Her eyes are shimmering with tears, and I swallow back my own. "We're having a baby," I whisper. I slide my hand over her still flat belly. My heart is racing so loud, I'm sure that everyone in the room can hear it.

Emerson nods and smiles as a tear rolls down her cheek. "I didn't know."

"We know now," I tell her. I bring her hands to my lips and kiss each palm.

"What the fuck is going on here?" Forrest's voice is low, and I can tell he's barely containing his anger.

Standing, I lean over the bed to kiss Emerson softly on the lips. "Love you, baby girl," I whisper.

My words are just for her, before I stand and turn to face Forrest.

"I love you, man. All of you." I let my eyes land on each of the guys before coming back to Forrest. "You're all like brothers to me." I glance down at Emerson, and she reaches up, taking my hand in hers. "I can't breathe without her. I tried to do it. I tried to stay away from her, and then we tried ending it, and we were both miserable."

"You knocked up my little sister?" Forrest seethes.

"I'll give you a few minutes," Dr. Jacobs says, stepping out of the room.

"No. I made a baby with the love of my life. With the woman who owns every piece of me."

"You're ten fucking years older than her."

I nod. "I know."

"She's a baby."

"Forrest," Emerson chimes in. "I'm an adult. Weeks away from turning twenty-one. I love him."

"Get out," Forrest tells me.

"No. I'll sell out my ownership of the shop. I'll keep my distance from you. I'll do anything but that. I won't walk away from them. I won't give them up." I look down at Emerson. "She's my everything. You and our baby are everything."

"I know." Emerson nods. She places our joined hands over her belly. "We love you too."

My knees go weak and my heart flips over in my chest. This woman, she's mine. We're having a baby. A piece of her and a piece of me. I'm having trouble wrapping my head around it.

"Like hell. Get out."

"I gave her up for you once, Forrest. I won't do it again."

"What the hell are you talking about?"

"Christmas. You gave me this big speech about how you wanted a better life for her, how no one would ever be good enough, and I ended us."

"He broke both our hearts that day," Emerson adds. "This is what we want, Forrest. I'm sorry that we hid this from you, but we needed time. Time to see where this was going, and time to be us without the pressure of my brother trying to stop what was already happening."

"How long?" His voice is gruff.

"Since spring break last year."

"What?" he roars.

"Hey." Legend steps forward. "Let's go outside and cool off."

"I'm not leaving her here with him."

"I'm going home with him." Emerson drops a bomb.

"No, you're not."

"You can't stop me, Forty," she whispers. "I love him. We're pregnant. This is happening whether you like it or not."

"I don't."

Emerson shrugs. There are tears in her eyes when she says, "I love you, but he's my future. If you can't be civil, you need to leave. When you've calmed down, and you're ready to talk rationally, you know where to find me."

Forrest rushes forward and gets in my face. Emerson releases my hand, and I keep my arms at my sides. Forrest grips my shirt and there's a blazing fire in his eyes. "You manipulated her. She's a kid, you motherfucker."

"Enough," Maddox says. "You're going to get us all kicked out. This is not the time or the place. She's going to be okay. Let's get you out of here."

"She's coming home with me."

"No, Forrest, I'm not."

He stands not even a foot away from me. His hands are fisted at his sides, and he's breathing heavily. Maddox has a hand on one shoulder, while Lachlan has a hand on the other. "Have a nice fucking life," he seethes, and lets Maddox and Lachlan pull him from the room.

The door slams closed, and Emerson sniffs. "We're going to step out to give you two a minute." Monroe links her arm through Legend's and they walk out of the room.

"I'm sorry." I don't know what else to say. I hate that she's hurting.

"He just needs some time. He'll come around."

I nod. My hand goes back to her belly. "A baby."

"Are you mad?"

"Mad? Why would I be mad? I told you I want to marry you. I believe I mentioned babies."

"That was down the road."

"I'd marry you today if I thought you would agree to it." I chuckle.

"You mean that, don't you?"

"Yes."

"I don't want a big wedding. Just our friends, my brother, and whoever you want to invite."

"You planning our wedding, baby girl?"

She shrugs. "My wedding."

"Em," I growl, and she laughs.

"Yes. When the times comes, if and when we get there, I want small and intimate."

"Oh, we're going to get there, baby girl. I was waiting for us to tell your brother and let the heat die down."

"We can't wait for him to live our life together, Rome. He either wants to be a part of this or he doesn't. He's the one who is being stubborn and is going to miss out on so much."

"I love you, future Mrs. Bailey."

"I love you too."

I press a gentle kiss to her lips. "I'm going to go get the doctor, so we can ask any questions you might have, and we can get you home and resting."

"Your place, right?"

"Our place. He knows, and I never have to spend another night sleeping without you next to me." I wink and walk out the door to find the doctor.

As I make my way down the hall, the opposite direction of where I know our friends will be, my heart threatens to burst open in my chest. It's overflowing with love for her, and our child.

We're doing this. She's mine, and that baby is a part of both of us. How is it possible to feel this deep, all-consuming love for someone you've never met before?

I hate that Forrest can't see what she means to me. I hope that once he calms down, once the news settles, he'll realize that no one can love her like I do.

It might be a long road to prove that to him, but I'm ready to travel it.

"CAN I GET YOU ANYTHING?" Roman asks.

I glance around and laugh. "What more could I need? You've made me a nice little nest." I have a bottle of Pedialyte, which the doctor suggested, a bottle of water, a turkey sandwich with carrot sticks, my Kindle, the remote, a blanket over my lap, my freshly filled bottle of prenatal vitamins, and my feet propped up on the reclining end of the couch.

"It's my job to take care of you."

"Rome, babe, I'm fine. I'm pregnant, not dying. Just relax."

Neither one of us slept well last night, and as soon as the sun was up, he was out of bed fussing over me.

He nods and takes a seat next to me on the couch. I'm getting ready to ask him if we can go upstairs and take a nap when there's a knock at the door.

Roman jumps up and goes to the door. "Hey," he greets whoever it is.

"Is she here?" I recognize my brother's voice immediately.

"Of course she's here. She's on the couch."

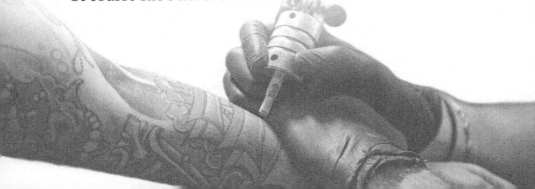

I hear footsteps and then I see Forrest appear. He looks apprehensive, which is a good sign. The anger he was full of yesterday at the hospital seems to have slipped away.

"Hi." I smile and wave. "Come sit?" I pat the couch cushion.

He takes a seat next to me on the couch. Roman takes a seat on the chair, after making sure my feet are covered with the blanket. They were in case you were wondering.

"Looks like he's taking care of you." Forrest nods to everything around me.

"He's taking excellent care of me. Even though there's nothing wrong with me. This is the 'Emerson is not allowed to get up for anything' station." I chuckle, because Roman really is going overboard, but I love him for it.

I love the way that he loves me. I know this is all coming from a good place, and I'm blessed, so very blessed, to have this man in my life.

"You're dehydrated," Roman chimes in. "You and the baby need lots of fluids and lots of rest."

Those are the exact words the doctor used. Luckily, he said for the weekend, and I could go back to my normal routine as long as I felt well on Monday. Thankfully, Roman has to go back to the shop tomorrow, so he called Monroe and asked her to sit with me. I laughed the entire time they were on the phone this morning as he was giving her strict instructions to not let me lift a finger. I have no doubt he'll call her again tonight to go over the instructions. He means well; it's coming from a place of love for me and our baby. He might be driving me batty, but I wouldn't change a thing.

I love this man.

I smile at him before turning back to my brother. "It's good to see you."

He nods. He's quiet for a long time, and we let him gather his thoughts. Finally, he looks at Roman. "You're really in love with my sister?"

"Yes."

"You want this baby?"

"More than anything," Roman says without hesitation.

"Em?"

"We fell in love, Forrest. It wasn't planned or a malicious attempt to hurt you. You don't get to choose who you fall in love with. I know you had this big, elaborate dream for what you thought my life should look like, but that's not your call to make. You never once asked me what I wanted. What I thought my life would look like."

"Tell me what you want your future to look like, kid."

It's with that question that I know everything is going to be okay.

If I'm being honest, I wasn't sure, and after his outburst yesterday, and the way we left things, I was fearful that we might not ever be back to the way we were. I thought that maybe our bond was actually broken. I hid that fear from Roman as best as I could, but it was there.

"I want to fall in love with a good man who will make me and our family the center of his world. I want a couple of kids, a house with a decent-sized yard where my husband and I can have some of the family gatherings at our place. I want to settle in this sleepy little town and raise my family here." My hand rests on my belly. I'm still coming to terms with the fact that we're having a baby.

I give him a minute to let that soak in.

"That's before I fell in love with him. Now, I want to enjoy the love of the good man who I've fallen in love with. I want him and me together, to love one another and our child and future children. I want to be the center of his world, because he's the center of mine. I want us to settle here and find a house that will support our growing family, and yes, I still want to host some family gatherings too." I swallow over the lump of emotion clogging my throat.

He remains quiet, letting my words sink in.

I keep going. "Forrest, Roman is one of your best friends. He fought this connection that we have. He fought it because he didn't want me to lose you. You know him, Forrest. He's been your best friend since you were five years old. He's your business partner. You trust him. I trust him. You love him, and he loves you. Roman and I... our love for one another grew. It changed and blossomed over time, and it's a love that I feel deep inside my soul. We tried to stay away from one another. We took a break for five months, and the minute we were back in the same town, we couldn't do it. My wish for you is that one day you find a love like ours. A love so consuming you don't feel like yourself without the other person."

Forrest has been so focused on taking care of me, he's put his life on hold. He bought that huge house to give me a home, when I would have been just as happy in a house a quarter of the size. He wanted to give me everything we didn't have with our parents growing up, but what he failed to realize is that he's always given me that. He's loved me unconditionally, and that's more than I ever could have wanted.

"Rome?" Forrest's voice cracks.

"Yeah, brother?" Roman answers. He too has a wobble in his voice.

Forrest stands and walks toward him. Roman stands too, but I remain seated. I can tell by my brother's body language that no punches are being thrown today. He's had some time to think about this.

"Welcome to the family. Officially," Forrest says. He offers Roman his hand as a single tear slides down my cheek.

"Thank fuck." Roman reaches out and pulls Forrest into a hug. "Love you, man."

They pull apart, and Forrest comes to sit next to me on the couch. "I'm sorry. Both of you, I'm sorry. I was caught off guard, and the age difference, and you're my baby sister, and he's my best friend, and I couldn't wrap my head around it all. Legend stopped by this morning, and he told me about your tattoo."

Roman lifts his shirt and shows him the ink. My heart melts every time I see it. He wanted a piece of me with him always. Even when he wasn't sure we would find our way back to one another.

"I've seen it, but I didn't know the meaning behind it. He told me how torn up you were. How you tried to stay away from her, but it was literally eating you up inside. Then I got a call from Monroe. She told me how hard the last five months were for you at school because you missed him so much."

"We have good friends." I smile, fighting back tears.

"We do. I'm sorry it took them to help me see what's been right in front of me. I see it now, the way you two look at each other. It's going to take me some time to get used to it, but I won't interfere."

"We appreciate that, man," Roman says.

"If you hurt her, we're done," Forrest adds. "She's my sister."

"She's my heart. My heart that's walking around this earth outside of my body, and she's carrying a piece of the two of us. There is nothing in this world that can pull me away from my wife and child."

"Wife?" Forrest chokes out.

Roman shrugs. "Not officially, but she will be. I figured I might as well give you time to get used to that too. She will be Mrs. Bailey."

"And I live here now," I tell my brother. "We're starting our life together."

That's something that we agreed on last night after Legend dropped us off from the hospital. We've spent enough time hiding and being apart. It's time to put that behind us and move forward.

"I figured." Forrest laughs.

"You're used to me being away at school. The transition should be easy for you."

"Me and that big, old, empty house," he jokes.

"You're just going to have to find yourself a woman, fall in love, and have some babies," I tease.

"Maybe." He shakes his head. "At least I'll have lots of room for my nieces and nephews." He smiles.

"Let's start with one."

"I'm sure the other three will eventually have kids too," Forrest tells me. He really does think of his four best friends as his brothers.

"You hungry? I just made sandwiches. I can whip you one up," Roman offers.

"Actually, yes. I didn't eat. I couldn't with knowing we were fighting."

"This one either." Roman points to me.

I stick my tongue out at him, pick up my plate, and take a huge bite of my turkey sandwich. I make a production of chewing my food and they both laugh.

"Good girl," Roman says huskily. He leans over and kisses me before turning toward the kitchen. "Come on, I'll make you one, and I could eat another."

"Can we cut back on the PDA, man?" Forrest groans as he follows Roman into the kitchen. I hear them laughing, and I relax for the first time since the doctor outed us with this pregnancy.

With one hand on my belly, the other works on shoveling the rest of the sandwich into my mouth. Everything is going to be just fine.

"I can lift a tote bag," I grumble.

"No can do, little momma," Lachlan says. "You sit your pretty little self on that couch. I don't need Roman going all hulk on my ass because you were working."

"It's my stuff," I counter.

"That you and your best friend packed with his help. He gave me strict instructions. You are not to lift a finger while he and the other guys make a trip to his place to drop off a load of your stuff."

"Frustrating man," I mutter.

Lachlan jumps up and rushes toward the kitchen. He comes back with a sliced apple and a big glob of peanut butter on a paper plate.

"What's this?"

"You were looking kind of hangry and I read that pregnant ladies need to eat lots of little meals."

"You were reading?"

"Yeah, I mean, I don't have any siblings, not blood siblings, so this is all new to me. I needed to know what was up. You know... in case you needed me."

"Lachlan, that's so sweet of you. Thank you." I stand and give him a hug just as the front door swings open.

"Why are you hugging my wife?" Roman asks.

"Not your wife," Maddox says, walking past him into the house. He heads toward me, and lifts me off my feet, hugging me.

"She's carrying my kid, and she will be," Roman explains.

"Gotta put a ring on it, brother. She's fair game until then," Lachlan teases.

"The hell you say?" Roman gently grabs my wrist and pulls me into his arms. "Tell them you're mine, baby girl."

"I'm all yours." I kiss him, and I hear Forrest pretend to gag.

"Can we get this over with so I don't have to watch any more of this? Rome, we talked about this. No PDA."

"Love you, baby girl." He kisses me again and follows the rest of the guys up the stairs.

Knowing better than to try and argue with any of them, I sit on the couch, prop my feet up, and wait. I hate that they won't let me help, but at the same time, my heart is overflowing with love for the five men who treat me like spun glass, and love me without question, each in their own way.

An hour later, I'm bored as hell just watching them do all the work when the five of them join me in the living room. "All done?"

"Yeah." Rome lifts me onto his lap, wrapping his arms around me, his hand resting protectively around my belly.

"Really?" Forrest grumbles, making us all laugh.

"Just wait," Roman tells him. "One day a woman is going to knock you on your ass, and you'll understand."

"If you say so." He stands and moves toward the kitchen. "If you can keep your lips off of my sister for five minutes, I have something for you."

"My wife," Roman calls after him.

"Stop riling him up." I swat Roman playfully on the arm.

"Just stating the facts, baby girl."

"I'm not your wife, Roman."

"Not in the eyes of the law, not yet, but in my heart you're more than that."

"Aww," Maddox coos.

"Laugh it up, fucker," Roman says without any kind of heat in his tone. "You fuckers will understand one day."

They don't get to reply before Forrest is handing me a small light green gift bag. "What's this?" I ask. I can already feel tears welling behind my eyes. These damn pregnancy hormones are going to be the death of me.

"Just open it."

Doing as he says, I reach into the bag, and pull out a small piece of fabric. At closer inspection I see it's a onesie for the baby. Opening it up, I read it out loud. "If you think I'm cute you should see my uncle." I hold the tiny outfit to my chest and offer my big brother a watery smile. "Forty." My voice cracks.

"I love you, kid. You too, Rome. And my niece or nephew will always know that they can come to Uncle Forty."

"Hold up." Legend raises his hand. "I'm the cool uncle here. We all know this."

"Keep dreaming," Lachlan scoffs. "You all know I've got this in the bag."

"Oh, no, you're all going down. That title is mine." Maddox smacks at his chest. The four of them bicker playfully back and forth, while it's all I can do to hold on to my tears.

"It's okay, baby girl," Roman whispers in my ear. "Don't fight the tears, beautiful."

I turn to look at him over my shoulder as one single tear slides down my cheek. "How did you know?" I ask, smiling at the man that holds my entire heart.

He reaches up and wipes away my tear with his thumb. "I can't explain it, but the best way I know how is you're a part of me, Emerson. I feel what you feel, baby girl, and I'm here." He kisses my cheek. "I'm always going to be right here."

I settle into his hold as the guys continue to talk about the things they are going to do for or with our baby to win the favorite uncle title, while Roman holds me protectively.

Does he know he's my dream come true?

EMERSON EPILOGUE

"IS THE BLINDFOLD REALLY NECESSARY?" I ask Roman.

"Yep."

"Can I at least have a hint as to where we're going?"

"Nope."

I'm ready to argue when the truck stops. "Are we there?"

"We are."

"Can I take this off?" I reach for the blindfold, but he stops me.

"Baby girl, just humor me, please. It's almost time for you to take it off."

"Fine." I pretend to be put out, but the truth is, I love that he's going to such great lengths to surprise me.

It's been three weeks since my trip to the emergency room. Living with Roman has been a dream. He agreed that the back bedroom would be the best for the baby, and since it's empty, I'm ready to get started. However, I know I need to wait until at least the second trimester before I can start.

We found out I was pregnant at six weeks, and from what I've read online, when you find out that early, it seems to go on forever. That's fine with me, though. I'm going to enjoy every moment of this next phase of our lives together.

"Stay put. I'm going to come around and get you."

I do as I'm told, and a few seconds later, he's opening my door and lifting me out of the truck.

"I can walk," I remind him.

"I can also carry you."

"Are we going up steps?" I ask, trying to find any kind of clue that I can.

Roman chuckles. "Patience, baby girl."

A few more steps and he's placing me on my feet.

"Now, I want you to count slowly to ten, and then open your eyes."

"Got it."

I start counting. When I get to ten, I peel off the blindfold and blink, letting my eyes adjust. That's when I see a banner, a huge banner strung across the room that reads "Welcome home, Mrs. Bailey."

"Rome?"

I turn to look at him, but he's not standing next to me. No, he's kneeling with the most beautiful diamond ring I've ever seen in his hand.

"You, Emerson Huntley, are the love of my life. Will you do me the incredible honor of being my wife? Will you marry me?"

"Yes. Yes. Yes." I nod as the tears start to fall. These damn pregnancy hormones.

Roman stands and slides the ring onto my finger, and it's a perfect fit. He kisses me soundly, before pulling away.

"Where are we?" I spin, taking in the huge open-floor plan. The kitchen has off-white cabinets with a marble countertop and what looks like new stainless-steel appliances. The open concept is light and airy and huge. Much larger than our house, or even Forrest's house.

"This is our new home."

I tilt my head to the side to study him. "You just moved me into your home. Our home."

Roman laughs, and my lips also tip up in a smile. "Yeah, baby girl, our home, but now we have a new one."

"Which is where exactly?" I ask. I didn't even know he was looking for a new house.

"Step outside."

"We just moved all of my stuff," I tell him.

"Yeah, and it's a good thing you've been slow to unpack," he teases.

"Hey! You're the one who kept telling me we would get to it and then distract me."

"And we will. When we unpack here. At our new home. Now, come outside with me." He nods toward the front door, and I do as he says. There is something he's not telling me.

I step out onto the porch to see my brother, Lachlan, Maddox, Legend, Monroe, and Roman's parents, as well as Drake, Lisa, and Lyra standing on the front lawn.

"Funny story," Forrest calls out. "Turns out I knew the guy who bought the Morgans' old place, after all."

"What?" I turn in circles, and sure enough, it's the house next door to my brother's that I loved so much. "What's he talking about?" I ask Roman.

"I bought it. I knew you loved this place, and I knew what we had planned for our future. It was a gamble because I didn't know if he would ever accept us, but I just figured if we were neighbors, we'd eventually wear him down."

"You bought us a house? Before you knew about the baby?"

"I bought us a house because I was dreaming of us with the baby." He winks.

"I love you."

"I love you too, baby girl."

ROMAN EPILOGUE

My EYES ARE GLUED TO the back door of our house as I wait for my bride to appear. Emerson and I decided we didn't want to wait to get married, so here we are, just four short weeks after asking her to marry me, getting ready to seal the deal with a kiss.

She's minutes away from being my wife.

My. Wife.

With the help of my mom and Monroe, we pulled off a small, intimate backyard wedding. My girl says it's everything she's ever wanted, and that's good enough for me.

Legend starts to play "Marry Me" by Train on the guitar and the back door opens. My breath stalls in my chest at the sight of her on her brother's arm.

At thirteen weeks pregnant, she has a slight bump, which is completely hidden beneath the loose dress that she's chosen. That's okay because we all know it's there. She started with morning sickness a few days after we got engaged, and it's been taking a toll on her. I offered to postpone the wedding, but she refused.

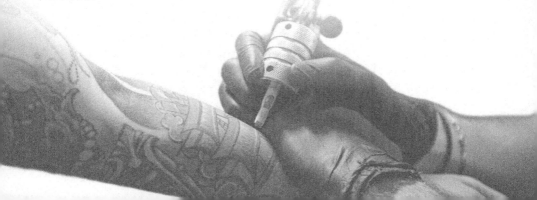

When they reach me, my dad, who got ordained for the occasion, asks, "Who gives this woman away?"

"Not me. Nope. Not giving her away. He's just borrowing her." Forrest winks at me, and I swallow back the lump in my throat. This guy, he's been my brother in my heart for years, and now, because I'm the lucky bastard his sister fell in love with, in the eyes of the law, he really is.

We all laugh, and Emerson kisses Forrest's cheek and sends him to his chair.

"You look beautiful, baby girl," I say, kissing her cheek.

"Hey, that's after. He's cheating," Maddox calls out, and Emerson giggles.

I nod for my dad to get on with it, and he does.

The ceremony is short and sweet, and fifteen minutes later, I'm kissing my wife for the first time. We turn to face our guests and cheers erupt. I don't know a moment where I've ever felt more fulfilled than I do right now.

Family and friends swarm us with hugs and handshakes of congratulations. The day couldn't be more perfect. The guys start talking shit about who's going to be the next victim to fall into the love trap, and I just grin.

It's not a trap, not even close. I've never felt more free. I smile at my wife, who blows me a kiss.

Monroe pulls Emerson over to my mom, and hers, and they start talking I'm sure about the baby and the nursery. I'm glad Emerson has Monroe and her mom, and mine is over the moon to have a daughter-in-law. I'm glad she has the support system as we enter this next phase of life while learning to be parents.

I'm going to be a dad.

I'm fucking stoked and scared out of my mind, but knowing that my wife is going to be by my side learning to navigate keeping a tiny a human alive, well, that eases some of the fear.

Forrest is talking to my dad, while Maddox, Lachlan, Drake, Lisa, and Lyra are standing in a circle chatting with drinks already in their hands. I scan the yard looking for Legend and find him sitting on the back porch staring down at his phone. I head over to him and take a seat next to him.

"Everything all right?"

"Yeah, just got a text from my mom. Her mom passed away."

"Oh, that's the grandma you never met, right?"

"Yeah." He's still staring down at his phone.

"I'm sorry, man. Do you need to go? What can I do?" I know he wasn't close to her, but she was still his family.

"No. I'm all good. She asked me to stop by because my grandma's lawyer sent me a letter to their place via certified mail."

"Any idea what it could be about?"

"Hard to tell. She never met me, so who knows." He shoves his phone back into his pocket. "Why are you over here with me when you should be with your wife?"

"Good question." I reach over and pat his shoulder. "You sure you're good?"

"Yeah, just weird, but I'll find out sooner or later what's up."

"I'm here."

"I know, man. Appreciate that. Now go. Your wife is waiting for you."

I grin as I stand and make my way to my wife. "Sorry, ladies, but I need to dance with my wife." I make eye contact with Maddox, and he fires up the tunes as I pull Emerson into my arms.

"How long until we kick them out?" I ask her.

"Roman!" she scolds. "We are not kicking our guests out."

"I need to make love to my wife."

"We have the rest of our lives, husband."

"That we do, wife," I agree. I kiss her, slow and sweet, ignoring the cheers and catcalls of our family. I block it all out and memorize this moment. I know in fifty years, when we're sitting on the back porch watching our grandchildren play, I'll still remember this. The day she changed my life by changing her last name.

We fought to get where we are. I'm grateful that everything worked out. It was a bumpy road, but our hearts led us to where we are today.

I can't wait to see what life has in store for us.

for taking the time to read ***Does He Know***.
I hope you loved Roman and Emerson's story.

Want more from the Everlasting Ink Family?
Look for Legend's story, ***Is This Love***, releasing March 2024.

Never miss a new release:
Newsletter Sign-up

Be the first to hear about free content, new releases, cover
reveals, sales, and more. kayleeryan.com/subscribe/

Discover more about Kaylee's books here
kayleeryan.com

Did you know that Orrin Kincaid has his own story?
Grab ***Stay Always*** for free here
kayleeryan.com/books/stay-always/

Start the Riggins Brothers Series for FREE.
Download ***Play by Play*** now
kayleeryan.com/books/play-by-play/

Facebook:
bit.ly/2C5DgdF

Reader Group:
bit.ly/2OoyWDx

Goodreads:
bit.ly/2HodJvx

BookBub:
bit.ly/2KulVvH

Website:
kayleeryan.com/

Instagram:
instagram.com/kaylee_ryan_author/

TikTok:
tiktok.com/@kayleeryanauthor

MORE FROM KAYLEE RYAN

With You Series:
Anywhere with You | More with You | Everything with You

Soul Serenade Series:
Emphatic | Assured | Definite | Insistent

Southern Heart Series:
Southern Pleasure | Southern Desire
Southern Attraction | Southern Devotion

Unexpected Arrivals Series
Unexpected Reality |Unexpected Fight | Unexpected Fall
Unexpected Bond | Unexpected Odds

Riggins Brothers Series:
Play by Play | Layer by Layer | Piece by Piece
Kiss by Kiss | Touch by Touch | Beat by Beat

Entangled Hearts Duet:
Agony | Bliss

Cocky Hero Club:
Lucky Bastard

MORE FROM KAYLEE RYAN

MORE FROM KAYLEE RYAN

Co-written with Lacey Black:

Fair Lakes Series:
It's Not Over | Just Getting Started | Can't Fight It

Standalone Titles:
Boy Trouble | Home to You | Beneath the Fallen Stars | Tell Me A Story

Co-writing as Rebel Shaw with Lacey Black:
Royal | Crying Shame

There are so many people who are involved in the publishing process. I write the words, but I rely on my team of editors, proofreaders, and beta readers to help me make each book the best that it can be.

Those mentioned above are not the only members of my team. I have photographers, models, cover designers, formatters, bloggers, graphic designers, author friends, my PA, and so many more. I could not do this without these people.

And then there are my readers. If you're reading this, thank you. Your support means everything. Thank you for spending your hard-earned money on my words, and taking the time to read them. I appreciate you more than you know.

SPECIAL THANKS:

Becky Johnson, Hot Tree Editing.

Julie Deaton, Jo Thompson, and Jess Hodge, Proofreading

Lori Jackson Design – Cover Design (Guy Cover)

Emily Wittig Designs – Special Edition Cover

Wander Aguair – Photographer (Guy Cover)

Chasidy Renee – Personal Assistant

Jamie, Stacy, Lauren, Franci, and Erica

Bloggers, Bookstagrammers, and TikTokers

Andrea, and Stacy - Graphics

The entire Give Me Books Team

The entire Grey's Promotion Team

My fellow authors

And my amazing Readers

Printed in Great Britain
by Amazon

31652898R00159